TRIAL RUN

J RUSTY SHAFFER

J Rusty Shaffer

Trial Run

© 2020 J Rusty Shaffer. All Rights Reserved.

Self-published

Cover Design by Victoria Davies

ISBN: 978-1-7351894-0-6

LCCN: 2020910866

Special thanks to Julianne Mertz and Shelby Shaffer for their amazing editing efforts. A very special thanks to my family who has supported all my entrepreneurial efforts.

Published in Reno, Nevada, USA

To my late father, John W. Shaffer, who told me throughout my life that I could be anything and do anything that I wanted. He'd often say, "If you can dream it, you can do it."

PREFACE

The United States, China and Russia have consistently been viewed as the world's main superpowers since the end of World War II. Respectively their populations today are 328 million, 1.4 billion and 145 million. With regards to land mass the United States has 3.8 million square miles, China has 3.7 million square miles, and Russia has 6.6 million square miles. Russia and China are communist countries. They do not hesitate to use their military or influence to invade or bribe other countries in order to gain strategic control of additional land and shipping lanes. The United States is a democracy with a doctrine of using its military to support and defend freedom for itself and its allies around the world.

With populations continuing to increase, competition for resources amongst these three superpowers is becoming fierce. Whether it be natural resources, economic resources or political resources, there's one undeniable fact – the planet is not getting any bigger. In light of this, two of these countries are on the move to fulfilling their long-range plans of global dominance.

PRINCIPLE CHARACTERS

United States of America

Parker Jane Hall – Intern/Dept. of Homeland Security employee

Timothy Chen – Chinese-American bio-research scientist, college roommate of Parker Hall

Josh Bennett – Dept. of Homeland Security employee

Elliott Myles – Ex-National Security Agency employee and neighbor of Parker Hall

Jarod Short – Parker and Tim's former Georgetown economics professor and good friend of President Andrew Hunter

Margaret Short – Jarod Short's wife

Nathan Hall – Former State Department employee and Parker's father

Andrew Hunter – President of the United States

Alden Scott - Chief of Staff to the President of the United States

Admiral James Reed – Chairman of the Joint Chiefs of Staff

Roger Thomas – Director, Homeland Security

Robert 'Bob' Harrison – Hong Kong National Security Agency station chief

Jordon McKenna – White House spokesperson

Frank Stackhouse – Interim Director, Dept. of Homeland Security

Forrest 'Hap' Wilson – Army Brigadier General, logistics
Dr. Abraham Schaul – Senior bio-scientist
Dr. Martin Ricci – Bio-scientist
Dr. Kabir Anand – Bio-scientist

People's Republic of China

Li Wei – Politburo member, educated at Stanford University
Huang Fu – Senior Politburo member
Zhou Shou – Politburo member
Wu Xin – Politburo member
Zhang Min – Politburo member

Gao Tang – Chinese military assistant in Ops Center
Liu Xiang – Li Wei's office assistant

Dr. Ho Min – Senior infectious disease scientist and 'secret lab' supervisor and Li Wei's close friend
Yuan Xi – Chinese Research Lab supervisor, 3rd floor
Faan Jun – Chinese Research Lab senior supervisor, 4th floor
Li Na – Dr. Ho Min's assistant, young woman
Sam Ji – secret lab researcher, Tim Chen's new friend

Tao Hanwen – Head of Manufacturing in China
Mao Qiang – Head of Infrastructure in China
Zau Fang – Minister of State Security
Wang Lei – Head of the Civil Aviation Administration of China (CAAC)

Islamic Republic of Iran

Dr. Ebrahim Heydari – Senior Lab scientist
Dariush Karami – Iran's Minister of Infectious Disease

CHAPTER 1

Present Day. Beijing, China.

L i Wei sipped his tea. "What is the news from the west Tang?"

"It is business as usual in the United States. Media reports are back to normal. Not much coverage on the virus. Virus coverage includes the typical blame that either it was an over-reaction or they didn't act soon enough in preventing deaths. They are once again acting divided, in-fighting and focused on their stock market."

"It is amazing that such an industrious nation does not learn. It is quite peculiar that as individually smart as they can be, as a nation they are lethargic. They certainly can be dangerous but for the most part they are too busy with individual pursuits and spouting their ideological arguments. Democracy is fraught with peril."

"Since I have been monitoring them for the past year and a half, I have learned much about the Americans. I am amazed that after such an event they are once again so passionately divided. Is it time to put Phase Two in motion?"

"Almost Tang, almost. Our trial run is finally coming to a close and I will approach the Council soon with my report."

"Very good your excellency, I will await your instructions."

1.5 years prior to present day. Beijing, China. Closed door Politburo meeting.

Huang Fu, one of the most senior Politburo members, was sitting quietly listening to his colleagues. After a few minutes he decided to speak. "This is becoming a problem. U.S. President Hunter is tougher than the others. He is over halfway into his first term and his economic attacks on us are relentless. He is winning the effort to neutralize our trade deficit and in doing so, their economy is growing like wildfire. For over forty-five years we could count on tough talk from whoever was the American president, but it always resulted in their political leaders' submission because their business leaders were too addicted to our low-cost manufacturing."

"This is the new reality Fu. I don't see that we have many choices," Wu Xin seemed resigned. "We have tried to infiltrate their media and recruit some of their more popular reporters. Our plan to create internal pressure in order to sway the American president's supporters has fallen short. Those who we have co-opted have stirred the pot as we have desired but the stronger the capitulation by one side of their population, the stronger the other side resists against these media personalities, news outlets, and philosophy."

Zhang Min, another senior member then interjected, "Maybe dear friends it is time to modify our long-range plans. I do not see a way to keep the decades-long status quo. This United States president is popular enough to be allowed to pursue his agenda against us. Even our influence via our Russian friends did not result in the stifling of the new American president."

It was then that Zhou Shou spoke up. "Colleagues. I cannot accept this new reality."

"But Wei, what can we do? War is not an answer and I do not trust the American war machine anyway. They are formidable when attacked."

"Remember the goals that were handed down from our fore fathers," Wu Xin spoke. "The eventual and complete domination of worldwide markets and supply chains. We have been patient for hundreds of years. Our citizens have been loyal participants playing their part at all levels over many decades. Our country has progressed according to this plan. However, we now face an opponent in the new president of the United States that may cause an interruption to that plan. I am afraid that for our term in this Chamber, we will not be remembered as good caretakers compared to that of previous regimes."

Li Wei took the opportunity to address the council with his thoughts. "Colleagues, I would like to now talk to you with closed doors. What I am about to discuss goes no further than this room. I have thought many long days and nights about this problem and I believe I might have a response to halt the American aggression toward out trade policies. I say might because, as is true with all we plan and do, more than a year is needed to fully execute this plan."

Zhang Min, another senior member of the council, nodded approval to Wei. "Wei, you may talk freely."

"Dear Friends, in order to truly defeat the United States, it is important to understand the psychology of the American citizen. We see, on a daily basis, that the American citizenry is not a contiguous body. America is divided into two political ideologies, conservative and liberal/progressive. The political classifications are Republican and Democrat respectively. As we watch their citizenry, their news broadcasts and their political rallies, it would appear, and one might conclude, that they might easily be headed for another civil war. As you well know, our efforts during the last decade to help sow the seeds of discontent in the United States have not produced this civil war or the results we have desired as fast as we would like. Their society is too advanced for armed revolution amongst their citizens for they are, for the most part, a law-abiding society and they employ a substantial police force across their country. And although this divide might seem like a sure way to conquer and crush their country, they have an uncanny way of coming together as needed. I have concluded that individually, Americans have too much to lose, namely their lifestyle, which is why it is unlikely that

Americans would ever cross over into armed conflict against each other."

"Yes, they love their Netflix and take-out pizza. Continue Wei," Min smiled at his own clever remark as the others gave a half-hearted chuckle.

"Remember World War II. Remember the 9/11 terror attack. Look at their vast fascination with sporting events including the Olympics. Even though it can be assumed that they are divided with regards to many of their strongest beliefs, all of you would be hard pressed to identify different ideological individuals at a sporting event or in their military. They are odd like this. From the Americans that we have spoken to and used as double-agents, they talk about words like underdog, American dream and freedom, and they possess a willingness to fight and coalesce for causes that rise above ideological differences. It does appear that they *can* come together, in extreme crisis, especially in war. Sports for the American is simply a form of war that doesn't end in death."

Wu Xin was growing impatient. "Yes, yes, we know this … so what do you propose?"

"I'm getting to that Xin, please indulge me a few minutes more. Fu is correct. War, armed conflict as we have known it for thousands of years, is not the answer – certainly not at this point on the earth. However, the American does have a weakness. It took me many years of studying the Americans and their lifestyle in order to identify this weakness. As I have said they can come together for a common cause like war and sport, but short of that, they live their lives divided into their ideologies. At first glance, it would appear that they are divided only over politics and their founding document, their Constitution. However, to truly understand the American mind, one must look deeper into their lives. I have found that American lives revolve around the economic level they have attained as individuals and families. And because of that fact, they are divided economically and when crisis strikes it can bring an economic contraction of their American lifestyle."

"I'm not sure we fully understand your insight. Can you give us an example of this Wei?" Min asked.

"To understand the American, is to understand their lifestyle. They are very materialistic. They define their lives by the devices they own, the size of their home and the cost of their automobile. They spend lavishly on holidays and vacations, restaurants, clothes, TV's, and more and spoil their children. They pay their professional athletes significantly more than their best teachers. Here's a good example. The influx of illegals from their southern border has accelerated over the decades. American children are taught that they do not need to work menial or laborious jobs. These jobs are filled by the illegal population. This labor arrangement is standard for Americans. Their children are too busy at higher paying jobs, sports or not working altogether. Americans look the other way at the invasion of these illegals because they can pay a cheaper wage to illegal laborers instead of paying an American laborer a much higher wage to do the same thing. The average American owes over $10,000 American dollars in credit card debt. Many individuals live month to month, from paycheck to paycheck. Unlike our culture, they believe in immediate gratification. Most do not save money. They are materialistic and their lives revolve around their material wishes, wants and aspirations. Essentially, their demand for a very luxurious and comfortable lifestyle has priced America out of being able to manufacture cheaply in the U.S. or perform cheap labor within their country with U.S. citizens. Therefore, my friends, my plan is as follows. As you are aware, our bio-weapon labs have been making great progress on an invisible weapon, and I was informed that there has been a breakthrough in recent months. Our scientists have fabricated two such viruses. The first one has a very high rate of infection and transmission, though it is not as deadly as other viral strains that the world has seen. The key to this virus is the speed of infection, which is faster than ever seen before. The second virus is extremely deadly and though very contagious, it is slower to spread than the first virus.

"I'm still not following Wei. Get to the point, please," Wu Xin wanted the bottom line.

"I believe that a rapidly spreading infection unleashed on the world can cause worldwide infection and panic. I believe the American media and health officials will drive this panic. This panic and the ensuing government response will also cause great economic interruption and hardship. My plan would include starting this infection using the first virus, Virus One, amongst our own citizens and allowing it to spread throughout the world naturally. We will help the spread to the U.S. by deliberately sending infected Chinese citizens to the U.S. We will of course keep news and information of the virus from being disseminated until enough citizens are infected and have traveled around the world. This would allow us to naturally shut down our factories thereby shutting down the U.S. supply of goods. My hope is that their stock market would immediately and dramatically decline and their people would panic, not only as a response to the unknown quick-spreading virus, but they would panic as to the declining economic circumstances and response of their government. Supplies would run short and though their total number of deaths would be rather small as compared to say, their seasonal flu, my guess is that the ensuing panic and the resulting blame of their leaders, especially President Hunter, would force their citizens to seek a new leader during their election next year. If America elects a new president, the candidates at present for the opposing party would be friendly again to our overall goals. We have worked with one of them before. Only if the current president is re-elected would we put Phase Two into effect.

Xin then asked, "What is Phase Two?"

"Phase Two would consist of—"

"Wei, I'm sorry," Fu said, "I must ask you a question. Your plan is interesting so far but I want to remind you of the Swine Flu pandemic which the world experienced in 2009 and 2010. If I recall correctly, the American media and citizenry themselves barely gave any notice to this crisis, though as we know, people were infected and died from the virus. Approximately 35,000 of their citizens die each year from the flu and I have never heard or seen any panic from their citizens or their government over these deaths. Why will this virus, Virus One, have such a dramatic and different effect?"

"I believe I can answer your question," Wei patiently responded. "First, the swine flu was interpreted as just another kind of flu. People understand, and especially Americans, that variations of the flu come and go. Their health and human services agencies, through local doctors and pharmacies, even offer their citizens a "flu injection" each season. Americans see this injection as the "fast food" answer to letting them go about their lives each flu season. Secondly, social media was nowhere near as widespread or prolific as it is today. We know that much commentary on most social media platforms is not rooted in common sense or fact, but in political correctness. Facts rarely get transmitted and it is easy for any person to hide behind their electronic devices and spread false opinions worldwide. As we have seen, these weak individuals can propagate blatant lies and many individuals accept this commentary and opinion as gospel. Thirdly, and maybe most importantly, the political climate in the United States has never been as extreme or confrontational as it is today."

Min was curious, "What do you mean 'extreme'?"

Wei paused to sip his tea before responding, "For many decades now the political ruling class in the United States has operated under the conclusion that their citizens are, for the most part, too busy with their lives to rise up and truly revolt. I have watched the American political class and though they argue and attack each other in front of the cameras, they share meals and cocktails behind the cameras. They are even so bold as to vote themselves pay increases, and though the media and some people complain, nothing is done to stop them. I have interacted with these politicians and they are all self-interested for the most part. Once a newly elected politician 'joins the club,' their true goals are to stay in power. The conclusion I have drawn is that Americans want their political leaders to be aligned with their individual ideologies, yet they expect nothing to really change in their government. They expect a certain amount of gridlock, but as long as their stock market keeps moving upward, as long as their shores are not attacked by an invading army, and as long as their restaurants, bars, gas stations and shopping malls remain open, they are content to cede power to keep the status quo. This was the case for decades until President Hunter was elected. This man does not have a political background and has not acted like any other elected politician."

"Explain please." Xin asked abruptly.

"Each political group has its respective media pundits. Again, that is nothing new. However, during the last administration, when the Democrats where in charge, their president and Congressional leaders 'over-reached' when proposing and adopting various laws and social programs which are at the heart of their particular ideology. This angered the Republican citizenry and especially the Republican media. Unlike the Democratic media and the Democratic politicians who act in concert and in lock-step with each other, the Republican media began to contradict and call-out the Republican politicians who didn't act against these Democratic measures and policies. This is of course culminated in a political up-rising of the Republican citizenry who voted Andrew Hunter, a non-politician, into the presidency. This is the capitalist businessman we are forced to deal with today. Colleagues, in 1900, about 73% of U.S. citizens voted in their presidential election. In their last election of President Hunter, only 55% of their citizenry voted. Americans are basically apathetic and most of what goes in America regarding their government is political theatre."

Fu turned to Wei. "I have an additional question of your plan. If the infection you plan to use, this … Virus One, is not as deadly as other viruses, why use it?"

"For several reasons. Virus One is a trial run. The purpose of the trial run is to prepare for our next move. The Americans, by way of their reaction to Virus One, will dictate this next move. As I stated earlier, either a new President will be elected in the U.S. who will be friendly to our government or, if President Hunter is re-elected, we would enact Phase Two. Phase Two would call for the subsequent release of a much more lethal infection, Virus Two, that would bring the U.S. to its knees. Either way, we will change the U.S. government's behavior toward us in order to resume our long-range world strategy. Secondly, we assume some of our citizens will die in the trial run. This must happen in order for the world to see that we are as vulnerable as any other country. Thirdly, if we decide to enact Phase Two, I am told by our researchers that we can immunize most of our population by putting a vaccine into our water supply ten days prior to the release of Virus Two. Lastly, we are not yet prepared for a new America that will be reduced to half its size and power. Our manufacturing needs to contract, to feel the lessening demand from the U.S. and adjust accordingly. While this contraction is happening during the trial run we will educate and diversify our people and their factories so that they can prepare for an America that is just another customer and not our biggest customer."

"How many of our people do you anticipate will die?"

"Between 25,000 and 100,000 during the trial run, Xin. During Phase Two, even though we can immunize most, approximately another 10,000 will die. We believe that this second attack will have devastating results on the world, especially America. We estimate 100 million deaths in the United States alone and over 65% unemployment as their economy and businesses are ruined."

"You make many assumptions, Wei. How do you know that America won't retaliate against us after the trial run and simply diversify their manufacturing?"

"Fu, America will not know that we are responsible for the trial run. Our media will put forth a story about our horrible wet markets and that it is but a typical zoonotic virus that unfortunately jumped from animal to human. Also, America gets 90% of its products from us. Not only their consumer toys and recreation products and tech devices, but their medicines, their construction materials, their necessities, even their medicines–nearly everything. Also remember that the World Health Organization is in our pocket. They will also corroborate our 'innocent bystander' story as well as tout us as the leaders in cracking down on the spread of the virus."

Xin was skeptical. "And because of that won't *our* economy be hurt greatly by the reduction of demand and the diversification from the West?"

"Gentlemen. The philosophy of capitalism demands that business has one true goal–profit. America begun under this premise and has grown to be a great Super Power. This is true of most of the world as they are also mostly capitalistic. They might diversify some of their manufacturing to satisfy Wall Street or media scrutiny or even political correctness, but their businesses will always seek the lowest cost for a reasonable quality. This I know. Having studied at their Stanford University as a young man, I have experienced their teachings, their views on entrepreneurship and their business mentality. This is especially true of low to moderate priced goods. Their economy is generally fragile and what I mean by that is that 50% of their people live month to month. Their population cannot afford a significant rise in consumer prices and their businesses are drunk on the profits from manufacturing at such a low cost in our country. My friends, ask yourself one question: What country will they turn to for their manufacturing? What country has a labor force as large as us? What country can better control their citizenry like we do? What country has the manufacturing capability and can deliver the quality that is demanded? There is no other country on the planet that can rival us or match us with regards to our labor and manufacturing capabilities." Wei sat back in his chair.

"Wei, how do you know that the Americans and the U.S. government will panic? I don't understand, why would they panic over what will certainly be labeled just another version of the flu, especially if Virus One is not as deadly?"

"Fu, do you remember in the late 1970's when

Americans lined up for hours at gas stations? At that time gasoline was priced in America at $1.00 USD per gallon and Americans panicked. They stayed in line for hours to purchase gas for their automobiles. At that time there was limited television news and only newspapers. They thought then that the world was ending. In today's climate of biased cable news and social media, the 'unknown' of the virus will surely initially cause a panic among their citizens. Of course, today, gasoline is much more expensive and they do not line up. They are a people prone to initial stress and panic. Remember, our friend is their media. They will create and propagate the panic better than any subversive effort we might undertake because their news organizations are now, as opposed to fifty years ago, capitalistic profit centers for their owners. Their media sensationalize all news. They alter ordinary news stories to create biased interest in their viewers. They benefit from increased viewership which in turns means increased revenue from advertising, and they feel no shame or remorse for their actions. I'm sure you have all seen every single minute of every single day they leave their 'Breaking News' graphics on the screen. We know this is ridiculous but they have seen viewership rise over the last couple of decades since their Gulf War and since 9/11. The news organizations, who for years were isolated factual reporters of news whether good, bad or indifferent, discovered that if they changed their reporting to being more biased and opinionated about 'the news', they could increase viewership, advertising and ultimately revenue. The one response we cannot predict is to what degree their government and people will panic. Again, my friends, this is the reason for the trial run. There is a third option we can take after the trial run. If during the trial run, we do not see the response we need to see from their government, we can then decide to do nothing more. Life will go back to the way it was." Wei was starting to convince Min.

"Yes, this is all starting to make sense."

"We have the greatest workforce on the planet. Because of our communistic heritage, our people understand hardship. We have blocked much of the west's internet sites and materialism for years because we understood that freedom is also a sort of 'infection' to our people and our way of life. Our main religion also reinforces this ideal. The afterlife, frugality and honor to country are ideals we instill in our culture. Americans are loyal to the dollar and what it can buy them. Religion in America is not as popular as it was fifty years ago. American capitalists will have no choice but to continue to purchase manufacturing from us. As I stated earlier, there is no other manufacturing option in the world as well suited toward the goals of capitalism as China.

"You are very wise Wei. But I must ask, have you considered what can go wrong?"

"Yes, of course Xin, I have considered what could go wrong and that is precisely why I am suggesting, and I have planned for, the trial run first with Virus One. Either way, we hurt America without taking the blame. If for some reason, I am wrong on my prediction of how I believe America will react, we will simply do nothing more. No one will ever find out our plans."

Xin kept pressing. "I still must ask, after the trial run

won't America prepare themselves for a next possible virus and be better suited to handle such an event?"

"I am glad you asked. This gets to the heart of the trial run. Remember, though Virus One spreads rapidly, it is designed to be only deadly to their most vulnerable and elderly who for the most part have underlying diseases and medical issues. I suspect America will do the following upon the trial run phase. They will initially be slow to react and then they will over-react bordering panic. This is the American nature of both their people and their government. They have always believed that bigger or more is better and their response will show that. Once Virus One is no longer perceived as a threat, most likely in about six months, their media will begin to debate the government's reaction. Some will say it was too slow and some will say it was too harsh. This is what we want. Yes, they will make some changes to their infrastructure to deal with a contagion of this sort but their media will make a point to embarrass the government. They will point to institutions that closed or the events that were cancelled and they will conclude that this indeed was an over-reaction to the virus and they will blame President Hunter for 'disrupting' their economy. The next time a virus is reported, they will be very reticent to over-react again and their lack of action and delay will truly decimate their country before they can even understand what is happening. According to a famous American fable, their government will metaphorically 'Cry Wolf' during the trial run. They will ignore the 'real wolf', Virus Two, a year later.

"So … my friends, are we in agreement that Wei's plan is sound and we should move forward?"

"I still have hesitations Xin. America is

unpredictable. I can envision a scenario where they successfully combat the trial run infection and they do prepare accordingly and then we are hurt because of their eventual manufacturing diversification."

Wei worked on Min. "Min, that is the benefit of the trail-run. If we do not see the exact reaction we want, nothing more needs to be done. If we do not want to enact Phase Two, we do not have to. We will not be blamed for the trial run; we will co-exist amongst the world community and be seen as being hurt just as much as any other country and we will feign our support for America. As I said earlier, they may be planning to diversify their manufacturing anyway. This is ok because *we* don't want our factories as dependent on American manufacturing either for our long-term future."

Zhang Min and the other Politburo members nodded their heads in agreement and so the plan was adopted.

Li Wei left the meeting and went back to his office. As he sat down, he leaned back and looked out the window at the beautiful Peking Willow trees that line the sidewalk. His eyes closed as he took a deep breath. *Could this be his legacy? Will this action permanently ink his name as an important Chinese historical figure?* He's always believed that he was special. That feeling comes from the west – his education did influence him but his culture and Chinese heritage always tempered showing that outwardly. He knew this was a bit out of character for a Chinese Politburo member. He should do as his colleagues and be happy to simply be a good steward of China's thousand-year plan. He should not want for fame. He rationalized his behavior because *they* sent him to the west to be educated. *They* sent him to learn the mindset of the American and understand the culture. He has been a loyal soldier. He continued to tell himself these truths in order to make himself feel better as to his own life. More importantly, his plan, which had been brewing in his mind for years, was now accepted.

CHAPTER 2

P arker Jane Hall poured her coffee into her new travel
mug, put her phone in her purse, and hustled out the
door. It was Monday morning and she immediately realized
it was cold and that she forgot her coat. She quickly turned
around, pushed the door open, and grabbed her pea coat
which was hanging by the door. She started her used Nissan
Maxima and put it in drive. Her commute was only about 25
minutes but it all depended on traffic. She hopped on I-295
and headed north. Parker Hall was a senior at Georgetown
University and had gotten her internship at the Department
of Homeland Security through her tenured economics
professor, Jared Short. Short had a friend at Homeland
Security and pulled a string for his best student. This is the
way it worked, especially in Washington. Parker knew this
and was grateful. She learned how to play the game from her
father. Nathan Hall served for over a decade at the State

Department under two presidents. Parker saw firsthand how the business of politics worked. She found it slightly distasteful but it didn't really bother her. Her ambition, to succeed and make her father proud, was more important than any feigned glad-handing she'd have to do.

Parker had set up her internship to be full-time, three days a week with all her classes taking place on Thursday and Friday. Parker figured that Friday was a waste day in government service–early beer call or people not even in the building; and Thursday, well, she'd miss one day but she'd be there for three days at the beginning of the week which was all that counted. Just then her phone rang She steered with her knees as she put in her Bluetooth. "Hello Josh."

"Hi Parker. Are you on your way in? There's something brewing here."

"I'm just passing the Washington Navy Yard, be there in fifteen."

"Ok, just come to the conference room on the fifth floor, we're gathering in there."

"What's up?" she asked.

"Just come to the fifth floor."

"Will do. Bye"

Though Parker was an intern, she had been highly recommended by Professor Short. For Homeland Security Director Roger Thomas, Jared Short's word carried a lot of weight. Parker had only been on the job for a couple of months, but had shown leadership and an uncanny knack for spotting potential issues. Ms. Hall was also easy on the eyes and Director Thomas wished he was twenty-five years younger. He was fully prepared to make her a full-time offer after her internship came to a close and she graduated Georgetown. In fact, he made a note on his calendar to call Jared Short, thank him again, and find out where her mind was on her aspirations after school. Roger Thomas was a lifer and so hiring new young interns was something he looked forward to every year.

Parker whipped into the parking garage and by some miracle found a parking spot on the first floor. She usually had to head up to the top of the seven-level parking structure in order to find a space. She smiled pulling in, *maybe it's my lucky day.*

———————————————

Tim Chen had graduated from Georgetown earlier that spring. He graduated with high honors and received a degree in International Business and Medicine. He was a first-generation American, having been born in Roanoke, Virginia. His parents had come to the U.S. originally on work visas. His mother and father were both college graduates of Peking University, Beijing China. Peking University is ranked number two in China and is known for its prestigious research facilities and programs, especially in the areas of science and chemistry. His mother and father both found jobs at an international pharmaceutical company located in Shanghai and their quick rise within the company, and their fluency in English, made them a perfect choice for a transfer to the pharma's office in Virginia, USA. Tim followed in his parent's footsteps, pursuing his education in the sciences. During the summer between his junior and senior years, he had flown to China's Shandong province where his grandparents live. The town, Jinan, is about a four-and-a-half-hour drive from Beijing. He'd made the same trip with his parents about five years prior, but he was so young he couldn't take advantage of the culture or the nightlife. Tim spent time with his grandparents but he also made sure to take advantage of his freedom as a college student to explore Beijing and its growing millennial population.

Though Tim loved his American upbringing, he had always been fascinated by his Chinese heritage. His parents raised him in a typical, upper-middle class home where he and his sister were always home for family dinner. Tim's parents were good teachers and always taught him to be humble in all his endeavors. He worked hard as his cultural work ethic demanded. He flourished academically in high school and was admitted to Georgetown after having applied for early decision. During his freshman year at Georgetown, Tim went to his share of parties but he was never really comfortable. He was not a big drinker; neither were his parents. He understood why his friends partied but Tim was concerned about, and distracted by, other things. Sometimes this internal conflict made for strange interactions with his friends, but they all knew Tim as a nice person, intensely focused on academics, like most Chinese-Americans. But there was one friend that 'got him.' Tim met Parker Hall when he was a junior and Parker was a sophomore. Tim was attracted to her intelligence but often, he admitted to himself, there was something else that made her special. Parker would often come over to Tim's dorm room to study, even though they only had one class together. Tim would often catch Parker staring off into the distance. He could relate to this kind of trance because he often daydreamed, especially in class. He knew that he and Parker would always be friends because as the Chinese would say, they were 'old souls.' Even though Tim knew Parker was an attractive young woman, he was happy with their relationship being strictly platonic.

After graduating from Georgetown, Tim followed his heart and accepted a position in a biological research facility outside of Beijing. He'd only been in China a few months but the Sunhexiang Bio Research lab was already keeping him busy working endless hours. Tim had much to learn but his supervisors were very pleased with his progress, and he was given more and more responsibility as a result. He liked his job; he was learning much, and although he couldn't put his finger on exactly why, being in China made him 'feel' very good.

When he left work for the day, he looked forward to meeting his friends for 'hot pot' at a local restaurant. Tim lived at the northeastern edge of Beijing. His apartment was modest but he was still close enough to the inner city to ride mass transit to the bars and restaurants. Because his commute to Sunhexiang was only about 20 minutes, he had purchased a small motorbike to make the rather quick trek. Some of his co-workers also lived near him so if the weather wasn't conducive to riding a motorbike, he'd hitch a ride with one of them. He liked the fact that he traveled against the traffic to and from work. For the most part, Tim Lee was happy living and working in China. He had followed his calling, and though he missed his friends in America, he was proud of his work and his continued exploration of his heritage.

CHAPTER 3

Parker walked into the fifth floor conference room. She recognized most of the faces, but there were a few people she didn't. She did recognize their security badges–one person from State and the other from NSA. Her boss, Homeland Security Director Roger Thomas, was there as well. He was a holdover from the previous administration. He had come up through the ranks like a good government employee. He thought that after the new administration came into office a few years prior, he would have been booted. It was fairly normal for a new administration, especially one from the opposing political party, to clean house at the director level. The current president was apparently so busy with other tasks that he decided to leave him in place. For the most part, Roger Thomas had kept his head down and avoided the limelight so there was really no controversy surrounding his role as Director of Homeland

Security. He was very loyal to the U.S. government. He liked the bureaucracy and the pace. Even though he was the Director, his decisions were based for the most part on collective thought. He was not a cowboy and so he'd been able to fly low, under the radar, even after making or going along with poor decisions. Parker nodded a hello and took her seat.

"You're late."

"I'm sorry Sir, the traffic was murder."

Just then Josh projected a map of China on the screen.

Director Thomas continued. "This is the city of Tianjin. It's located along the northern coast of China. The metropolis is the largest coastal city in the country, and it is one of four municipalities and one of five of China's national central cities. As of 2016, the reported population was 11.6 million. It's probably up to 15-17 million by now. Currently, we're getting some intelligence from an agent we have in China that there's some kind of viral outbreak in the city and the Chinese government is taking steps to involuntarily quarantine people."

"Outbreak? What do you mean?" said the woman from State.

"Some sort of flu strain has got everyone's panties in a bunch and is having an effect on a lot of the people there."

Josh Bennett had worked at Homeland Security for about a year, so he felt comfortable speaking up. "There are reports that people are becoming infected rather quickly, many are being hospitalized and they're reporting some deaths."

Once again, the woman from State chimed in. "What does the CDC think?"

Roger Thomas replied nonchalantly, "Ma'am, we've got a call with the folks at CDC in about an hour. I suspect that they will report that this will blow over and simply be confined to the area of the outbreak."

"I'm not so sure." reflected the guy from NSA. "Has the White House been informed?"

Director Thomas smiled. "Way too early to put this on their radar. This may be just the seasonal flu."

Parker finally spoke. "Has anyone contacted the Chinese Ambassador?"

"We've reached out to him and we should be meeting later this afternoon," the woman from State responded.

Director Thomas then concluded, "I'm putting this in the mix for us because, who knows, it might become a thing or it might not."

The man from NSA started to rise from his chair. "Ok, keep me in the loop and I'll do the same."

"I'll let you know what the Chinese Ambassador has to say. Other than that, the Secretary has a full schedule and we're all slammed at State, so I'm going to resist telling her about this right now until we know more."

The conference room cleared except for a few. Director Thomas began to speak but stopped and waited until the door closed. Parker gave the Director a puzzled look. She obviously did not know that every conference room at Homeland Security and most other sensitive government agencies was soundproof.

"I'm too busy to deal with this, but I'd like you two to poke around and see if you can gather any intel like how this 'flu' started. Understood?"

Parker and Josh responded together. "Yes, Sir."

"Sir, can I ask a question?

"Sure, Ms. Hall, make it fast."

"Why do you think this is a Homeland Security matter at this point?"

"I don't. Someone at State does. The question you want to ask me is, 'Why do I think it *might be* a Homeland Security Issue?' The CIA and NSA have known for years that China's bio-weapon program was robust, like many countries including ours. Add to that our lovely new president who is like no other. He has single-handedly decided to take on China over trade. Don't get me started on that subject."

"I don't get it Sir, what does that mean?"

"What that means, Mr. Bennett, is that the U.S. is poking the bear. There was an NSA meeting last Friday suggesting that China may not simply roll over at this point in history. A Chinese historian made a point of giving all of us in the meeting a little lesson on Chinese history and how their culture, and more importantly their government, views China's roll on the Earth. So . . . it means for you two that someone decided that China is on our radar in a big way and even though this 'outbreak' is probably just a bad strain of the seasonal flu, we cannot just take it as business as usual. I want weekly briefings for a while, even though I'm confident you're not going to find anything devious. That's for fiction novelists."

"We're on it. Sir, can I ask you one more thing. Do you personally believe the Chinese government had something to do with this outbreak?"

"No. I don't, Ms. Hall. I also don't believe we should be in a trade war with China. They are a manufacturing partner and a damn good one. Have you ever been over there?" He asked rhetorically. "They eat weird things like bats, snakes, pangolins–turns my stomach. I think this was something that was born out of their 'wet markets'. How serious this is I have no idea. Even though the 'historians' say that China wants to rule the earth, I don't buy it. It's the twenty-first century. China produces half the crap the world buys. They don't want this anymore than anyone else. I for one don't want to pay fifty bucks for a pair of flip-flops either. Off you go."

Li Wei walked in the brisk fall air with a purpose. He was on his way to the Politburo building but not for a council meeting just yet, that would come later this morning. As he walked in, he turned right instead of left. He proceeded down a corridor, stopped, inserted a key into an elevator control panel. The elevator opened and as he got in, he made sure there was no one behind him. The elevator took him down three floors. As he stepped out, he turned left and walked to the end of the hall where there were two armed guards in front of a door. He presented his identification and then put his fingers on the fingerprint reader. As the internal laser scanned his fingerprint, he glanced over at the guards. Though they appeared to pay no attention, they could see his every move through their peripheral vision. Just then the door clicked open and as Wei stepped into the operations center, it looked like a spaceship. Monitors were everywhere and three people were at consoles with headsets on. Gao Tang was a mid-level soldier in charge of the ops center. Of course, every mid-level soldier desired to be a higher-level soldier someday so Tang snapped to attention and immediately walked over to Wei as soon as he spotted him.

"Good morning, Sir. I hope all is well with you this morning."

"Good morning Tang. How are we doing?"

"It would appear that all is going well so far. We have successfully infected an animal in one of our live wet markets and the bio-weapon has reacted just as our scientists have predicted. The virus has jumped from animal to human. It looks perfectly natural."

"What are the numbers?

"It's early Sir, but 500 infected, 25 dead."

"It's killing faster than I thought."

"It's killing the weak among us. The scientists that I spoke to at the Sunhexiang Bio Research lab said this might happen. The virus is very contagious and spreading rapidly. The researchers said that it might have an adverse effect on the elderly population."

"Very good Tang, exactly what I wanted. This will further scare the west. Their culture does not take death easily. They believe in keeping their elderly alive even through extreme pain." Wei shook his head, "That is not our way."

Gao Tang showed no emotion as he listened to Li Wei. Tang knew what Wei meant. Chinese culture celebrated their elderly, but avoided keeping them alive to experience unnecessary pain. In their culture, it was better to leave this earth with your faculties intact than to be kept alive in a vegetative state. Respect and dignity carried high importance in Chinese culture. After spending considerable time reviewing data and maps projected on the monitors, Wei left the room and proceeded to his regularly scheduled Politburo meeting. He allowed himself a smile as walked to the meeting. He wondered what part of him was smiling, the Americanized part or the Chinese part. He would have liked to think further about that as it was indeed an intellectually interesting question, but just then he entered the Politburo Chamber and had to vacate his thoughts in order to update his colleagues on the plan.

As Parker arrived home after work, she turned the ignition off and just sat in her car. She was already thinking about her plan of attack. She knew she had to dig deep into Chinese social media to uncover what was happening on the ground. This wouldn't be easy because the Chinese government had a stranglehold on the Chinese people's freedom to post negative information on the internet. As she exited her car, her neighbor, Elliott Myles, exited from his front door in a robe and walked to his mailbox. He looked like he just got out of bed, scruffy beard and all. Parker knew a little about him from talking with her dad and briefly talking to Mr. Myles when her family bought the townhouse three years ago that she now lives in. It was unclear as to what Mr. Myles did at the National Security Agency or the area in which he worked, but the rumor was that he got canned, or actually asked to retire some years ago. Parker's dad had told her that Elliott Myles had an undergraduate degree in biology and a Master's in Public Health. She waved to him and mouthed *Hi* as she unlocked her front door and walked in.

Elliott smiled and waved to Parker, got his mail, and walked back inside his home. He knew that his work at the NSA had caused him to be secretive and suspicious which didn't lend itself to personal relationships. There were many times that he lamented his path in life and wondered what his life would be like if he hadn't answered that ad thirty-some years ago to work at the NSA. He often thought that he didn't accomplish much in life. Of course, that fact was exactly the opposite. Elliott had begun at the NSA as an intelligence officer which in those days was another name for data compiler and 'coffee getter.' He didn't mind as it was easy work and he was learning. After a couple of years, he was promoted to an Information Management Specialist, which simply meant he was the one who *asked* the intelligence officers to compile data and get coffee. Before he knew it, he was elevated to Director of Information. The post was still a few rungs below real insider status, but he took the promotion happily. This post included some travel and for that he was grateful. He loved to travel and missed it. As a teenager, his father worked for a major airline and he often remembered flying 'standby' with his dad, enjoying First Class on many flights. His travel for this post mainly consisted of meeting with local NSA data analysts posted around the world, but his particular responsibilities mainly took him to Asia about ten times per year. Elliott had amassed quite a bit of knowledge (not to mention frequent flyer miles) about Asia and the Asian culture over the years he traveled. It was this knowledge would eventually lead to his being fired by the NSA.

CHAPTER 4

Over the course of the next several weeks, Parker worked longer hours than normal trying to figure out if there was any evidence that China released the virus on purpose. She first had to figure out if they made the damn thing. It was apparent that she was getting frustrated and Josh wasn't helping.

"Can we stop for tonight?"

"Just one more site. I'm trying to find—"

"Seriously. I'd like to go get a drink before the governor orders all bars closed. They say that might happen tomorrow."

Parker was typing and talking at the same time, "You think they'll do that?"

"Where have you been? Haven't you been watching the news? California, Florida, New York and Texas have all virtually shut down. It's crazy. A lot of my friends have already been laid off. You think we'll lose our jobs?"

Parker was still focused on her computer screen, "Uh … what? When? Wait–what did you say?"

"I asked you if you thought we're going to lose our jobs?"

"No."

"Parker! No, what?? Do you know something I don't?"

Parker finally looked up from her computer and leaned back in her chair. "No, I don't think we're going to lose our jobs. We're the only ones on this project and it's pretty important."

"Yeah well, I don't know. We haven't found anything yet. I guess I could deliver pizzas."

"C'mon. Let's grab that last drink, I've got a theory I want to run by you."

Wei was pleased with himself and knew the members would be as well. "Good morning, gentlemen. I trust you have all seen the news coverage from the West."

"Yes, but it is hard to watch. It's hard to know what is fact and what they are making up."

"Yes, Shou, I told you that is a huge fault of their media. Anyway. I'd like to start us off with an update on Phase One, the trial run."

"Please proceed, Wei."

"Thank you, Fu. As you are aware, we released the Virus One bio-weapon into the targeted live wet market approximately four weeks ago. The virus has now successfully jumped from animal to human and is spreading throughout our country. Early numbers indicate five hundred infected and twenty-five dead."

"How many are hospitalized?"

"I do not know that, Xin, but I will find out."

"It seems rather pedestrian so far. How will it get to America and the rest of the world?" asked Min.

"Our scientists have informed me that biologicals, like this virus, spread slowly at first but then speed up exponentially infecting many more day after day. To make sure, we have purposefully infected some of our agents and sent them on airplanes to America and several other countries."

"When is it projected to hit America?"

"It's already there, Min. They are trying to figure out what is going on. They only have very few reported cases at present."

Fu asked the group, "So we wait?"

"Yes. I will report back in ten days. We should have more significant numbers at that time." Wei slowly sipped his tea while eyeing the members.

———————————

Parker and Josh were seated at a local watering hole. It was busy, but there was an eerie feeling in the bar.

"Should we be scared of this? Isn't it just a bad case of the flu?" Josh asked as he handed the waitress his credit card.

"I have no idea. I watch the news just like you. Tough to tell if they are embellishing or not."

"I'm more worried about my job."

Parker stared at him. "Stop. We're not going to lose our damn jobs. Ok, so let me tell you my thoughts so far."

"Go ahead, don't mind me, I'm just going to drink my beer and enjoy our last bit of freedom."

"Seriously, just listen! So of course, I've been getting nowhere with the regular Chinese government sites. They seem to be downplaying the virus."

Josh responded while scanning the bar. "We've known that for a couple of weeks now."

"I've been tapping into some 'black' sites. Sites that the government hasn't closed down. And people are reporting some strange stuff."

"What do you mean 'strange'?"

"Like people are saying that they've been going to wet markets for years and they are well aware of possible infection and they know how to handle themselves and the animals."

"So?"

"Soooo, don't you think it's odd that the Chinese government, who we know lies all the time, has put out the story that this virus originated in one of their wet markets?"

"I think I've had too many beers. I'm not following."

"Pay attention, Joshua! China hates to look bad about anything to do with their country. Their wet markets have been a source of attack by some journalists for years, claiming they are cruel and unsanitary. If this actually started in one of their wet markets, wouldn't China put out some other story to deflect people thinking badly about their wet markets?"

"Ok, I'll play along. You think that because China lies about the truth, and because they are saying that the virus started in a wet market, that *must* not be the truth? Right? That's your logic?"

"Yes, exactly. I've also read reports that the alleged wet market where this supposedly happened was closed *prior* to the outbreak. They are also saying that none of the people that worked there can be located."

"So it's a bit peculiar. I'm still not making the leap to a bio-weapon."

"I get that. But … it's getting interesting."

"Ok, well you keep going and I'll keep playing along."

Josh was a little buzzed and wasn't really listening. He was a viral young man and was too pre-occupied checking out the local female persuasion. But Parker wouldn't have noticed anyway. She opened her iPhone 11 and tapped the mail app. She started writing.

Timothy, how are you? I miss you! I hope you are well and safe during this time. Tell me what you are doing. How is work going? Reply soon!

– Hugs, PJ

She tapped send and a few seconds later closed her phone. She loved a good mystery and she wasn't one to exaggerate, but she was very curious. Call it women's intuition, but she felt that the Chinese government was hiding something. She would gage Tim's reaction, though she instinctively knew it would be metered because the Chinese government was monitoring their citizens' emails, texts, and social media posts.

Just then she realized Josh was no longer sitting next to her. Parker scanned the bar and spotted him flirting with a tall blonde. She approached Josh and the girl and interrupted their conversation when she tugged on his sleeve. "C'mon Casanova," she said. "We have an early morning and it is time to get you home."

CHAPTER 5

It was now three months into the trial run and Li Wei was in his office looking at the daily numbers. It's happening, he thought to himself. What Wei was seeing was a worldwide pandemic developing. News reports from around the world were covering the story. The stock markets throughout the world, including the U.S.'s Dow Jones Industrial and Nasdaq, were dropping like rocks. President Hunter was being criticized by his rival's media for not taking action soon enough, but Wei knew that was just rhetoric. The U.S. president had actually stopped flights from China to the U.S. six weeks earlier, but it didn't matter. China's actions were those that only a communist state could take.

Though Wei predicted that China would lose citizens, they had to show the world that they were concerned about the spread. The government went through the public exercise of building an additional hospital in the infected city in seven days. They quarantined whole prefects of their population with armed guards and gates. Their people were only allowed out of the their 'area' for food and then just once per week. In some cases, the military even welded shut the doors and windows of persons they knew to be infected. Wei had seen to these measures so that the world could witness China reeling from the crisis and trying to do the best they could. Wei knew that many of his countrymen were simply sacrificed for the greater good and it didn't really matter what the hospitals and doctors did to try to alleviate the symptoms of the infected. If your body was weak, or inflicted with another underlying disease, you probably weren't going to live. Once a person was sick to the point of needing to go the hospital, it was too late–especially if they were elderly.

Doctors tried various known flu remedies and breathing machines called ventilators, but it was mostly to no avail. Wei looked outside his office at some of the leaf-less trees, living through their yearly shedding of leaves to be re-born again in spring. Wei made a mental note to contact the lead virologist and his long-time friend at the Sunhexiang Bio Research lab to thank him again for his team's effort in creating Virus One. As the days passed and Wei watched the response of the world, and especially America, he knew that option three, doing nothing after the trial run, was becoming less of choice. China would resolve this now one way or another. America would be driven to its knees and China, once again, would be the only world superpower. He had to calm himself. His Americanized side wanted to rejoice and get excited, but the devout Chinaman that he was echoed one word inside his head, 'Patience.'

America and most of the world was on lock down. People were told to stay inside their homes. Businesses were closed, some supplies were getting scarce, and there were long lines of frustrated customers at food stores. The U.S. reported a dramatic rise in unemployment and, most significantly, was treating this as potentially being worse than the 1918 Spanish flu, even though only a few thousand people had died so far from Virus One. Wei was actually a bit surprised that the U.S. reacted so dramatically. He thought to himself that the American people were strange. He was actually disappointed that his plan was creating so much panic. For him, it made no sense to panic over 3,000 deaths when the seasonal flu kills 35,000. Wei shook his head. The U.S. and most of the rest of the world were destroying their economies much like one would scuttle a ship. When a ship sinks, it tends to do so slowly, but you know it's sinking and it's hard to watch and nearly irreversible. Nonetheless, the hopeless feeling of not being in control while something dies is an odd feeling. Americans were watching their fortunes, jobs, and businesses die a slow death and they were doing this to themselves. Remarkable, Wei thought. China was reeling too. Wei knew this would happen, but he also knew that the Chinese people were much more resilient than Americans. The centuries of strife and struggle in China had created people that knew what suffering was and they lived their lives accordingly. Other than the Americans that fought in various wars, Americans were soft. Suffering for them was having to wait for the latest release of a video game or not having Wi-Fi for an hour. Li Wei understood that America knew nothing of suffering, but she would soon find out as the weeks and months progressed.

"Fifteen minutes, sir," an aide said to President Hunter. The President didn't respond. He was sitting behind his Oval Office desk looking at his notes. He was at his best when he spoke from his own notes. He didn't remember when he became relaxed about speaking, maybe from his years as an entrepreneur. He certainly credited his law school training with being able to feel extremely comfortable at not only speaking in public but fielding questions. As an attorney, he knew he inherently had a leg up on any media person for the age-old adage was true, never argue with a lawyer–unless you're another lawyer. He stood, donned his jacket, and headed out to the Rose Garden. He knew he had to instill hope and confidence for the American people, yet at the same time, balance the realities of the quick spreading infection and demolished economy.

He had been engaged since the first public reports of the outbreak in China. He'd also remembered watching the movie, 'Contagion,' and though it was a movie, he knew that movies and so called 'science fiction' novels had a way of becoming reality, or at least some of it becoming reality. He was a controversial leader. He knew that. He was a strong constitutionalist which certainly rubbed those on the 'left' the wrong way. More importantly, he was a logical thinking leader who apparently made sense to many

Americans because he got elected. In response to this crisis, he had to try do everything a government could do, short of waving a magic wand, to curtail death while at the same time figuring out how to not completely ruin the economy. When he was first alerted to the outbreak several months ago, he started doing some research on his own about the 1918 Spanish Flu pandemic. Interestingly, at that time, the federal government really didn't do anything close to what the current health experts had advised him to do. At that time, the U.S. government was totally consumed with World War I. He knew that approximately 105 million U.S. citizens were infected and of those, anywhere from 500,000 to 675,000 people died. No businesses were shut down, no state governors mandated 'shelter-in-place' orders. His thought process on this was two-fold. One, even though about 10,000 U.S. citizens had died so far, was shutting down the economy an overreaction? He knew that there would be debate on that for millennia. He also knew that the political and social media climate these days was not even close to what was happening in 1918. No good answer either way.

"Sir, we're ready," the aide said.

The President snapped back to reality, walked to the podium, and began to address the nation.

Parker, Josh, and many other employees were now working remotely from home. Zoom meetings filled their days. Most

Americans were adapting to the new routine. Get up, make coffee, work in sweats till your first Zoom video call for which you had to change into a nice shirt, hop on the treadmill or bike, back to the computer, shower, hit the store for some food if necessary, back to the computer, then dinner. Since the meeting with Josh in the bar, which coincidentally did happen to be the last night before the governor shut down all non-essential businesses, Parker had not made any real headway with her investigation. Tim Chen had responded to her email cryptically, and Parker really didn't give it much thought. She simply advanced the notion that Tim was avoiding alerting the Chinese email monitors. She needed to talk to him though; it had now been over a month since she sent him the email. Parker was about to pour her coffee when she got a message from Josh on her secure chat.

"Come into the office ASAP. The Director wants to see us."

As she finished reading the text, she tried again to pour her coffee, but abruptly stopped. She switched from the cute oversized mug her Dad had bought her while they were vacationing in South Carolina last year to her trusty travel mug. She finally poured her coffee, grabbed a light coat as it was now March, and headed for the door. As she grabbed her keys, she went into slow motion and stopped in her tracks. Her laptop was in her bag, but she didn't need it. Her message would be short. She started typing on her phone.

Timothy, I miss you! How are you? Remember the time we went to the Nationals game and you caught

that foul ball? That was so much fun. Talk to you
soon.

– Hugs, PJ

She tapped send, put her phone in her purse, and ran out the
door.

Li Wei headed over to the operations center in the Politburo
building. He wanted to see the infection map first-hand on
the big monitor. Normally, he should have been able to pull
it up on his desk computer, but Wei instituted strict
lockdown procedures of digital assets with regards to the
trial run. He did not want 'prying eyes,' as the West would
say, to interrupt their plans. He also needed the exercise.
The walk to the Politburo building was only about a quarter-
mile, but it would do him good to stretch. As Wei entered
the secure room, he immediately started asking questions.
"Show me the infection numbers and deaths." A man in a
military uniform immediately started typing and pressing
keys on his keyboard. Wei made a mental note of the
figures. 200,000 infected and 8,000 deaths. Not bad, Wei
thought to himself. Those other 192,000 Chinese would
recover and develop herd immunity. The 'herd' concept
basically states that if a healthy person gets the virus,
survives and develops anti-bodies naturally, the virus will

have nowhere to go. The recovered person will not infect an otherwise uninfected person. Wei thought to himself that he didn't want to report those numbers to the World Health Organization. He barked an order and Gao Tang snapped to.

"Yessir."

"Send the daily report to the W.H.O. and state the following numbers: 82,345 infected and 2,750 deaths."

The young man nodded as he wrote down the numbers and immediately left the area. Wei knew it was time to turn the panic up on the U.S. He would begin to vastly underreport the infection and death numbers. At first this would give the U.S. and the world hope that the virus was mitigating naturally. In reality, even though China's numbers would be increasing, it would appear to the world that the U.S. was the new epi-center of the outbreak. Wei could imagine the U.S. media reports. *China is leading the fight as to the virus. Their initial and immediate lockdown procedures mitigated their infection and death rates. Our president was late to the game and now has blood on his hands due to the continued increase in infections and deaths across the U.S.* As he walked back to his office, he shook his head. He actually felt a little sorry for the Americans. When he was at school, he did have American friends. These were ordinary people that were nice to him and he enjoyed their company. However, Wei always thought that they were in many ways ignorant. They called him 'Lee.' They didn't understand that 'Li' was his last name and 'Wei' his first. Whatever. He didn't care. But he did take note. He was being taught at their finest university and he was also getting an education from ordinary Americans and their behavior. He understood the bigger picture, but still couldn't help thinking about some of his former classmates. Once back at his office, his lunch was brought to him. Traditional Chinese wonton soup. This was not the fake U.S. version that he was forced to eat time and time again while at school. His soup was steaming and he knew that the broth had simmered for days, the vegetables fresh and the wontons handmade today. As he sipped his soup from a traditional Asian soup spoon, he made a loud slurping sound. He remembered how this unnerved his American friends. He friends never understood that this method of sipping cooled the soup as you took it into your mouth. He muttered under his breath, *fools*, as he refocused his mind to the issues at hand. Yes, he said to himself. It is time for us to begin our retraining of our factories. He called his assistant, Liu Xiang, into his office.

"Xiang, please contact Mr. Tao Hanwen. Please tell him to come to my office now."

————————————

Elliott Myles was at his computer. There was really nothing to do, as the state was under a lockdown order. He had a treadmill, one of the fancy ones with a monitor that had the instructors who encouraged you and led you through a workout. He hadn't used that in months; he just didn't feel like working out and found himself cussing at the instructors in the video when it got too hard. It's not that he was worried. He knew what was happening better than anyone.

When he was at NSA and traveling around the world, Elliott saw first-hand plenty of virial outbreaks and plenty of 'quarantine type' measures put into place. He was actually surprised that this crisis, this virus, didn't happen sooner in the U.S. He'd been warning of this type of outbreak to his superiors for years. Unfortunately, SARS, MERS, and the Swine Flu were all infections that never really took hold in the U.S. It was a cruel joke by mother nature herself. These infections were serious in other parts of the world and those countries and populations heeded steps to avoid being infected. He'd been in Hong Kong and China twenty years prior and seen many people wearing masks as a common everyday occurrence. These countries had gone through these infections and, although a country can never be fully prepared for an outbreak, Asia understood them and had procedures and processes that needed to be put in place as soon as an infection was to strike. The U.S., on the other hand, didn't see large numbers of deaths from these worldwide outbreaks. Because of having an ocean on two sides of the four sides of the country, the U.S. was naturally semi-quarantined. Also, the U.S. has never even gotten mildly upset at the 35,000 plus people that die every year of the seasonal flu. He had always thought though that this was a ticking time bomb, either form a natural occurrence or a deliberate one. Elliott still had some ways of getting information, be it classified or otherwise. He typed in a website and began reading. His facial expression immediately began to change from one of relative indifference to one of grave concern.

CHAPTER 6

T im Chen was relaxing after breakfast. It was Sunday and thank God, he didn't need to go to work. Many in China were ordered to stay home because of the crisis, but he was still needed at work. His work was deemed essential to the Chinese government. He had fun driving his motorbike as the weather was getting a bit warmer, but more importantly, there was no one else on the road. In actuality, there were a few cars and trucks, but nothing like the ordinary traffic he'd become accustomed to. These days he tried to enjoy his ride into work.

Tim was watching a movie, a DVD he brought with him from the U.S. when he moved to China. He knew he wasn't going to be able to watch Netflix in China, so he thought bringing a few classic movies he loved might help him if he got lonely or felt isolated from his parents or American friends. He'd seen this one many times, but he didn't care because it was an awesome movie. It was Die Hard with Bruce Willis.

Bruce was just about to say his classic line, 'Yippee-Kay-Yay Motherfucker,' when Tim's phone beeped. It was an incoming email. Probably one of the many he'd been receiving on a daily basis consisting of further instructions regarding social distancing, which prefects were going into lockdown, and which ones were coming out of quarantine. Tim hesitated before hitting the pause button. What the hell, he thought, I should look at the email. The movie will be there when he was done.

Tim picked up his phone and saw it was a message from Parker. He hated it when she called him Timothy; no one called him that except for her. As he read the email, he was confused at first. He thought to himself, *I never caught a foul ball at ...*, then he realized what it meant. Parker was speaking in code. They used to use code when they were both at a party and wanted to leave, but didn't want to seem rude or not cool. He immediately understood it to mean that *she wants me to use an alias email to contact her and then she would have further instructions*. Tim grabbed his computer. He launched an incognito browser and went to a website where he had an email account that he rarely used. He typed a message and sent it to Parker's alternate Gmail address.

I still have the ball I caught. Ready to go to the game.

There was no signature and he didn't leave a salutation. He would now wait for Parker to figure out a secure way they could talk. He closed his laptop and paused for a minute. He knew Parker pretty well; she didn't cry wolf. He also knew she worked at Homeland Security. He thought that he should be more aware at work, after all it was a bio-research facility. He wasn't aware of any weaponizing of any bio agents. The lab had many floors, labs, and employees so he certainly didn't know what was going on everywhere. His team was focused on agricultural viruses from insects and possible vaccines for them. He'd wished he was on the team that was working on the vaccine for the current human virus outbreak. He knew he could contribute to finding a cure. As he pressed play on his remote and the movie resumed, he put aside his thoughts and once again focused on the comfort of knowing exactly what was coming next in the movie.

"Sir, Mr. Tao Hanwen is here to see you."

Wei responded immediately, "Send him in Xiang." Tao Hanwen walked in. He was a tall man with a long background in manufacturing. He was appointed to the government position of Head of Manufacturing nearly a decade ago. He had helped implement the tremendous surge over the last twenty years of U.S. companies using China factories for their products. He helped guide big and small factories alike from the north to the south and everywhere in between. His techniques for helping Foxconn and Apple work through huge assembly line issues and distribution needs were well known. Wei asked him to sit.

"Hanwen, how have you been?"

"I've been staying healthy, but I'm concerned about our factories. They are losing business."

"I realize that as does the Council."

"We must get our factories producing again. When do you—" Wei raised his hand. Hanwen immediately stopped talking.

"We have evaluated the current problem and we believe that this crisis might be a blessing for us. We believe that there is too much dependence on American companies and the quantities of the products they want to produce. I want you to put a plan in place that allows our factories to temporarily downsize and pull back from doing as much business as we previously have done before the crisis."

"With all due respect Sir, we don't have to put a plan in place. The virus is taking care of that for us. Our factories are not working or certainly not working near their previous capacities."

Li Wei knew he had to be careful about how he pitched this to Tao Hanwen. Hanwen was not in the inner circle and was not aware of the trial run plan. He was simply reacting to what he thought was a natural disaster. Wei had a great deal of respect for Hanwen and his experience with factories and manufacturing. He needed to be tactful with his demands and allow Hanwen to embrace the change on his own, as a wholly separate plan in reaction to the crisis.

"Hanwen, I think I am not making myself clear and

I apologize. Let me express myself in this way. How much of our manufacturing, as a percentage of factory capacity, on average, is used for U.S. companies?"

Hanwen thought for a second looking upward. "Probably on average 20% as a percentage of world exports to the U.S … but … there are certain sectors of manufacturing that account for much more. We have been blessed that our country manufactures 90% of the world's rare-earth metals. These metals are used in a wide array of products including computers, phones, electric motors, electric guitar pickups, and many other hi-tech components so that is why the 20% number might be misleading. These metals are also used by the U.S. military in their air-to-air missiles and even their stealth technology. Everyone gets these metals from us, whether we do the manufacturing or not."

"I see, the 20% number is indeed misleading. Nonetheless, it has been discussed by the Politburo council and we believe that there is an opportunity to divest some of our manufacturing from the U.S. and into other countries. I would be curious to your thoughts."

"Sir, this is a very interesting thought. I have believed for many years now that we are too reliant on the U.S. Of course, that is not what the West reports. The U.S. always sees itself as the center of the universe. Those in their country that oppose our partnership are always reporting that *they* are too dependent on us. This current crisis has already caused a contraction of our business with the U.S., as well as most all countries. If you would have come to me six months ago, the process of lessening dependence on the U.S. would have had a two-step component. The first step would have been to deliberately contract and the second step would have been to reconfigure to a lower production rate while actively finding new customers in other countries. However, we have been given a gift with the natural occurrence of this virus. Step one has been taken care of for us, naturally. If we are to lessen our dependence on the U.S., our responsibility now is to *not* accept new manufacturing from the U.S. We shouldn't completely turn off our manufacturing to the U.S., but aim to drastically reduce it."

"I knew I could count on you for a very reasoned analysis. Let me ask two additional questions. In your opinion, first, how do our factory leaders react to the U.S. orders, and two what will be the U.S. companies' reactions?"

Tao Hanwen raised a finger signaling to Wei to please give him a minute to think. Hanwen pondered the question. He was a thoughtful man and had always conducted himself with professionalism. He led his life this way and it has served him well, whether he was talking to Li Wei, a Politburo member, or a small factory manager.

"Sir, thank you for giving me a minute to think about your questions and answer you thoughtfully. I believe the answer to your first question is rather simple and natural, given the current crisis. We can train and counsel our factory owners and managers to say that because of the virus, they just do not have the manpower necessary to accept orders at the previous volumes as before the crisis. That should be very understandable and natural at least for three to six months. After that, we will need another answer as to why a factory cannot increase production. As for your second question, I am not totally sure what the U.S. will do. My best guess is that they will seek manufacturing elsewhere. They will find some, but they will not be able to match the prices, quality, or delivery that we have given them in the past. That also means that we might be able to raise our prices for whatever level of production we are providing them."

Wei smiled to himself. Tao Hanwen adapted to the situation better than Wei could have predicted. Interestingly, Wei was unaware that his Head of Manufacturing had felt this way for years. He must make a note to himself to have meetings with various managers of different departments. Otherwise, Wei was very pleased with the response.

"Thank you for your input. This is a terrible crisis that has caused us all to think about our country and how to make it stronger moving forward. Please put a plan together, as described, and a timeline to immediately enact the training and counseling."

Parker was at home making herself some dinner before settling into an additional hour or two of work. Her phone dinged, indicating an email. At first, she didn't recognize the tone, but then she realized that the tone indicated that she had an email from an account she rarely used. She signed into that account and, as she suspected, the email was from

Tim Chen. He obviously recalled their time in college and he responded accordingly. Now she had to navigate a secure connection with him so they could communicate effectively and transparently. She knew that the conventional methods, even personal VPN and other secure types of internet connection and communication, wouldn't be up to the task. The Chinese monitoring systems employed at this time in history were incredibly good. The only option to ensure that this type of communication remained undetectable was a government secure system. At first she thought that maybe she should try to meet Tim in person somewhere, but she knew that with the travel bans and real possibility of being infected, that was an impossibility at present. She was about to make a decision that could ruin her career, but she did have a directive from the Homeland Security Director. She even thought that maybe it could be a crime to use the government's secure communication system with someone in China. She had to risk it. If Tim knew nothing, or could confirm that this virus wasn't a weapon, she could end the secure conversations, disable the account she'd have to create for him, and all would be back to normal. She went to the storage closet upstairs and found an old textbook in a box of her college things. It was the book she and Tim used for the only class they had together. She began to look up various pages and make scribbling notes on a piece pf paper. After about fifteen minutes she went back downstairs to her computer and began creating a secure account for Tim Chen in the Homeland Security communications portal. After all of this, she logged in again to her rarely used Yahoo email account, the one that she had asked Tim to respond to, and began typing a message:

> *So nice to hear from you, especially during these*
> *troubling times. I can't help but remember our time*
> *in college and the economics class we had together.*
> *Do you remember the textbook we had to use? It*
> *was so thick and heavy!*
>
> *Anyway, tell me about your life, what are you doing*
> *for fun? I wrote a crazy poem the other day. Tell me*
> *what you think:*
>
> *57 people were standing in a row, waiting in line for*
> *a dime. 17 responded with a deal and the others*
> *were left to steal. Only those below the row fought*
> *to avoid the widespread crime.*
>
> *I know it's kinda stupid but you know me.*
>
> *BTW – did you hear about Frank E. from class? I'll*
> *have to tell you all about it. Have a great day!*

She double checked her notes looking back and forth from
the email to her white pad of paper. She hit send. She hoped
that Timothy remembered the fun they had one semester
with cypher codes and cryptic messages. Parker knew odds
were 60/40 that he would understand. She knew that they

didn't really put any of this down and actually practice this like a government would. It was merely another distraction during college and was interesting.

———————————

Elliott Myles rose from his computer and went to his front window. It was almost dark but he stared outside anyway and watched the wind rustling the trees. Leaves and blossoms were starting to grow and for a second, he was amazed how nature just kept chugging along despite a worldwide pandemic. He grabbed his phone and made a phone call:

> "Hey, it's me, can you talk? … I saw the report online … Yeah, I know I shouldn't have but these are crazy times … ok, just confirm one thing for me … what's the confidence level? … Really! … ok, thanks."

Elliott tapped the red 'end' button on his cell phone. He thought for a second. He tapped the message app on his phone and started typing:

> *Hey, it's Elliott Myles next door, I was wondering if you have a few minutes for a phone call sometime today? Thanks.*

CHAPTER 7

The worldwide pandemic was now in full throat. It was late spring in the northern hemisphere and nearly every country on the planet was affected. Heading into spring, over five million people worldwide were infected and nearly fifty thousand people worldwide had died. Virus One was doing its job better than Li Wei could have imagined. Ten million people in the U.S. alone had lost their jobs and were seeking unemployment. The U.S. Congress passed a bill that gave every American $1,200, but really that was drop in the bucket compared to what Americans were losing. Worldwide businesses were shut down, hospitals overrun, and the world was grappling with measures to prevent further spread. Military troops were sent to borders of states and countries, only letting people enter that actually lived within the border they were protecting. For some reason, toothpaste in the U.S. was flying off the shelves and was scarce. People all over the world were waiting in line at food stores to buy essentials. Armed police and security guards were now a regular sight at these food stores worldwide. The combined factors of the virus and, more importantly, *human actions in response to the virus* were quickly thrusting the crisis to a horrible zenith. If infections and deaths continued, and humanity continued its lockdown, Virus One would become the single worst event in human history. While world leaders and their health officials were immersed in the crisis and their medical models predicted mass future infections and deaths, ordinary citizens were beginning to question the lockdown and the continued deliberate scuttling of the economy. Popular radio show hosts were publicly starting to question the continued economic destruction of not just the country. but of ordinary individuals.

Though the 1918 Spanish Flu killed nearly 100 million people worldwide, the economic toll at that time was nowhere near what was happening at present. Li Wei remembered his U.S. college days and how his dormitory had movie night every Friday. He thought about one movie in particular, an old Godzilla monster movie from the mid 1950's. At the time, he remembered thinking that if 'Godzilla' were to ever happen, *that* would be the end of the world. He never imagined that the *voluntary response* to a virus might dictate the world's end. In the U.S., President Hunter extended the lockdown another thirty days. Though he was listening to his medical experts, the American media couldn't resist blaming him for all ills. Americans came together for the initial lockdown, but there was a growing feeling amongst many that at some point citizenry would have to revolt and go back to work and their lives, whether they had permission or not. Wei wondered if they would even need to release Virus Two. Virus One might be enough to rebalance the scales of power being sought by China.

————————————

Tim Chen got to work early. He parked his motorbike in the secure parking lot and proceeded to the third floor lab where he had a cubicle. Prior to actually doing any work, he needed to go through the sterile protocol necessary to work in the lab environment. It only took about fifteen minutes but it was necessary for a 'clean' environment. He proceeded to enter a locker room where he could change and don his PPE, Personal Protective Equipment. As he put his personal items into his locker, his phone made a sound that indicated an incoming email. He took a quick look out of curiosity and saw that is was from Parker Hall. He didn't have time now to read it so it would have to wait until after work. He donned his cap first then shoe covers, gloves, N95 or higher face mask, gown, shoe covers, and lastly, a second pair of gloves.

After this procedure, Tim approached the double door airlock and the first door opened automatically. When he stepped inside the airlock, the first door automatically closed behind him. A disinfectant spray was released from the sides of the airlock washing him in the mist. The disinfectant stopped after about seven seconds and then the second door opened. He then entered the actual lab. His lab was a bio-level 4 lab so it was kept at a slightly negative pressure relative to the adjacent areas. In other words, an inward directional airflow was established by exhausting more air than is supplied. This prevents any contaminates from spills or releases from migrating outwardly from the lab into surrounding rooms. As Tim got to his lab area, he looked around and paused for a moment. *Was there indeed something going on here that he was radically unaware of? Something with an evil intent?* He shrugged his shoulders. *No way, I'm not that oblivious*. Just then his boss entered his area.

"Good morning Mr. Chen."

"Good morning Sir."

"You have been a quick study and your work has shown it."

Tim was surprised by the comment from Yuan Xi, but not by the content. He knew he was smart and dedicated to his work. "Thank you, Sir."

"There is a project that we have been working on upstairs in the fourth floor lab that I want you to be involved in. They are pushing to finish this within six months and I think you can be of great help."

"I'm at the lab's disposal, whatever is needed. Can I ask what the project is?"

"You will be involved in finding a vaccine," Xi said.

"Ahh, for the current virus I presume, that is a worthy—"

"No, this is another vaccine that is very important to China. Please report immediately to the fourth floor lab, and

you will get more details. You are to report there every day
until told otherwise," Xi ordered.

Without hesitation Tim answered, "Yessir."

There was no way to go from his sterile third floor
lab to any other area in the building without re-sterilization.
He proceeded to go back to the locker room, undress,
shower, then re-dress for the entrance into the fourth floor
lab area. He thought for a moment about looking at the
email from Parker, then decided against it. It would take
long enough to re-sterilize and he didn't want to disappoint
his new temporary boss in any way. As he was re-dressing,
he continued to think about his new assignment. *What could
be more important than a vaccine to the current horrible
virus?* He didn't have an answer. He was now very curious.
He would make sure to get home as soon as his shift ended
and read Parker's email.

———————————————

Li Wei was headed to a Politburo meeting and was late. He
and his assistant were compiling new numbers and he
wanted to be as accurate as possible with the council
members. As he walked into the meeting, everyone was
already seated and waiting for him.

"I apologize gentlemen. Please forgive me."

Fu spoke first. "That is okay, Wei, please sit." Wei
took his seat and arranged his papers while Zhou Shou
began to talk.

"Colleagues. I begin with a discussion on the

current worldwide crisis and the status of our country medically, economically, and politically. Wei can you give us an update on the first two areas?"

"Absolutely. I will first start with the infection and death numbers. In general, our country is doing better than others in the world. We have total infections of approximately 250,000 and total deaths of 10,000."

Xin looked puzzled. "Excuse me, but those numbers are not the same as what is being reported by the world media..."

"Yes Xin you are correct. When we began the trial run and Virus One started spreading in our country, I made the decision to deliberately withhold updates to our countries infection and death numbers as well as deliberately lower them both for worldwide consumption."

"... and your reason being?"

"Two-fold Xin. First, we want the world media, including our loyal friends at the World Health Organization, to report that even though the outbreak began in our country, we, the Chinese government, are responding to the outbreak and taking the measures needed to suppress and eradicate the virus. Secondly, we want the world to see the U.S. numbers surpass ours so that the U.S. and other world media can report that the reason the U.S. numbers are larger is because the U.S. government, more specifically the U.S. American president, is not doing enough, or did not react quickly enough."

Shou spoke up. "And what of our economy and factories?"

"Our economy has contracted, as expected, but our

people are resilient. I have put into place a plan for our factories nationwide to adjust to the new production levels. This will take a few months but we will be able to succeed. As the U.S. begins to overcome the virus and return to a sense of normalcy, our plan also prepares our factories to *not* accept what will certainly be a flurry of orders coming from American companies."

"Thank you, Wei. Colleagues. Politically, our country is strong and is on the 'right' side of this virus. Wei's brilliant plan accounted for any possible negative political ramifications. Given the astonishing success of Phase One, we have had glowing praise from around the world as a leader in the pandemic response," Shou spoke with pleasure.

"Wei," Fu Said, "do you think we will really need to implement Phase Two, even if the U.S. president gets re-elected later this year?"

"I do not know, Fu. As we sit today, Virus One may have wounded the U.S. enough that no matter who is president, they will not be able to resume business and life as usual. To date, their reaction to Virus One has eradicated the economic gains made since the current American president was first elected three years ago. Depending on how much longer the crisis remains in the U.S., their economy will continue to suffer and we just may not need to do anything more. Time will tell."

CHAPTER 8

Tim Chen's shift was over and he was tired. The work on the fourth floor was much more intensive than the work he had previously been doing on the third floor. Not that he was complaining, but there was a very different atmosphere in that lab than to what he was normally accustomed. He hopped on his motorbike and proceeded to drive home. The wind was whistling through his helmet's face shield, but he could hardly hear it. His thoughts were on the email from Parker. He almost felt guilty that he didn't answer it immediately, but his shift, and duty, called. He instinctively knew though that this email would be different. This email would be like none he ever received. He'd need time and privacy to decipher it. It was a challenge he was excited to undertake as soon as possible. As he parked his motorbike at his apartment complex alongside many other motorbikes and traditional bicycles, he quickly locked it and made his way to his apartment.

Once inside, he immediately pressed the power button on his laptop. As it was booting up, he went to the fridge and grabbed some leftover noodles and vegetables that he'd made the day before along with some hoisin sauce, chopsticks, and a glass of water, and then he sat down at his computer. He logged in and read the email from Parker focusing on the section he knew was coded into three parts:

He identified the first part of the code which read,

Do you remember the textbook we had to use?
It was so thick and heavy!

This he understood immediately. She wanted him to recall the damn textbook from that class and that would be where she hid the cipher. He knew she would have kept that textbook in her possession, but he no longer knew where his was. He thought he could probably find it online and sure enough, after doing a little searching on the Georgetown website, he found the class and noticed the book was the same. That didn't surprise him. Professors didn't like to change books because it meant they had to read the damn thing. They were so predictable. His alumni status allowed him to get a 'student' price for the book. He purchased it with a few clicks.

So far so good, he thought. The second part of the code was the hard part and read,

57 people were standing in a row, waiting in line for a dime.

17 responded with a deal and the others were left to steal.

Only those below the row fought to avoid the widespread crime.

He had to laugh. He knew Parker pretty well and she could sometimes get carried away with intrigue and the mystery of codes and ciphers. He also thought to himself, *she's just an intern and she's learning, but there's no way this would fly in the real spy world!* Nonetheless, he continued to work talking out loud to himself.

First line, page 57, tenth line of the book. Easy.

Second line, page 17, but then what? A deal? A deal on what? A deal on a dime ... no ... a deal ... meaning *one* deal, maybe the first line. Keep going. *Others were left to steal.* What the hell does that mean? Others ... what others ... other people ... other parts of the code ... other parts on the left, Yes! Those parts were on the left-hand side of the page opposite page 17. Of course, page 17 was on the right hand side of the book and page 1 was on the left side. So, the answer was page 16, line 1.

All be dammed he thought, maybe this wasn't so elementary.

> Third line, *below the row* … the next line down … no … think Tim, think … look at the whole sentence. Could it be that simple? Wow, she was good. She was trying to tell him to go back to page 57, down one line in the book to line 11.

All in all, it took him about thirty minutes to decipher. He stopped there and once the eBook downloaded to his local disk, he turned to the pages he needed and started looking at the lines. They had always joked at school that normal codes and ciphers could be better. Once they were cracked, or figured out, anyone could simply apply the cipher and read the code. But Parker always wanted to be smarter. He remembered her saying that what if a cipher was just a clue to get to another clue that there was no actual cipher for? In this way, only two people, the creator and receiver, could fully decipher the coded phrases, clues, sentences, or passages. With that in mind, he started to write the 'lines' down on paper indicated by the cipher. Another, *Wow* came out of his mouth. He read the lines and instantly knew what they referred to because he *knew* Parker. *Cool!* came out way too loud and he reactively put his hand over his mouth.

Onto the last coded part of the message–the third part of the code read,

BTW – did you hear about Frank E. from class?

Now he was pretty sure he remembered the people in the class and there was no Frank E. What did this mean? A person in the book? He instantly went to the glossary. No Frank E. Wait. He remembered that they used to sign their coded messages with fictitious names. Frank E. was not her name because she didn't sign it as her own. She asked if he remembered Frank E. Maybe she was telling him to use that name. That was it. The cipher gave him a secure web address to register the name Frank E. He immediately typed in the URL and within a few seconds, there was a registration screen that had a single text box for a name. He typed 'Frank E.' He instantly got an error message. *What the hell?* he mumbled. He tried again without the period after 'E.' Wrong again. *Shit.* He thought. The error message said he had one more try and if he was wrong again, he would be locked out. He had to think. He was mad at himself for wasting the second try. He had made the second attempt too quickly, without thinking it through, and he should have known better. At this point he had only taken a few bites of his soup, which was now cold and uninviting. He pushed it aside and continued to think. After a minute he concluded that the best way to do this was to start saying the name out loud.

> *Frank E. (spoken slowly)... Frank E. (a little faster)... FRANKIE!*

That had to be it, but he couldn't risk another wrong try. He thought about it for another minute and then decided to go for it. He entered the name, 'frankie.' Bam! He was in. The page refreshed to another page that had one entry near the top with a drop down 'carrot' or arrow. He clicked the arrow and as it rotated in place to a downward direction, the body of a message appeared.

> *Hi Timothy, you made it in! I hope you are safe. I needed to set up this secure messaging with you because I've been tasked at Homeland Security with finding out if the Chinese government deliberately released this virus the world is dealing with? My investigation from here has only turned up bits and pieces of anecdotal information that the virus may not have originated in a wet market. I don't know if you can help but I wanted to reach out to you. You can use this system to message me back. BTW-- Don't pull up the URL on your phone browse. They've been having some kind of security issues with the URL on a mobile device, so only use it on your laptop–that's secure.*

Tim began typing a response:

> *Hi Parker. I forgot how clever you were with those ciphers we used to mess with, but I still cracked it in well under an hour! Anyway, if you had asked me this question yesterday, I would have said no, nothing unusual. However, today I was asked to work on a vaccine in a different lab on another floor. When I asked if it was for the current virus*

*pandemic, my supervisor said no, something more
important. That made me curious. I will keep my
eyes and ears open. BTW–are you dating anyone?*

Tim hit send. He just had to ask. He knew they didn't have
that type of relationship but he did miss their friendship.
Male and female friendships like he and Parker had enjoyed
were not quite the same in China. It was just a different
culture. Just then he realized that he was really tired.
Between the job and the mental exercise of decoding the
message, he was ready for sleep. Tomorrow was another
day.

Parker Hall woke up and realized instantly that she
shouldn't have had that second glass of wine. She was a
lightweight and she knew it. She had drifted off to sleep
while the TV was on and didn't hear the text message come
in from Elliott Myles the night before. She really hated
missing messages, no matter what time of day or night. She
grabbed her phone from the nightstand and started typing a
reply:

*Hi Mr. Myles, so sorry I didn't reply earlier. I had
my phone on mute and didn't hear your text. Let me
know a good time to talk today.*

She wished she could sleep in, but she knew she had work to do. She popped out of bed and began her new routine. Sweats, coffee, computer. That was it. If she had to be on camera for a video call, she'd hop in the shower. As the coffeemaker gurgled and brewed, she was already on her computer and had logged into the secure server at Homeland Security. There was a link to a news page on the home page that these days was filled mostly with virus information. On average, she awoke to about twenty-five secure emails. Most of these were departmental announcements regarding human resources or events. The email section of the server was not as robust as say Microsoft Outlook. This was typical for government. In order to save a nickel, they hired a company to build the email functionality rather than simply employ the best private sector option. Oh well. She scanned down the messages and saw one from 'frankie'. *He figured it out, cool!* She opened the message and read. *Hmmm.* She had no idea if what Timothy said meant anything, but she had to temper her enthusiasm. She knew this was a character flaw she had to work on. As enthusiastic as she took her work, she wanted her work to be fruitful, to result in a positive outcome. She had always been like this. Not that she necessarily wanted to find that China deliberately released the current virus. Part of her hoped she would find that they were responsible, but a bigger part of her wanted to find out that they would never do something like that. What was important to her was that she be proved right. That her effort resulted in *something*. She didn't want to spend all this time exploring potential leads and other trails only to find out she had wasted a bunch of time. Timothy's last comment in his email wasn't lost on her. She knew he found her attractive, but nothing ever got weird or even close to weird in college. She thought he might just be lonely. It was flattering anyway. She quickly typed a reply:

> *Ok, understood. And BTW--NOOOO, I'm not dating anyone ... why do you ask?*

After hitting send she decided that she would update Josh and keep going. No need to update Director Thomas just yet.

Elliott Myles had been awake for hours. He was normally an early riser from his days at the NSA. Just then his phone made a sound which signaled an incoming text. He didn't get a lot of texts anymore, so the sound surprised him. It was from Parker Hall. He immediately replied:

> *How about now?*

He wondered if his sense of urgency was a bit over the top. He had been listening to the news and reading the reports, and part of him wondered if this crisis could tip. From his days at the NSA, he was trained to see and forecast many different scenarios. This type of thinking always served him well and by thinking this way, he knew he would never be caught off guard with his jaw hanging down. The virus was certainly infectious and, even though the death of anyone was bad, the deaths so far were not even comparable to the seasonal flu. This crisis has done something that previously no one thought possible. The reaction by governments to essentially halt economic life set a countdown clock in motion. This clock was counting down to eventual mass hysteria. It was not predetermined and certainly the 'clock' could be shut off, but only if the world returned to near normal. He knew that significant economic damage had already be done.

Some of the initial scenarios he had thought about were no longer applicable. In the beginning of the outbreak the world didn't really take it that seriously as it was limited to China. He had to admit, he really didn't give it much thought either until it started occupying the media full time. Everything had accelerated since that time. The NSA had trained him on the science of group behavior. All of that training came rushing back. The Asch effect, group think, group polarization, social facilitation, etc. The studies were numerous and the NSA spent much time and expense on this. He knew governments understood that you can't always use force to get what you want. Using the psychology of group behavior, the NSA, the CIA, and even the FBI were able to manipulate individuals and even countries to get what they wanted. This was done all the time. This behavioral training also included human psychology and panic. The urge to survive is what causes a drowning man to unintentionally pull their rescuer under with him; this was well documented. At present, he saw that citizens were indeed complying with the 'stay at home' orders that many states in the U.S. and countries around the world had implemented. He knew instinctively that this would only last so long–the clock was ticking. He knew that unless people got back to work and moved about, that panic would eventually ensue. Certainly, enough Americans owned firearms that survival instincts would set in as people ran out of money to pay for food and the entire situation could 'tip' to mass chaos. His phone made another sound. It was another text.

> *Can you give me a minute and I will call you?*
> *Thanks.*

Tim Chen was working late these days. The new assignment required a nearly 12-hour work day. He had been more tired than usual by the end of his shift the last few days and he could already hear his parents from 7,000 miles away, *you've got to take care of yourself. Balance work with relaxation and exercise.* He knew they were right, but he just had to find the time. The actual work he was doing was procedurally the same as he did in the other lab, one floor below. But something was different. There was a sense of urgency amongst the people working there. He knew by their reputations that he was working with the best scientists in this lab. That was a big reason why he initially applied for work here. He wanted to eventually work with the best. Not that the researchers were bad or in some way incompetent on the third floor, but it was just different. The seriousness with which the people on the fourth went about their work was borderline intense. Everyone was working toward a goal, but unlike the third floor where they were *hoping* to find good results and eventually a vaccine for some agricultural diseases aimed at plants, the researchers and scientists on the 4th floor were working toward what felt like a foregone conclusion–that they already *knew* they would indeed create a vaccine. But a vaccine for what?

He dragged his feet, booties on, into the airlock to begin the de-sterilization process. All he could think about was laying down and getting some sleep. He wasn't even that hungry. Because he was new to the lab, he wanted to be methodical about his work. That meant going a tad slower than the other researchers who had already been working for months on the project. Because of this, he was one of the last ones to leave the lab at the end of the day. He usually bounced out of the third floor lab, excited to be going home. Today was different. If it weren't for the fact that he was walking so slowly, his view aimed downward, he might have missed it. Coming into view on one of the researcher's stations was a folder titled **Virus Two, Human Vaccine Trials**. His eyes opened widely, but he couldn't make his body stop moving forward. His brain said stop and take a look, but his body said keep moving. As he entered the airlock his focus turned to completing the task at hand. Dressing into his street clothes in the locker room he started to think. *Virus Two,* he thought, *Human Trials. What the hell was that about?* Was he indeed working on a vaccine for the current virus outbreak? Why would that be secret? Every country in the world was working on a vaccine. *Why keep it secret?*

By the time he got home is was nearly dark. He hated that he was working into the dark hours. Leaving work with the sun still shining made him feel his entire day wasn't spent at work. He opened his computer, logged into the secure Homeland Security site. He saw that he had a message from Parker. It was a short reply simply acknowledging that she had received his email and congrats for cracking the cipher she put together. *Oh God*, he thought, she also engaged him on the dating question. He was too tired to play along tonight; he'd skip any reply she hoped to get on that topic until another day. He began typing:

> *Long day at work, very tired. Long story short I was moved to another lab. Not given reason or what we are doing except for working on a vaccine. Unclear what for. Upon leaving just now I saw a folder, labeled 'Virus Two–Human Vaccine Trials'. Not sure what that's about, but they told me when they moved me last week that the lab I'm in now was specifically **not** working on a vaccine for the current outbreak*

> *– frankie*

He hit send, made sure it actually did send, closed his laptop, and then laid down on his couch. He was completely asleep in less than five minutes.

———————————————

Parker poured another cup of coffee and then dialed Elliott Myles. Normally, she'd would have just walked next door, but because of the social distancing rules, she figured she'd call.

"Hello?"

"Hi Mr. Myles, it's Parker. How are you holding up with all the social distancing and stuff?"

"I'm good, thanks. Please, call me Elliott. How are you doing?"

"Good, working a lot, and bored."

"I hear you. Listen, I wanted to talk to you because I know you're at Homeland Security and I wanted to ask you some questions."

"Mr. Myles, you know that most of what I know and do is confidential, and I know that you used to be with the NSA, but I'm not sure I can tell you anything material."

"I do get that and I appreciate you honoring the confidentiality. How about I just ask questions and you answer what you can, alright? … and Elliott, please."

Parker thought he was fishing around for news on the current outbreak, what the government response was going to be, when they thought the lockdown would end, that sort of thing. She'd answer what she could and move on. She really wasn't privy to that kind of info anyway so she knew most of her answers would be an honest, 'I don't know.' She was dead wrong. "Sure, go ahead, I'll answer what I can."

"Great. Ok, first question. Do you know if the government has concluded that the virus originated from a wet market in China?"

She thought to herself, *somewhat ordinary question.* She responded, "I don't know, not in that department but that seems to be the public consensus when officials are talking on TV."

"Do you know of any reason that our government would think otherwise?"

Parker instantly thought, *that question hit too close to home–where is he going?* She responded cautiously, "Uh, well I think the answer is again, 'I don't know,' but we're getting into an area that I probably shouldn't talk about."

"Ok. I get it. Parker, just listen. I'm going to stop dancing around. I know you're an up and coming star at Homeland Security and your dad and I go way back, so I want to give you some info that I've found–don't ask me how I know or where I got the information, and I won't have to lie."

She thought to herself, *Holy crap, what's this about?* She once again responded, "Sure, go ahead."

"I have conformation that the wet market story is a ruse. I'm not saying I know the real origin of the outbreak, but that info about the wet market I do know to be false. Now I can add two plus two, Parker. For all my years of training and working at the NSA, I think someone needs to take a closer look into this situation."

Parker thought to herself, *WOW–he nailed that. Now what do I say?* She began slowly, "Well … you may have a point there … Maybe we should not talk on the phone."

Elliott smiled because he knew he called it! He still had it. He responded, "Good idea. I'm not sick, can you come over for dinner tonight?"

"Sure, 6-ish?"

"See you then."

She smiled. She *wasn't* wasting her time. Thank goodness. Just then she saw an email from Tim. She opened it and seemed to lean into the computer as she read. *Hmmm ... What to make of that?* she said quietly. She'd respond in a bit, but she wanted to first talk to her dad. Trust is a weird thing in Washington, DC. It's like currency everywhere else. She would ask her dad what he thought and whether she should engage Mr. Myles tonight. She knew she said yes to the dinner invite, but she'd make her final decision on whether to bring Mr. Myles into the inner circle at the dinner meeting depending on what her dad thought.

CHAPTER 9

Li Wei was at home thinking about his answer to Huang Fu at the Politburo meeting earlier in the week. The fact that the U.S. was over-reacting to the crisis in a way that he never expected was a sort of 'game-changer,' as his U.S. college roommates would have put it. On the one hand, they could certainly do nothing more with regards to Phase Two and call it a 'win.' One could even argue that that moving forward with Phase Two might not add much and only risk exposure. On the other hand, warfare doctrine dictates you finish off your enemy. The lack of that mindset cost the Japanese the war during WWII. It was well documented that Japanese Admiral Nagumo, who led the Japanese carrier battle group on the attack on Pearl Harbor, December 7, 1941, decided against launching a final, third wave of airplanes from their carriers to finish off Pearl Harbor and to destroy the U.S. warships, dry docks, the oil tank farm, maintenance shops, and other support facilities.

Wei took a sip of Baijiu from his shot glass. It felt warm as it slid down his throat. He had enjoyed Baijiu since his mid-twenties, after coming home from earning his degree at Stanford University. Baijiu was a traditional Chinese drink distilled to be anywhere from 40-60% alcohol and could produce one hell of a kick in Westerners who 'thought' they were tough drinkers. The Chinese had a tradition of swilling the drink at after-hours business outings. Many U.S. businessmen would attempt to drink toe-to-toe with their Chinese hosts only to be overmatched and out-witted. They typically paid the price the next morning. Doing business in China was a throwback to a golden age. Email and video conferencing were great, but China really did most of their business the old-fashioned way–person to person. U.S. corporations would send their representatives to China to inspect factories, approve prototypes, correct production flaws, negotiate orders, and otherwise oversee all aspects of the manufacturing of their products. Their Chinese hosts, the business owners, looked forward to these meetings very much. Golf, drinking, karaoke, and even mistresses were all acceptable hobbies for Chinese businessmen. Adding in an inexperienced drinker from another country was too good to be true. The Chinese knew they could push their 'partying and culture' a bit when entertaining their U.S. counterparts. Make no mistake, this ritual was also a test. If a Westerner rejected their food and their hospitality, then they risked being shunned and their business would most likely suffer.

A typical evening out went as follows: American businessmen, assuming there was more than one traveling to

China, would attend meetings all day that would conclude sometime in the afternoon. A driver from the factory would take them back to their hotel to 'rest' before dinner. A few hours later, the Chinese business owner or his driver would pick the businessmen up from the hotel to go to dinner. In many instances, the passengers in the car would include the Chinese owner, a couple of his close managers, and possibly even the owner's mistress. Once everyone arrived at the restaurant, the American businessmen would be paraded into a room where they would be seated around a huge, round table where others from the factory, the managers and other friends, joined the dinner as well. Dinner guests would consist of the American businessmen and between eight and fifteen other people.

The table would have a large Lazy-Susan that reached out to within a foot of the edge of the table. Beer and other alcoholic drinks would be brought to the table by the case, and food would start coming immediately. Within seconds, all of the glasses, the size of small orange juice glasses, would be filled with beer. One of the middle managers of the factory on the other side of the table would stand up with his filled glass and say to the leader of the American contingency, 'Ganbei'! This would be an invitation no proper guest would refuse. This was the Chinese way of asking, really demanding, that everyone drink down their beer in one continuous sip as a toast of friendship and successful business. 'Ganbei' literally means 'to drink a toast' in Chinese. The American businessmen would swill the relatively small amount of beer, remember college days, and not think that much of it at first. But then the glass would be immediately and without being asked, filled again, and the process would be repeated with a different person at the table standing and saying, 'Ganbei'! This would continue all night. Those Americans that would smartly be aware of what was transpiring instantly did the math around the table and realized that they were not only outnumbered by the Chinese, but that the Chinese celebrated like this several nights a week and were quite used to it! It was a foregone conclusion that for Americans to do business in China, this would be the toll that needed to be paid, and nearly all American businessmen visiting their Chinese factory partners paid it happily.

Wei took another sip. His 'Ganbei' days were virtually over, but he still enjoyed sipping the drink at night before retiring to bed. He thought back to the question at hand. It was an interesting dilemma. The Japanese Pearl Harbor lesson was hard to ignore. He played out the scenario of phase 2. With all of the mass confusion from phase 1, and the fact that neither the U.S. nor any other country figured out yet that China was responsible for putting Virus One into the eco-system, he didn't think there was much risk of China being negatively exposed. Sure, China would lose more citizens, but he knew from history that people served their countries in many ways. The more he thought, the more he wanted to eliminate the bigger risk– that the U.S. economy would rebound and discover that China was somehow responsible for the pandemic. He finished his drink. *Yes*, he thought, *China will finish what it started in order to guarantee its world dominance*. He had convinced himself. Now he only had to convince the council members.

Parker left work early. She needed some privacy to call her father and determine whether she was indeed having dinner with Elliot Myles tonight. Parker had always been able to talk to her father, whether it was boys and dating, career advice on choosing a college or even a bit of coaching on the side during high school volleyball. Parker always felt very close to her dad and she knew that he would giver her the straight skinny on the topic at hand while at the same time making her feel like she came to any conclusion or decision on her own. She often thought that his listening and conversing skills must have been a huge benefit for him at the State Department. She wished that she was more like her father in that way.

On the contrary, Parker's relationship with her mother had been basically like oil and water for most of her life. Not that she didn't love her mother, she was simply *too much like* her mother. Even after Parker's mom had died, Parker thought kindly and smiled often when she thought of her. Her mother was driven to succeed in her career. She was ambitious in wanting the best for her family, and she was even tenacious about the necessity of Parker being prepared for her future, whatever that might be. One minute Parker and her mom would be laughing and discussing something and the next minute it was an all-out argument. Her memories of her mom were now primarily focused on the good times, but she always realized that she got a lot of traits from her mother, which was a plus and a minus. She often wondered if their tumultuous relationship would have naturally settled down with age. A tear slowly rolled down her cheek because she knew she'd never have the chance to find out. As Parker wiped her face, she picked up her cell phone and dialed.

"Hi, Dad. How are you?"

"I'm fine honey, just staying inside."

"Got a minute Dad?" Parker asked tentatively, not wanting to interrupt anything.

"Sure Parker, shoot."

"Mr. Myles asked to talk to me yesterday and we just finished a phone call," she began. "He asked me about some stuff that has to do with my work that borders on confidentiality, and I'm having a hard time figuring out how far to take this."

"Can I ask for some more details?"

"Well, it has to with this virus and China. I just—",

"Stop," her father interrupted. "I think I can guess where you're going. So, what did he specifically ask?"

"Well, he kinda hit the bullseye of what my current task is at Homeland Security," Parker spoke cautiously. "He wasn't probing, you know, he was just asking. He said he had independent information that actually might aid my task and was concerned, like we all are, about this crisis."

"And you're asking me whether you can trust him?"

"Jeez Dad, you continue to be the smartest guy I know," she laughed.

"I don't know about that, but thanks sweetheart," he chuckled. "I appreciate hearing that from you. I think the short answer is 'Yes, you can trust him. What you don't know about Elliott Myles is that he took one for the team."

"I don't understand, what do you mean?"

"Please don't repeat this honey, but Elliott Myles was very high up in the NSA," her father explained. "After the SARS epidemic happened in the early 2000's, he started analyzing Asia's response as well, specifically looking at China. During the next few years, he put together an amazing report of a coming attack. Not one that included planes, ships, and armies, but one where the enemy was virtually invisible. His report detailed an attack from China using a biological weapon."

"Oh my God, so he kind of predicted this in a way?"

"Well sort of. During that time in the late 2000's, our government was well out of 9/11 and many thought that the protective measures that we employed due to the terrorist attacks went too far. Also, we elected a new president who was of a different mindset. His thought was that because our country had exhibited such a capitalistic attitude where profit was of utmost importance, that in a way, we brought the attacks upon ourselves," he explained. "That President believed that it was no surprise that the U.S. was knocked down a rung on the geo-political ladder. He actually went to other countries giving speeches and basically apologized for America's perceived arrogance. That President was considered a 'globalist' and believed that we, the Earth, should simply be viewed as one community. To this end, he also believed that China was not only our friend, but a vital ally for the future of our manufacturing. He even proclaimed that manufacturing and the jobs that it created were not coming back to the U.S., so we all needed to get over it."

"I knew some of that, so keep going."

"When Elliott submitted his report, it was like he was crucifying a friend," her father continued. "None of his higher-ups wanted to hear about the possibility of a 'bad acting' China. The more he pushed for his report to be recognized as accurate research, the more it was panned within the NSA. He eventually went around his superiors, outside the chain of command so to speak, and tried to get us at State to take it seriously. I remember reading it. I remember thinking that this was not only feasible, but maybe even probable. He laid out the case for the U.S. to immediately put in measures to combat the possibility of a chemical or viral attack. One, begin to pull back China's manufacturing of essential medical supplies and medicines needed in the U.S. Two, begin to limit travel to China by restricting or eliminating the frequency of flights from U.S. airlines. And three, re-negotiate our trade policy with China."

"WOW! He really foresaw this, huh?"

"Yes, honey he did. He eventually got fired when my higher-ups at State got wind of the report and complained to NSA about a 'rogue agent' peddling fear mongering over a future flu bug. The NSA fired him and ruined his reputation. He's been pretty much a hermit ever since. I can't help but think that now, he's due a pretty big apology for the way he was treated–on all fronts."

"Ok," Parker sighed. "Well, I certainly understand more than I did. That's exactly what I needed Dad, thanks."

"Honey, I don't know the answers to any of what's going on right now. But I'll tell you this. If Elliott Myles believes something is amiss. I would trust him. He's never been one to embellish or stretch the truth or even fudge research. He's the real deal. And I certainly wouldn't have allowed my only daughter to move in next to him if I thought he was a kook. I love you too much."

"Awww, Dad, I love you too! Thank you again and talk to you soon."

"Hope that helps! Bye Honey."

Parker hung up the phone. She had her answer. She rationalized that after hearing her dad talk about Elliott Myles and what Elliott himself had said to her on the phone, she would take the risk and bring him into the fold but only in person–over the phone or computer/mobile device was too risky. Since he lived next door she could simply go knock on his door. She'd make a point to do just that later in the afternoon.

Li Wei was walking into his office when his desk phone rang. He had asked Tao Hanwen to phone him when he had the plan finished. "Good morning Hanwen."

"Good morning Sir. I have the plan ready."

"How long before all of our factories are performing as required?"

"Sir, I believe that it will take six months to

completely educate all of our factory owners and managers as to our new directives. Of course, we will begin with the largest factories and work down to the smallest. My plan also includes reaching out to other countries and other customers to instill further confidence that our country is ready to start producing their products again soon and that we are ready for any expansion they need."

"Very good Hanwen, very good. We must begin immediately. I would like updates monthly."

"Yessir. I will begin the plan. Thank you for trusting me, I will not let China down."

"You're welcome Hanwen, good luck my friend." Wei thought to himself, ... *let China down? Just don't let me down.*

CHAPTER 10

Seven months prior to current day, Mid–September

It had been about ten months since Virus One was released by the Chinese into the wet market the previous November. The world had gone through a lockdown from March to July. In order to save lives, many world economies took a huge hit. China was the first nation to reopen in late April. What the world didn't know, and what China hid very well, was that China deliberately re-opened early in order to get a public relations boost regardless of possible further infections. If the world really knew China's death toll and the total number of people infected, they probably would have condemned China politically and that may have hurt their overall plans. The truth was that China had over three hundred thousand dead by mid-September. They burned the deceased bodies they could and shipped other bodies in refrigerated trucks to be buried in China's vast and virtually uninhabited lands to the west. Their mobilization was astonishing, but not surprising. China's Politburo wasn't pleased with the death toll, but they knew that they had the numbers to sustain such a drop in population. It was getting to the point by mid-summer where further closure would create a death of its own economically and so therefore. most countries were forced to relax their 'stay at home orders' and 'non-essential business closure orders' by July 1 even though there was not a vaccine yet for virus 1. In about three months' time of economic inactivity. the world lost decades' worth of economic growth. Trillions of dollars were lost in gains and business progress.

Different countries employed different strategies for reopening their economies. The U.S. government and businesses in particular underestimated the public's response to the new normal. Though the virus had been tempered by the lockdown and social isolation efforts, people were still tenuous to put themselves in any perceived harm's way. The media still reported cases and deaths, not at the rate they were during the initial months of the outbreak, but they were still happening. Many people still wore masks and avoided unnecessary travel and outings. What was previously acceptable before the virus was almost frowned upon now. Social norms took on meanings. No more shaking hands, no more gratuitous hugs, and many people still voluntarily tried to distance themselves from each other. As businesses re-opened, those that thrived on group gatherings were still shuttered either voluntarily or because individuals didn't want to be confined indoors with others.

Professional and college football games, airports, air and train travel, casinos, concert venues, amusement parks, movie theatres and playhouses, and even popular beaches were affected. The government had talked about having a National Immunization Registry once a vaccine was discovered. The registry would allow a user, once they had been vaccinated to give access to a public webpage in order to prove to any business or individual that needed it, that they weren't contagious and were healthy. HIPPA laws (Health Insurance Portability and Privacy Act) were immediately amended to allow for this important national database. Of course, this took longer than estimated and revised estimates by government officials called for having the National Registry by the following summer. It was a moot point at this time because there was no vaccine yet. Reports from the government and a few pharmaceutical companies were that they were close to a vaccine. As a result, the venues that controlled these social activities demanded huge amounts of insurance from their organizers or leagues, larger than reasonable, so as to insulate them from the liability of being seen as purposefully putting people together and dramatically increasing the chances someone would get sick and possibly die. These athletic and entertainment activities subsequently took a backseat to health, at least for the near future. Entire professional and some college sports seasons were canceled and salaries of the professional players were cut. Sports TV and sports radio downsized accordingly because there was essentially nothing to talk about. Other situations happened that became a part of the 'new' normal of society:

- Concerts went completely on-demand for the foreseeable future.
- Casinos opened up, but had limited gambling machines based on social distancing rules. Ultimately, it didn't matter since not many people wanted to crowd around gaming tables or in casinos. Because there were no sports to bet on, Sportsbooks were empty.
- Amusement parks tried to open, but without a vaccine, people were just too nervous to be in crowds and get on rides.
- Airlines and trains stayed open, reducing routes and frequencies, and parking unused airplanes. Without proof of health, airlines flew half-full airplanes and handed out mandatory masks. Meal service was indefinitely suspended. The government agreed to bolster the airlines financially because they were deemed critical, so the airlines didn't mind flying half-full. They were even so bold as to raise their prices and those that had to fly paid it.
- Rules were put in place so that all new hire interviews were done via video. Companies avoided spending on travel for any area of their business and invested in video conferencing. Those companies that produced products overseas invested in robot video conferencing where a robot with wheels and an iPad could be guided by the user to different areas of a factory in order to talk to a worker, a manager, or just oversee the manufacturing process.
- Commercial real estate took a hit because businesses realized that they really *could* let many

of their employees work from home and they didn't need the physical imprint of such large offices. In turn, leases were broken and companies moved to smaller spaces. New office configurations consisted of shared spaces and few conference rooms. Employees now worked at least 50% of the time remotely.

- Employees took a hit, too. Businesses had the opportunity to re-hire only those they wanted *and*, in many cases, at a reduced salary. Why? Because they could. The pandemic became a built-in excuse for companies to start fresh from the ground-up. They viewed this as an opportunity to streamline their operations and make up for losses.
- Businesses big and small took the social distancing rules and applied them to their restaurants, bars, gyms, retail stores, grocery stores, etc. Only a certain number of patrons were allowed inside at a given time. Apps popped up to allow reservations for shopping at particular stores.
- Schools and universities changed. Universities went 75% remote. They reconfigured their dormitories for the students who decided to stay on campus, but charged a higher price. Students were forced to sign-up ahead of time in order to sit and eat in any cafeteria areas. High schools practiced social distancing in classrooms and events and had 'left and right lanes' in hallways for students to walk. Graduations either went online or were performed

outside, but even then social distancing rules were still mandated.

- The legal system had its challenges as well. Courtrooms experimented with going online. Lawyers wore suit coats, shirts, and ties with shorts because only their top half would show while on camera. Jails were subject to social distancing norms as well, and prisoners rotated their time 'in the yard' for exercise.

- Malls became a thing of the past. No one wanted to be in a crowded place near other humans who might potentially infect them. Most malls remained closed and businesses either left, shut down, or provided an entrance and exit from the outside of the mall rather than from the inside.

- Because of the masses of individuals that were able to work remotely and the reduced frequency of flights, gasoline became cheap. It was basic supply and demand. Cars were driven less, fewer airplanes flew, and the world enjoyed gas as low as $0.75 per gallon in some areas.

- Credit rating agencies which had enjoyed a monopolistic stranglehold on individuals for decades were now subject to severe change or a 'new' competition. As many people became unemployed to no fault of their own during the lockdown, people were forced to choose between paying their bills or buying food. Millions were trashing their credit rating to survive and rightly so. As a result, the housing market and the automobile companies put pressure on the credit rating agencies to change or not 'ding' someone's credit during this time. A person's credit rating became a joke. No one trusted them to accurately report an individual's credit worthiness. New credit apps popped up measuring a person by other metrics besides finances. Because the credit rating agencies were stodgy and stubborn and resisted change, mortgage companies, automobile financiers and other lenders started to adopt the new criteria. It did lenders no good to hold onto their money–their business was lending.

- The TV networks that broadcasted live had plenty of viewers during the initial weeks and months of the shutdown. But as people adjusted to the new normal, on-demand TV viewing took the lion share of profits. This had already been changing before the crisis. People didn't necessarily have the same routines anymore. Get up, go to work, come home, zone out to TV, go to bed. Because people were stuck in their homes÷ for months, when they were effectively 'let out' as countries allowed businesses to re-open, they took this re-opening as a chance to change. If you were going to spend time in front of the TV, you could access on-demand platforms and pay for no commercials. The days of mindless channel surfing were gone. People reacted to the overabundance of TV during the outbreak, watching every minute of every day, to now rejecting TV. They still got their news, TV shows, and movies, but when *they* wanted. As a result, networks fully adopted the on-demand business model and, except for real emergencies in which a network could always 'break-into their programming,' there was no more live TV needed.

- Even dating changed and most initial dates were via Zoom or other video conference platforms. Bars mandated social distancing so it was difficult to 'meet' anyone and carry on any kind of meaningful conversation.

- If a person wasn't wearing a mask in public, people gave him or her a look like, *what is wrong with you, you're going to infect me!* Survival instincts had kicked in and it was perceived by many that though things were open, life wouldn't be the same until a vaccine was found and administered to all.

- Stock markets around the world were generally up and had been since countries began re-opening. However, only a few stock traders were allowed on the floor of the exchanges. Various sectors were still down while others–healthcare, healthcare supply, distance learning and communicating, home delivery, etc. –were up.

- Politics had even changed. The U.S. presidential election was a couple months away, but it was a forgone conclusion that President Andrew Hunter would get re-elected at this point. Neither political party had held a convention and even though American citizens were passionate about their politics and political leaders, the sentiment was that the election and the political banter surrounding it took a back seat to human survival. Each political party took a bit of a hit as the U.S. tried to get back to some kind of normal or new normal. The Democrats were voted out as the leaders of the House of Representatives. During the crisis, they had tried to slip through various stimulus bills, ridiculous spending measures, which were immediately rebuffed by the Republicans and many American citizens. Although Republicans were forced to swallow some of these spending items, the voters took note and acted accordingly. The left's continual rant about the border being some sort of 'discriminatory object' was exposed during the crisis and even the most liberal politicians couldn't endorse open borders any longer, certainly not for the foreseeable future. Conversely, citizens demanded that the Republicans fight to approve huge spending bills to beef up the current healthcare system so that hospitals would be ready for the next outbreak and not be caught off guard. This meant spending for supplies, medicines, and machines that once manufactured, would sit idle in a warehouse until needed–if ever. A system would also be put in place to audit those supplies once per year, making sure they were operable and current and those that were not, like expired medicines or outdated machines, would be trashed.

- Oddly enough, as the world practiced social distancing, people became more intrusive at the same time. Cameras were everywhere including peoples' homes. People started to record everything and post it on YouTube. Strangers could use the internet to insert themselves into a family's life and watch them eat dinner. They could watch someone clean his garage if they chose to do so. If they desired to watch someone fix her dishwasher, they could. As weird as that sounded, the live streaming aspect of this went a step further. Rather than just watch someone else from a recorded video, you could live stream with them and *virtually* interact together. YouTube videos became works of art. With video software becoming more point-and-click, anyone could put a slick intro and graphics into their videos to build their 'brand.' Videos weren't just posted on YouTube; they were produced.

All in all, the U.S. and other countries around the world were recovering as best as they could. Fear was still prevalent and people were upset. Though everyone inherently knew that once a vaccine was found life would improve, questions which could never be answered were asked. Did there need to be a lockdown? Could there have been a hybrid course of action where some worked and some didn't? This was leading to a bigger debate than 'who shot Kennedy.' There was no way to prove what would have happened had there not been such an economically devastating lockdown. Because of this fact, millions of people concluded that the reaction to the virus was indeed an *over-reaction* which had irreversible consequences for individuals economically. Ultimate blame was laid upon public health officials who were seen as speculators at best, flip-flopping on medical policy week to week. A new distrust of anything a public official said was the norm. None of their calamitous proclamations regarding death toll numbers came close to becoming reality. As countries, and especially U.S. businesses, we're trying to re-open and pull out of the economic dive, people decided to trust in themselves rather than any health official or doctor. This led to an unfortunate result. There was a feeling that was continuing to permeate the world's individuals. It was common thinking now that health officials had essentially 'cried wolf.' That conclusion was hard to refute but this also meant that if, for some reason, there was another, more deadly pandemic in the future, many, including politicians, would ignore any future warnings as just another, 'cry wolf' moment.

CHAPTER 11

P arker and Josh had survived the government layoffs which happened over the summer and Parker had even received a permanent job offer from the Homeland Security Director which she eagerly accepted. She graduated *summa cum laude* from Georgetown but unfortunately, with the crisis still raging, there was no public graduation or any pomp and circumstance surrounding her achievement. Her father had surprised her with some balloons, a cake, and a few small gifts, but it was just her and her dad. She wished her mom could have been there and so she teared up for a few seconds while her dad was cutting the cake. Her mom had succumbed to cancer several years earlier. Even though her mom was focused on her career, she had always the anchor that her and her father depended on. She had worked in the financial sector early in her life, climbing the ladder and paying her dues. She then leveraged that experience into further success as an independent financial consultant. Even with all her mom's success, Parker mostly admired her parents for their amazing relationship. Her parents had been happy and worked at their relationship. They took the time they needed to get away and simply enjoy each other. Parker hoped she would someday have that kind of marriage.

After her mom passed, she worried about her father. He was still young, in his late 50's. Nathan Hall left the State Department after his wife had died and it took a year for him to really figure out what his life was about after losing his wife. Money wasn't an issue as they were good savers and planners early on and while he wasn't considered rich, he was comfortable. The home that he and his wife enjoyed had been paid off years ago as was their car. He tried consulting for the government, but he felt like he had 'been there, done that.' He tried teaching a government class at the local community college, but that wasn't really fulfilling. He was still bouncing around and Parker couldn't help but be worried about him. She knew that her father was hopelessly devoted to her mother and that he had loved her very much, but Parker also didn't want him to be alone. She had more than once reflected on her father's recent unrest about finding 'his niche' and what she perceived as a lonely life. She knew that she'd inherited her father's quality of 'not being satisfied with the status quo' as evidenced by her tenacity to find underlying truths. However, she also knew that she'd inherited a mission like devotion to work that she was passionate about, much like her father's love and devotion to her mother and years of public service.

Parker and Josh were still working on their directive to investigate the virus which everyone knew originated

from China, but the Director had also given both of them
additional, more pressing work. Homeland Security was
adjusting to a new normal as well. There were new rules in
place for people coming into the country and traveling to
and from other counties. The borders of the country were
not just a political football anymore but a much more
pressing issue as far as testing and qualifying foreigners and
citizens as healthy or sick who were coming into the
country. Parker was certainly busy but she still was able to
devote a few hours here and there to her and Josh's initial
investigation. She had been in communication with Elliott
Myles and Tim Chen over the summer and their thoughts
and even anecdotal evidence still pointed to the crisis being
some sort of deliberate attack; she just didn't have the
required proof yet. She had kept the Homeland Security
Director in the loop from month to month but because he
was busy turning his attention to other issues, he really
didn't pay attention anymore to the theory that this virus
was a deliberate attack. The director figured that if the
media hadn't found something by now, there was nothing *to*
find. He knew there might be no 'smoking gun' in this
instance and that this 'exercise' simply might end up being
the aggregation of circumstantial evidence, which could be
interpreted differently but would be used by this
administration to negotiate tougher trade terms. If was off
his radar.

     Parker Hall wasn't necessarily discouraged about
her progress, but she was becoming impatient. Her last
email with Tim Chen was about two weeks prior. She was
so hopeful months earlier when Tim had initially reported

that he was working on a vaccine for an unknown virus, but since that time he got busy, she got busy, and there was no new information for him to report. What she didn't know, or really what she had forgotten, was that Tim Chen was incredibly methodical in everything he did. His character didn't lend itself to panic or embellishment. What she was about to find out was that he was still as engaged as ever and had made progress. He had to be careful about his 'snooping around' in the lab. Tim knew that China was still a communist country and some of the personal freedoms he could count on in the U.S. didn't apply in China. He had no choice but to be very discrete. His initial discovery of the folder was an accident, a natural occurrence. There was no suspicion because he didn't do anything out of the ordinary. He knew that the lab was under surveillance all the time but he had found a way to gather information that didn't alert his superiors. Parker decided she would reach out to him again:

> *Frankie, how are you? What is latest from the lab? I'm hungry for any progress you can report. Thanks.*
>
> *– PJ*

_____

Li Wei objected strenuously which resulted in him raising his voice to a level which no one ever did inside the Chamber. "Colleagues. Please listen again to my logic and my argument. We must initiate Phase Two by next spring in order to guarantee our future desired world status."

Xin seemed to be Wei's nemesis at this juncture. "I still do not understand. Your implementation of Phase One has been brilliant—as you say, 'better than expected.' I'm not convinced we shouldn't leave well enough alone."

Huang Fu spoke up as the elder statesmen. "Xin, I too was skeptical, but I believe that Wei has made a compelling case for moving forward with Phase Two. I believe the reward far outweighs the risk."

Zhou Shou had his own take on things. "I am on the fence colleagues, but not for the reasons you think. Wei's plan was brilliant and I believe has worked. However, if we leave the West to their own devices and to come out of this crisis on their own, it is unknown what strategy they will take, what laws they will pass, and what actions, whether deliberate or unintentional, might befall us. It is for these reasons that I believe Wei is correct in asserting that we should move forward with Phase Two. At least we know that we are controlling the situation."

"Shou, you are wise and that is why you are on the council," said Zhang Min. "Your reasons are the best yet that I've heard for continuing into Phase Two. However, I too wonder, are we not being too paranoid about the West? Why do we believe that anything they do will hurt us? My understanding from Wei is that our factories are all focused on our new agenda and direction. The U.S. in particular has resumed production and they are understandably upset about new 'lack of capacity.' But Wei told us that this would be their reaction. What am I missing gentlemen? Haven't we achieved our objective?"

Wei forced himself to speak calmly. "My esteemed friends. I push for Phase Two because I believe we have only achieved half of our objective. Yes, our factories have been realigned to operate with less U.S. production dependence and increased worldwide dependence. But, as Shou has offered, we don't know what is coming next. For example, what if the U.S. realigns their society for manufacturing? They were once a manufacturing force decades ago; they could be again. What if they align with another country or two or three and create a relationship like they previously had with us? Americans are peculiar. Put a rock into a stream and the water will always find a way around. The lesson here is that the rock, not the water, becomes irrelevant. We are the rock and we believe that we are indispensable as to manufacturing the earth's goods. The U.S., given no other choice, might simply adopt the 'deviation' and make it a new normal. Yes, our country is strong, but in order to be the world's leader, we need to *ensure* that no other country or countries can become strong and attempt to rival us. Phase Two would guarantee that scenario, giving us decades as the new world leader with the ability to dictate economic terms to the rest of the world."

The members pondered in silence. Li Wei knew that this was a powerful argument. He had to exhibit patience. After a minute, members started to nod and Zhang Min, the elder leader spoke.

"Members of the council, it is decided. Phase Two shall be implemented per the original plan. It is what is best for China."

All nodded. Wei smiled inwardly. He did not dare show any bravado that he had out-argued his fellow Politburo members. That was not the Chinese way. The meeting broke and Wei would head back to his office to finalize the Phase Two timeline. He hadn't heard from the Sunhexiang Bio Research lab in over a month, and he knew he couldn't move forward with Phase Two until a vaccine for Virus Two had been finished. He must remember to call Ho Min, his longtime friend and the most senior at the lab, when he got back to his office to get an update.

CHAPTER 12

Two months prior to the current day. Mid-January

Tim Chen locked his motorbike and proceeded into the building. He'd been allowed to sleep in for a few hours because he worked all weekend, but it still felt like he was late for work. Security was tighter than usual, so he kept his identification in his hand as he passed through several checkpoints. Once in the locker room, he proceeded to go through the routine that he'd become accustomed to for nearly a year now. He had been working in the new fourth floor lab for about nine months now and understood the routine and the comings and goings of the various researchers and supervisors. Over the summer he'd made friends with a few of the other researchers near or at his pay and experience level. As he got to know them over the previous months, he took the opportunity to innocently ask them questions about work. He certainly made sure to do this outside the lab. He asked questions on the way to and from work and he even got together with some of them for a drink. China had opened up its economy earlier in the late spring and so by now, in January, life was almost back to normal. He took his time in gathering information and he knew that Parker was not well suited for this amount of patience. *She's just going to have to wait*, he reflected. He needed to proceed at his own pace. Most of the people he talked to knew nothing. They kept their heads down and performed their work. But there was a breakthrough. He had gotten together with a co-worker about a week ago. He'd met this particular co-worker, Sam Ji, in the locker room after his shift one night. Sam actually worked in another lab that Tim didn't have access to.

They were finishing their third beer and as they were talking Sam said, "Dude, enough with the formalities. Just call me Sam, everyone does."

"Okay, Sam, no problem."

"I don't know about your lab, but it's amazing that we're working on this."

Tim didn't react, he just played along. "Working on what?" He took a sip of his beer while leaning back, but he tried to also keep one eye on Sam to gauge his reaction.

Sam emptied the bottle and signaled to the waitress for two more. Tim could tell he was getting buzzed. "I mean … it's amazing that some of the protocols of testing are being skipped."

"What do you mean?"

"I'm mean we're testing, testing mind you, this

'vaccine' on human beings and they completely skipped animal testing. When did that become normal?" Sam was really feeling the effects of the alcohol, now into his fourth beer.

Tim continued to indulge his new friend. "C'mon, no way! What are you talking about?"

"Yes, it's true. I'm serious. We may not be doing that testing at our lab, but I know for a fact that we are sending our samples to another local lab where they are doing human trials."

"What reason would anyone have for skipping the animal trials and peer review of that data?"

"I don't know," Sam said. "I overheard my boss on the phone say that there was some deadline we all were working under. I think I overheard February or March or something like that."

"Hmm. I don't know pal, sounds weird to me. I haven't heard anything."

"Well you wouldn't. This project came from the Politburo and they've been pretty hush-hush about it. See all the security? That's what I'm talking about."

Tim got what he needed and now he knew where to look. He quickly changed the subject and he and Sam began talking about other things. A little bit later, their 'beer fest' concluded. Tim begged off on karaoke and headed home. After he unlocked his front door and stepped into his apartment, he immediately opened his laptop and logged onto the secure Homeland Security communications portal. He saw that he had a message and read it. As fast as he read it, he started typing:

All good here, getting back to normal. Discovered interesting information about my project. Chinese gov seems to be fast tracking and skipping protocols. Already at human trial stage. Apparently, February or March deadline. Still not sure what it means or adds up to, but now know where to look further. Be back soon.

– frankie

He clicked the send button, waited a few seconds, and then closed his laptop. He needed to get into that other area where Sam Ji worked. He asked himself a question, *why would the Chinese government issue a directive to make a vaccine, with a completion deadline of a month or two from now, and skip to human trials? Any scientist knows that might cost the lives of those trial patients and eventually compromise the vaccine.* He leaned back in his chair. *Wait a second,* he thought. *We don't even know what virus this vaccine is for? If someone was testing a potential vaccine on human beings that meant that those humans had to have the virus for which the vaccine was created, right? –Holy shit!* he thought. He understood government secrecy, but the indications were now there. He knew that a government would only act like this if what they had could be a potential weapon–and its cure.

Elliott Myles continued to monitor the situation through the summer, the fall, and into the new year. He had gotten some more anecdotal information from close sources, but nothing definitive. He appreciated Parker's candor and he concluded that her father must have given her the 'Ok' to confide in him. He had known Nathan Hall for many years and always thought of him as a straight shooter. He never minced words, which wasn't easy to do working at State or anywhere in DC. Words were like bullets for all those that worked at State, including the Secretary. Elliott wondered, *come to think about it, how did Nathan survive all those years being a straight shooter?* Oh well, a question for another time. Elliott certainly saw those qualities in Parker though. He never had kids and it was nice being a sort of 'mentor' to her. Although of late he felt like it was a one-way street of information and he was going the wrong way. Getting good intel had hit a wall. Just then his phone rang. "Hello?"

"How do you *not* know it's me? My name and face are staring right at you?"

"Oh, right. Hi Parker. Old habit I guess."

"I've got something significant. Be over in 20 minutes?"

"Ah, sure. 20 minutes. See you then." Elliott instinctively looked around the room to make sure it wasn't a mess. He was an old dog and his mother always taught him to clean up before any guests arrived. He was like any single male. Pick up clothes off the floor, especially underwear, brush your teeth, put dirty dishes in the dishwasher. Pretty standard checklist for a single guy no matter what age. His place was pretty clean actually so after he brushed his teeth, he had a few minutes before Parker came over and decided to check something. He sat at his laptop and logged into an NSA secure site, where he wasn't supposed to be. He just wanted to see if there was any news or confidential communiques coming out of China in the recent days. He scanned the topics. *What is this?* he mumbled. He began to read a report that had been compiled by the Hong Kong Station Chief as to Chinese factory production levels and capacity. Normally it wouldn't have piqued his interest, but he knew the Station Chief and also knew that his research was impeccable and trustworthy. The headline just rubbed him oddly. It read, '**China factories declining further U.S. orders based on country directive**.' The report was multiple pages, so he scanned it quickly. After a few minutes the doorbell rang. *Crap, Parker*. He only said that because he wanted to have read the entire report prior to her coming over. Oh well, he'll summarize and read detail later. He opened the door.

"Hey, come on in. Can I get you anything to drink?"

"Got beer?" she quipped.

"Sure. Wow. You must have something important if you're asking for a beer?" Elliott was teasing her but he really loved her swagger.

"Timothy Chen finally found out some more info." She handed him a print out of the email so she didn't have to read it.

"Interesting … interesting. When did you receive this?"

"Just now, well, sometime this morning. What do

you think? I have my own ideas."

"At NSA we never played that game. It was dangerous. But since we're not at the NSA right now, I'll speculate out loud. It appears that China, by government directive, was fast tracking a vaccine. Now, normally, one might conclude, 'how could that be suspicious or evil?' But because it's China, I know, as does most of the NSA, CIA, and FBI, that in these kinds of scenarios China is lying or hiding something. Christ, it's almost passé at this point. Everyone knows it and accepts it. But in our case Ms. Hall, it might just be a key to what they're up to."

"That's sort of what I thought, but I'm not sure I can conclude much more from his email."

"Well, lesser trained minds might be stumped, but as is known in many circles, I, on the other hand, am not a lesser trained mind."

Parker smiled, "OK Professor Plum, I get that you're smart–spill the beans please."

"Look at what he says. 'Apparently, February/March deadline.' Let me ask you–when has a research scientist or pharmaceutical company ever predicted with certainty or put a deadline date on a vaccine? That's not the way that particular science works. Follow me so far?"

"I'm with you. You're right, that makes no sense."

"Most vaccines are found at least twelve to eighteen months *after* a virus is discovered. And we know it's twelve to eighteen months because we know the typical research timeline and history of creating vaccines for viruses. So far so good?"

"I'm still with you, but I'm gonna need another beer if we keep going deeper."

"Oh, we're going deeper alright. Beers' in the fridge, you know where. So … let's play the analogy game. Just follow me. Let's say I wanted to make a lock and a key. I wouldn't build the lock and then fumble around for twelve to eighteen months figuring out the key, right?"

Parker grabbed another beer out of the fridge and twisted the cap off of beer number two, but she was so completely engrossed in the puzzle that she didn't realize the cap bounced on the table and then just fell to the floor. Elliott noticed, but he decided not to say anything. Once again, he smiled inside knowing his NSA level acuity was still there. He was typical ex-NSA, always validating one's skills.

"Right. That would be stupid. You'd want to know ahead of time what the configuration of the lock was that worked for the key you were making."

Elliott looked at her and smiled and pointed as if playing charades. "Exactly." He said in a soft voice. "The only way I could predict or build the key to a definitive date would be if I knew what the configuration of the lock was beforehand."

"Soooo. Recap for me please."

"The Chinese have a deadline to create a vaccine for a virus that they also created first. That's the *only* way they would be able to meet a deadline for creating the vaccine."

"OH MY GOD so that means—"

"Stop–stop right there. That's all we know. This could indeed be for a virus to kill bugs in agriculture and they wanted to complete the loop by also creating a vaccine."

"Seriously? You don't believe that. You're thinking what I'm thinking."

"Parker Hall, I may be thinking that, but my NSA training is now kicking in and there is a process to go through in even considering what you are thinking. Let's be careful here. I know you have the ear of the Homeland Security Director, but you don't want to speculate; you want to conclude logically. Think Spock from Star Trek."

Parker hated Star Trek, Star Wars, and all those space movies. She wanted to jump to the 'win.' She took a breath, thought about her father, and decided to keep listening.

"So how do we *logically* proceed?"

Elliott didn't respond to the sarcasm because this now was getting serious and he knew it. He didn't want to scare his young mentee, but all-be-dammed if she didn't stumble upon something that might be earth changing. He kept his cool and fell back on his training.

"We need some additional pieces of information to confirm what this is." He spent the next ten minutes telling her what was needed and then they both took a deep breath, smiled, and she politely excused herself and started to leave.

"Thank you for the beers."

"My pleasure. OK, Goodnight."

Parker said goodnight and started to walk out his front door.

"OH SHIT—WAIT!" Elliott said loudly.

She turned and looked at him.

"I almost forgot," he said, waving her back. "Come

back in for one second." She retraced her steps and stepped inside.

"What?"

"Right before you came over, I found a classified report from Hong Kong on the NSA secure site. I need to read the full report, but it basically said that Chinese factories were now declining further U.S. orders ... per China government directive."

"And how does that fit into the puzzle?"

"I don't know yet. Let me finish reading it and I'll get back to you."

"Okie-Dokie."

Elliott closed the door and thought to himself. He continued to be impressed with her, but things were different now. Had China developed a bio-weapon, and how did that relate to the virus that had just traveled around the world causing the most massive economic meltdown in Earth's history? He wished for one second that he was back at the NSA, in the fight. He shook his head. *Funny*, he thought. Here in his home, a newbie analyst at Homeland Security, a young researcher in China, and a washed-up NSA jockey might just be onto something bigger than nuclear war.

CHAPTER 13

The president had given nearly a hundred virus crisis briefings during the preceding nine months. These briefings were rapid fire, every day, mostly when the outbreak initially hit. Then slowly over the summer and into the fall, they started to be spaced out, one every few days, one every week, one every two weeks, etc. His last briefing was nearly a month ago. Things were slowly getting back to a new equilibrium. The media kept reporting the infections and deaths and would do so until it didn't 'pay' for them to broadcast those numbers. The president had always believed that ever since the news went 24/7 on cable, it stopped being about the news and began being about viewer ratings and advertising dollars. He labeled this the 'bad side of capitalism.' He had always thought that the problem with the news these days was that it inherently involved politics. Politics was another word for 'polarization.' He was always trying to give this lecture to unassuming visitors to the Oval Office. He loved analogies and he would tell those that would listen, "Imagine two companies with two nearly identical products. For example, let's say it's the iPhone versus the Android. And let's say that in an eagerness to sell their products, that one or both of the companies stretched the truth about their respective phones in their advertising, and in some cases flat out lied to consumers. Well you can imagine what the result would be. Users, who had actually had the phone in their hands, could verify or deny the various claims by the company to be true or false. If it was determined that a company flat out lied in order to make the sale, they would be rebuffed in reviews, online, and by their stockholders. Now here's the problem with the news. First, they don't sell a product, they sell words and speech. Those words and speech are fluid and it only takes an additional word or two to change a fact to an opinion. Secondly, because the news involves politics, most of their 'users' are biased in the first place and don't mind the lies if they are in their favor. They're essentially blinded so the news outlets continue to lie in order to play to the political emotions of their watchers."

Today's briefing would be fairly routine. He'd talk about the declining infections and death numbers. He'd talk about the progress on the vaccine. He'd talk about the needed hospital and health care worker supplies that were now being over produced and stockpiled and on and on. It wasn't that he didn't think this was all important information, but at this point he thought someone else could report to the American public. But his handlers had advised him that America needed to see his face and hear his words and feel his confidence coming out of this crisis. Make no mistake, the U.S. and other countries were recovering, but the virus was not 'done' and societies across the globe were still adjusting to a new normal. So long as there was no vaccine yet, the world would still be in recovery and adjust mode. As he walked out to the Rose Garden and proceeded to the podium, he squinted a bit. It was a bright sunny day. He didn't know why, but the brilliant sunshine instantly reminded him of a line from the movie 'Jaws' The Mayor of the fictitious Amity Island, Larry something or other, was speaking to the press on the beach, just a few minutes prior to another shark attack, saying, "It's a beautiful day, the beaches are open, and Amity as you know means friendship." The President chuckled to himself, *yeah, welcome to shark city*. He reached the podium and began talking.

———————————

Tim Chen was deep in his thoughts while on his ride into work. He was generally concerned now about what he'd surmised about the 'clandestine part' of the lab. He'd hoped Sam Ji was too drunk to recall most of the conversation or even think twice about it. He couldn't think about that right now because he was determined to find out more as soon as he could. As he arrived at the lab and locked his motorbike, he knew instinctively he'd have to take more risk to get more info. The key, he thought, was to know the risk and not make it any worse than it would be anyway. After dressing in the locker room, he contemplated simply walking into the restricted part of the lab and acting dumb. He knew he couldn't quite get away with that and besides, he didn't even know how to get in that lab. He had to figure out a way to be *ordered* to go into that area. He walked into his own lab and to his work area. His supervisor approached him and began talking.

"Good morning Mr. Chen. How are you today?"

"Good morning Sir. I'm well thank you." It was time to go for it. Tim took a breath and proceeded. "Sir, can I make an observation?"

Faan Jun was surprised for a moment. "Absolutely, Mr. Chen. Is there something not working to your satisfaction in your work area?"

"No sir, nothing like that. When I was transferred into this lab months ago, the pace of work was much different than my previous lab on the third floor. I am just curious; is there a timeline we are working on?" He cringed a bit inside. This could go one of two ways.

"An interesting observation Mr. Chen, and what conclusion are you drawing if there were such a timeline?" This particular supervisor loved any chance for a teachable moment. He was one of the senior supervisors and so he had some 'pull' in the building. He'd spent over twenty years working on bio-hazards and their cures. He looked forward to the new class of researchers every year and took it upon himself to include a mentoring component to his supervisory role. Faan Jun had plenty of seniority and with that, access to the entire building.

"Well sir … (Tim feigned like he was thinking). My

thought is that if my colleagues and I knew of the timeline we could plan our work accordingly and be more efficient."

"Yes Mr. Chen, that is a sound and correct observation. Let me ask this then. Why do you think you and your colleagues have *not* been told about any possible timeline?"

Tim thought for a second, *talk about a loaded question!* "Let me think sir ..." *maybe because we're building a weapon and people might not be too cool with that, duhhhh!* Thank God his thoughts were still private even in a communist society. "Sir ... I can only imagine that there is a good reason." He played dumb really well.

"Well Mr. Chen, yes, there is a good reason. But I hear your concern and I am delighted that you are thinking about your work and how you can do your job better."

"Thank you sir. I should get back to work." Tim gave it a good try. He knew there would be other times to try as well.

"Mr. Chen, wait one second ... just ... just come with me, I want to introduce you to someone." Faan Jun led him around the corner to a locked door he had never seen opened. He thought it must have been some kind of closet. To his surprise, Jun opened the door and it led to a short hallway which then led to another locked door. Jun opened it and inside was an entire lab. Tim thought, *this must be the lab Sam was referring to*. Tim was under the impression that there was no way to get from lab to lab without going through the locker room and all the sterilization procedures, but apparently, he was wrong.

"Dr. Ho, excuse me. I'd like to introduce you to Mr.

Tim Chen. Mr. Chen is currently working on 'the project' in my lab."

Dr. Ho Min smiled, "Ahhh, nice to meet you Mr. Chen."

"Yes Sir, thank you and nice to meet you, Dr. Ho. This is a very nice lab." He tried to bait Ho Min and it worked.

"If you have a moment, I will show you around."

"Yes Sir, thank you. I would welcome that."

Jun then addressed Min directly. "Min, do you mind if I use your office for a phone call?"

"Not at all, you know where it is, I will take good care of young Mr. Chen and see you in a few minutes, take your time."

Faan Jun immediately walked to a distant part of the lab and disappeared into an office. Tim played along.

"Ready, Mr. Chen, shall we?" Min held out his arm as if to signal 'after you'.

As they walked Tim was scanning the room looking for any evidence or paperwork of what they were working on. Min started speaking as if he were a tour guide, pointing out various areas, machines and tools. Tim listened with one ear in case Ho Min needed a response, otherwise his mission was clear. As they rounded a corner Tim saw three vials with liquid marked '**vaccine candidate**' and then a number next to each. He cataloged this information into his brain's database as they continued to walk. Ho Min was doing a fantastic job occupying himself on the tour. They wound around to different areas of the lab and ended up near Min's office. Faan Jun was still on his phone call, so Min felt secure in leaving Tim right there for the moment.

"Mr. Chen, please wait here for Mr. Faan to get off his call. I must quickly see one of my researchers." Ho Min walked away and Tim was left standing there, alone. Ho Min's office was mainly glass and it was easy to look inside. Faan Jun was positioned so his back was to Tim and that allowed him to thoroughly scan the room. Tim's scan paused at the credenza, to the left of Min's desk. He saw a binder along with other binders, but the spine of this binder was just labeled '**V2 characteristics.**' At that moment Faan Jun finished his call and began to rise from the desk chair. Tim immediately looked away and down. Jun walked out of the office and approached him.

"How was the tour?"

"Very nice Sir, it appears to be state-of-the-art in here."

"Yes, it is. Good. Let's say our goodbyes to Dr. Ho and get you back to work."

Tim nodded in agreement. At that moment Ho Min came into view, walking toward them.

"Are we all set?"

"Thank you Min, for the time and the tour. Mr. Chen is a rising star in my lab and I thought it was important he meet you."

"Is that so Mr. Chen? I look forward to seeing you again."

"Yes Sir, thank you. Maybe someday I will have the honor of working for you."

"Ah, yes. Maybe you can young man. Let me ask … Jun, I have a researcher whose father has passed and he must travel to the funeral. He will be gone for a couple of days later this week. Can you spare young Mr. Chen for that time? I will pair him with one of our senior researchers–he will be helping me out as well as learning about my lab's procedures."

"Yes. Yes, that is not a problem, Min. I will make Mr. Chen available to your lab. When do you need him, Thursday and Friday?"

"That is correct. Well Mr. Chen, it appears you will get your wish. I will send over a temporary access badge so that you can get in when needed. See you then."

"Thank you Sir, and thank you Mr. Faan. I will embrace the opportunity." *Boy, would he ever*. He went back to work. He had another seven hours and then he could get home. Once home he'd send another email to Parker and let her know what he found.

It was late and Elliott Myles was sitting at his computer. He rubbed his eyes. He'd been sitting there for over an hour re-reading for the fourth time the Honk Kong report on Chinese factory production. *Why am I fixated on this and what does it mean*, he pondered? He decided to get up and stretch his legs. Just then his phone rang. *Who the heck is calling at this hour?* he thought. The caller ID indicated a private number. *Christ, some damn robocall. What the hell, let's see who it is.*

"Hello … Elliott?"

Elliott was surprised it was actually a human and

further surprised that someone knew his name. "Yes?"

"It's Robert Harrison, I'm calling you from Hong Kong. We haven't spoken in years, but I hope you're well."

Elliot's brain went into overdrive. If it were a computer, one might have heard the hard drive spin up and the cooling fans kick on. After just a couple of seconds, he recalled the name and the who the person was. "Jesus Bob, how the hell are you? It's been at least five years, right?"

"More like seven. Now that this crisis is in recovery, I had a moment and I was thinking about you and how you predicted this whole damn scenario years ago."

Elliott's 'hard drive' was still spinning at high RPM, recalling all sorts of information on Robert 'Bob' Harrison. He was an American who had joined the NSA probably about seventeen years ago. He'd been stationed in Asia for quite some time and been in Honk Kong for the last five. As Elliott recalled, he'd been a pretty smart analyst but not aggressive enough to quickly move up the government career ladder. Elliott had originally met him about twelve years ago on one of his trips to Singapore. At that time, Bob Harrison had attained the position of Assistant NSA Station Chief, Singapore. Elliott recalled that he thought Bob had always been a better soldier than general. "Well, hell, I'm glad you did. How have you been? What's your position these days?"

"I've been the Hong Kong Station Chief for a few years now and the family is fine. Jake is nineteen, a sophomore at Cal Poly San Luis Obispo. When this crisis hit, he decided to stay there and continue with classes via Zoom. Emily is here and attending SCAD, the art and design University here in Kowloon."

Elliott's brain was whipping through lines of code trying to recall ... "And how is ... Susan, right?

"Susan is good. She's still with Cathay Pacific, primarily flying the Hong Kong-San Francisco route. She got furloughed for a few months then they re-called her. Thank goodness, too, because as much as I love my wife, we were gonna kill each other if she had been home any longer!" he laughed.

"Gotcha."

"So what have you been up to? Do you miss the grind?"

"Just hanging out, doing a little consulting and teaching, but not much else. But ya' know, yes, I do miss the rush a bit. Any good juicy info you can share ... about anything?" Elliott knew that Bob Harrison was a pretty straight shooter, but he wasn't above proving that he was 'in the know' and sharing things from time to time–at least that was what Elliott remembered.

"Naaaaa. Nothing juicy. We've had some of the cell phones of the Chinese Politburo members tapped for months now but nothing. Hey, that's confidential by the way."

"Of course, you know me, who am I gonna tell?" He knew if he asked about the factory report that Bob would know he'd accessed a secure site and that Robert Harrison might just shut down as to sharing any more information. Elliott had to be nonchalant about asking and he'd have to do it in a way that didn't raise suspicion. "Hey, speaking of China, I heard from a buddy at a company that makes products in China that they are having a hell of a time getting production back to the levels they were before the crisis. I didn't ask for details, but he seemed concerned to the point he was pissed."

"I feel for him. Yeah, I guess scuttlebutt over here is that China is taking their time ramping back up. Odd for them you know ... they usually overpromise and under deliver. Seems like the PRC doesn't want their factories playing so fast and loose anymore."

"Hm. Sounds like they are just being cautious."

"Maybe ... maybe."

"Hey, do me a favor? If you hear anything interesting by chance, give me a shout?"

"I will certainly do that–why, you know something I don't?" NSA agents were one of the few groups of people that were more suspicious than lawyers and Robert Harrison was no exception. The NSA pounded that behavior into its agents and employees during initial training. That's what made the NSA listen more carefully, scrutinize intel that much harder, and probably think the worst of situations rather than the best.

"No, no, just hungry for some action, you know me."

"Right. Will do. Gotta go, take care and let's not be strangers."

"You got it. Love to the family, thanks pal." Elliott had no idea if this would lead to anything but it was a 'another line in the water'. He did learn one thing. The NSA wouldn't be tapping Politburo members if they didn't have suspicions. Interesting.

CHAPTER 14

The weather in January is usually horribly cold and Li Wei usually rode in a covered vehicle to his party meetings, but on this mid-January day, it was unseasonably warm and the sun was shining. Wei stood tall as he walked across the Zhongnanhai compound which housed the Communist Party headquarters in the Imperial City. He had about thirty minutes before his next meeting and so he headed to the Water Clouds pavilion. The compound itself had an area of fifteen hundred acres and was located just west of the Forbidden City. Within the compound there were three 'seas,' the Northern Sea, the Central Sea, and the Southern Sea. They weren't really seas in the traditional sense, just big lakes. He enjoyed walking the compound nearly every day once the weather turned warmer in late spring. He especially loved the Water Clouds Pavilion which was located on an island in the middle of the Central

Sea. It was here that he did his best thinking. He would often bring his lunch of traditional Chinese noodles and vegetables and take in the beauty and wonder at what his countrymen had built for him and other party officials to enjoy. Wei had his cell phone with him all the time, like most people in the world today, but he made it a point not to take or make calls while on his walks or enjoying his lunch. He made sure to put it on vibrate 'just in case' so the ring wouldn't disturb the peace and serenity that he and others were enjoying. He knew he had much work to do, but it was Chinese custom, and he tried his best to adhere to the doctrine of balancing work with rest. 'Rest' to him meant being in a quiet area and allowing his brain to just think. He had done much thinking and planning in the last couple of years. He deftly negotiated the Politburo members to understanding and accepting his plan. Though he was a devout Chinaman and forever loyal to his country, his time in the U.S. had influenced his ego and as a result had challenged his traditional Chinese humbleness. He caught himself thinking about the future. Sometime after virus 2 was released and the West's eventual submission to China's dominance, would he be applauded as a hero? This thought was a direct result of his time in America and the influence of American culture. He was torn; he shouldn't think of such things but it will have been *his* plan and his plan alone that vaulted China closer to its long-term goals. At this point in his life he was comfortable. He didn't need money or material items. But there was a continuous yearning deep inside him for recognition. His cell phone buzzed and he answered.

"Ah Ho Min, my old friend, how are you?"

"I am good my friend, how are you?"

"I am sitting in the Water Clouds Pavilion on the Central Sea. The sun is warming even though it is still only about 7° C. It is warm enough to sit outside. This place is so serene and beautiful and normally I would not have answered my phone, but when I saw it was you, I smiled." Wei had known Ho Min for decades. They were school chums before Wei went to America to attend college. Their families knew each other and Min had always been a loyal dear friend to Wei throughout his rise in the Politburo. Wei had always respected Min and his passion for his work. He was a trustworthy fellow Communist and more than that, he was a brother Chinaman. In order to carry out his plan, Wei had to trust Min and let him in on the secret. Min was too smart to make a virus and a vaccine on a deadline and not know why. He had always been able to trust Min and there was no reason not to trust him with this. Ho Min was a consummate professional and he took the plan as a devout Chinese loyalist should-that it was in China's best interest and that was the only 'fact' he needed to know.

"I must apologize. In our last conversation two weeks ago, I couldn't provide you the information you desired, but I finally have news that the vaccine is nearing completion. It should be completed sometime in the beginning of March."

Wei was so relaxed and fixated on the beauty of the scene and his old friend's voice, that he forgot he was on an unsecure cell phone. "Very good Min, and what is your opinion on the pre-release time?"

"Ten days prior to release of V2. This is the time necessary for the vaccine to penetrate the water supply and properly promulgate through the system in order for—"

As Wei listened to Min's response, he noticed a military officer walking into the pavilion. Seeing the military officer caused his brain to instantly revert to his training and he immediately recognized he was on his unsecure cell phone. Normally, he would make these calls from his desk where the communications were routed through party intelligence apparatus on site or somewhere in the cloud, but more importantly it was secure. *Gāisǐ de!* he thought, *stop talking NOW!* Wei immediately interrupted, "I'm sorry my friend I must go. Goodbye." With that, Li Wei immediately ended the call. *Was anyone listening?* He knew he should have known better. He was sorry he hung up on his friend, but Min would have to understand. After another minute or two of second-guessing, he concluded it was too late to undo the call and so he refocused his thoughts. It was time for his meeting anyway and so while he walked, he began to sketch out the timeline. *Possibly mid to late March release of vaccine and then ten days later, the release of virus two.* Resolution is coming soon, he thought.

Parker Hall woke to another cold day. Frankly, she was sick of being inside and working remotely. Just like the government was a little slow to react to the crisis, they were slow to react to the recovery as well. Homeland Security as well as other governmental departments were still mandating as much remote work as possible in the name of safety. There was still no vaccine and even though many experts said that by now, nearly a year later, herd immunity had taken over and all was fine, other experts kept touting social distancing. It was very confusing. She could perform her routine with her eyes closed. Get out of bed, brush teeth, walk downstairs, make coffee, open laptop, open shutters, turn off porch light, get cream out of fridge, pour cream into cup, pour coffee into cup, and on and on. She finally sat down to her computer and logged into the Homeland Security secure communications site. As the system logged her in, she instantly saw that she had an email from Tim Chen–or 'frankie' as she had nicknamed him. She read it and nearly spilled her coffee. *What did this mean? This had to be something important!* She immediately started typing and filling him in on what she and Elliott Myles concluded the night before. Just then her phone made the incoming text sound. It was Josh. She replied, *sure, come over, I've got some updates.*

Twenty minutes later she was opening the door to let Josh inside. He'd brought his backpack which for Josh meant that he not only had his laptop but probably a few days of clothes, toothbrush, and God knows what else. Parker gestured for him to sit down.

"I was bored sitting at home." As he plopped onto her couch he said, "What's up?"

"Lots is up." She filled him in on the conversation with Elliott Myles and the email from Tim Chen. "Elliott said we still need some more information, but this could be big."

Josh got up and headed to her pantry while talking, "*What* could be big? The fact that China wants to dominate the world and when they concluded their military couldn't beat us, they released a virus on us and the rest of the world?"

"Exactly. Well, maybe. Can you be serious for a minute."

"I am! I was in the office yesterday and the Director was there, too. He was asking about any updates and I said nothing really significant, but that we had a mole in a lab in China working on a vaccine for an unknown virus."

"JOSH! You didn't–tell me you didn't say that?"

"I didn't say that." Parker sat back and exhaled as she was relieved. "What *did* you say?"

"We just chatted about things in general. He still doesn't believe there was anything 'funny' going on in China, but then he just seemed resigned to the fact that he's been in this business too long and that all the information he had pointed to this being a natural occurrence in their freaky wet markets. He asked me if I thought that we, you and me, should keep digging."

"And? … What did you say?"

"I said that I should talk to you before I answer that question. So 'as of now, we dig!' Ok, quick–what movie was that from? Huh?"

"Jesus, I don't know–but I do know why you don't have a girlfriend."

"*The Great Escape*. Awesome movie."

"Ok, that's great. Can we do some work please?"

Josh got his laptop out. "Ok, sure. What do you want to work on?"

"Find out anything about factories in China not renewing orders per China government directive."

"Okay, will do. And what are you going to work on?"

"I'm going to keep digging on what Timothy found, you never know."

And with that Josh logged onto her Wi-Fi and started typing. Just then, Parker closed her laptop and said, "C'mon–let's go."

"I just got settled. Where are we going?"

CHAPTER 15

E lliott Myles was growing impatient. Impatience was a quality he never attributed to himself. He rationalized that it was retirement added to the remnants of social distancing and the crisis. *Hell*, he thought, *maybe I'm just getting old.* He grabbed some coffee and opened his laptop. It had been about a week since his conversation with Bob Harrison, but it felt like a month. His patience was wearing thin. *Christ*, he thought, *I've had plenty of intel take months and even a year, what am I expecting?* He was toying with calling Bob. He knew that alone would raise a red flag. He decided to simply focus on something else. Just then, his doorbell rang. He looked through the peephole. It was Parker and Josh so he opened the door. "Yessss. Can I help you?" he said sarcastically.

"Bored are we? We heard from Timothy," she said as walked in with Josh following behind her, neither one of them waiting for an invitation from Elliott.

"Come in ... but I see you've already done that so, okay. What's up?"

"Read this," as she handed him the printout of Tim's latest email.

Elliott donned his cheaters and started to read. He was reading aloud, but mouthing the words so they were barely distinguishable. "Vaccine candidate and V2 characteristics. If it was 1944, I'd say V2 was a rocket launched from Germany over to England." Josh chuckled.

"Yeah, but it's not. What is with you men, always joking?"

Josh defended Elliott. "Lighten up Parker, we're just having a little fun before the end of the world."

"See—right there, we don't need that right now." Parker proclaimed.

Elliott took charge of the room. "Okay, enough. Let's think about this. We know that they are making a vaccine for a virus and they have some kind of self-imposed, excuse me, government-imposed deadline. Of the two pieces of information that your friend Tim has shared, the first one is pretty clear. It appears that he saw some vials marked vaccine candidate. Next, he saw a binder marked V2 characteristics."

Josh found a bag of chips in Elliott's pantry. "A second vaccine and its characteristics?"

Parker immediately shut him down. "No."

"You wouldn't need a binder on vaccine characteristics until you actually had the vaccine. Because the vial said vaccine *candidate*, they're not there yet," said Elliott.

Parker responded, "That sounds reasonable."

Elliott kept thinking. "V2 … char-ac-ter … that's it."

Josh bit into another chip and spoke. "What's it?"

"The answer."

Parker was growing frustrated. "WHAT ANSWER?"

Elliott sat down and leaned in. "V2 is a virus. The vaccine candidate is a possible vaccine for the 'V2' virus and 'characteristics' are the virus' attributes. The lab would have to know these attributes in order to craft a vaccine on a deadline."

Josh was annoying Parker by eating and talking at the same time. "Okay. But," he continued chewing, "how does this all add up?"

Elliott continued to think out loud. "2 … what is V2? … hmmm … second … number 2 … no! It can't be!"

"No, what?"

Elliott grinned. "V2 refers to a second virus."

Josh took another bite. "Soooo, what is the first virus?"

Parker couldn't take it anymore. "Will you stop eating those damn chips! For Christ's sake!"

All were silent for a minute. Elliott went to his computer, but Parker just stood there. Dare she say it. She'd hoped she wasn't jumping the gun but it added up. She knew it. Just then Elliott's phone rang. He looked at it–Bob Harrison.

Elliott put his finger in front of his mouth indicating for Josh and Parker to be quiet as he answered the call.

"Bob, what's up? It's late there."

"Hey Elliott. Yeah, I know, but I'm up and something interesting crossed my desk a few hours ago. As I told you, the taps on the Politburo phones had been a bust for months. Nothing of importance. Well, we intercepted a conversation that Li Wei, one of the Politburo members, had on his cell phone. Appears he got sloppy. Got a pen? I don't want to send this, even over secure email."

"Copy. Go." Elliott wrote feverishly on a white pad. Parker and Josh watched intently. Not only did this seem important by Elliott's reaction, but they were almost astonished that someone was actually writing on paper. "Ok, got it. Thanks, Bob–really appreciate it. Get some sleep. Bye."

Josh spoke first. "I can't read your scribbling."

"A Politburo member was speaking to someone in one of the Chinese medical labs," Elliott explained. "The lab person said that the vaccine would be completed around the beginning of March. Then the Politburo member replied, 'Very good Min, and what is your opinion on the pre-release time?'"

"Who is Min?" asked Josh.

"I'm not done. Then Min answered the question by saying, 'Ten days prior to V2. This is the time necessary for the vaccine to penetrate the water supply and properly promulgate through the system in order for–'", and then the Li Wei stopped the call and hung up."

Parker then said, "Josh, you asked what the first virus was? Virus One was what the world has just experienced for the last year!"

"Really?"

"That would be my guess guys. I'd like to know more about 'Min' though."

"What does this mean then?" Josh asked.

"If had to put this all together," Elliott began, "I'd say that we have some pretty strong evidence now that China released the first virus as some sort of test. To understand the world's reaction…"

Parker chimed in before letting Elliott finish, "…and you think that they are getting ready to release a second virus?"

"Maybe. Again, this is still speculation, but it's starting to add up. Follow me on this. We know that well over a year ago, before any notion of a virus, our president was hammering the Chinese on a fairer trade deal and he was making progress. Now, understand that China has always thought of themselves as a world leader. But President Hunter was succeeding in knocking them down a peg. Our own manufacturing was again on the rise, our economy was flourishing, and like I said, the president was sticking it to them daily."

"But if you were going to release a virus, why do it in your own country? Your people would die and die first and your country would take an economic hit," asked Josh.

They all thought for a few seconds and then Parker's eyes lit up. "Not if they *knew* ahead of time it wasn't that deadly."

"Bingo!" Elliott was delighted with the answer. "Look, China has a population of about 1.5 billion with a 'b'. As a communist country, they'd have no problem sacrificing twenty, thirty, fifty, even a hundred thousand people. Remember, China doesn't think like us. They think and plan decades and centuries at a time. We plan thirty days or maybe ninety days out."

"Also, releasing it on their own population first would take way any suspicion about nefarious behavior," Parker interjected. "They could win the PR war, too. 'Hey, look at us, our people are dying, poor China, we're trying to fight it along with the rest of the world.'"

"Right. So, let me ask you both this. Let's take all this to be true for a minute. Let's say you were China, and you did run a test. First, what were your original goals? Second, did this test produce those goals, and third and most importantly, if they did produce your goals, what would be the follow-up plans?"

Neither Josh nor Parker said a word. Elliott knew that even if they were right so far, what was going to happen next was complete conjecture. They needed more proof. They needed to take this to high government officials, which would not be easy, but they needed to have one more piece to the puzzle to be believed, or so he thought.

Once Parker was back at her house and Josh had left, she logged into the secure Homeland Security communications portal and began typing an email to 'frankie.' As she updated him on their collective thoughts, she knew that this particular email might put him in danger. She concluded her email by telling him they needed more proof. She was basically asking him to get it. She wondered what he would think of this now. Though he was an American citizen, he had a strong loyalty to his heritage and the Chinese people. She wasn't sure of his thoughts regarding the current Chinese government. She certainly didn't want to put him in harm's way, but her time at Homeland Security had opened her eyes to China. Every country was self-interested to a degree, and International relations and cooperation were basically a negotiation and balancing act. If the American people truly knew half the shit that was going on behind the scenes...she didn't want to go there. As she ended the email, she reiterated to Tim that he *must* find out more information. She didn't know why she felt that she had to write that. Timothy was smart enough to 'get' what she had said the first time. She was now believing more and more that China had indeed deliberately put the current virus into the world. She also believed that there *was* something else coming from China in the near future and she was starting to get scared.

———————————

Tim Chen woke up late. Even though his phone alarm had gone off, he tapped snooze four more times. It was Thursday, his first day in the 'secret' lab. He had put in some extra hours on the fourth floor lab so that he wouldn't leave his fellow researchers with a ton of his work to do as well as their own. The last two nights were especially rough; he'd gotten home close to midnight each night and was more than tired–he was simply exhausted. He was barely able to get his clothes off before his body fell limply into bed. Now, he was already borderline late and he had to hustle. He didn't have time to check his laptop for any messages, especially any from Parker Hall, but he'd check when he got home after work.

After microwaving something frozen, Tim bolted out the door and within a couple of minutes, he was on his motorbike and headed to work. Traffic had picked back up to near normal levels, so he'd have to pay attention and not let his mind wander as it had when he was the only one on the road. Sure enough though, he started thinking about work. He'd known of Dr. Ho's reputation and it would be an honor to work under his supervision. But his over-riding thoughts were around the mysterious vaccine which the lab was creating for some unknown virus. He wondered if his conclusions, about the unknown virus being a weapon, were too harsh. He'd hoped he didn't send Parker into a panic over his email. Rationally he knew that many countries had bio-weapon programs. Researchers that worked there specifically worked on viruses and bacterium that were deadly. It was actually a little scary to him, but it didn't shock him. He had always been of the mindset that he never wanted to work for those programs and in those labs. That was his choice. He wanted to work on cures for less deadly diseases that attacked everything from humans to plants to animals. He pulled into a parking space, locked his motorbike, and went inside the building. He noticed that lab security had been increased. By the time he entered the 'secret' lab area, he had gone through three checkpoints. If the lab was working on a bio-weapon, it would certainly explain the heightened security. He couldn't be sure. As he walked to Ho Min's office, he was actually kind of excited about working in this lab. Regardless of purpose, this lab was state of the art and run by a researcher/scientist whose reputation preceded him. He knew how the Chinese government did things. They would keep even the highest-level managers out of the loop if they could. He'd like to think Dr. Ho didn't know anything about a bio-weapon.

"Ahhh, Mr. Chen. Welcome young man. Let me introduce you to your lab-mate. He will show you your work area and the tasks that need to be done for today and tomorrow."

"Thank you Dr. Ho, it is my honor to be of assistance to you." With that, Ho Min introduced him to another researcher who would act as his partner but was really a kind of a low-level supervisor. As Tim followed his lab-mate, he noticed that the vial he had seen, the one that read 'vaccine candidate', had disappeared from a nearby work station. He and his lab-mate got down to business and within fifteen minutes, Tim was working at an adjacent station focused on the tasks for the day.

About nine hours later, Tim was parking his motorbike at his apartment complex. At least he was home at a decent hour. He had to catch up on laundry, email, and sleep. After putting some soup on the stove, he flipped open his laptop. After he logged-in to the secure communications portal, he read the email from Parker. He took his time, read it very carefully, and then read it again. He finally leaned back in his chair. He didn't want to believe what he just read, but he couldn't argue with the logic. Tim knew that the Chinese government was certainly capable of planning something like this and secretly, too. He just didn't want to believe that China would use a bio-weapon on an actual attack. He knew China had long-range goals as a country, but he didn't understand what would be accomplished by this action. The world's economy had been decimated and, though the world was working hard to 'come back' from the pandemic it had just experienced over the last year, he knew that China manufacturing had taken a hit, too. Maybe he'd had his head in the sand? Maybe geo-politics was really strained and there was more going on behind the scenes than he and the Chinese people were led to believe. He grew up in a free society and frankly, since being back in China, he'd really not felt the 'pinch' of Communism. His day-to-day life was almost the same as it was in the U.S.

At that moment, Tim made two decisions. He decided that he would attempt to get more info on what he saw in the lab. He didn't know how yet, but he realized that tomorrow might be his only chance as it was his last day as a temporary researcher in the 'secret lab.' His other decision might actually have even more importance than figuring out what was going on in the secret lab. He'd make a point of paying more attention to China's current Communistic practices and the political doings of the current Politburo. He loved China and its people. He never experienced any of the oppression that many spoke about. He'd start to learn more about China, its society, and why those opposed to communism would risk their lives in fighting for freedom.

CHAPTER 16

L i Wei took his seat. It was a regularly scheduled Politburo meeting and he knew from attending hundreds of them that they could boring, but this one wouldn't be.

"Wei, we are getting inquires now from the U.S. government regarding the resistance of our factories to ramp up U.S. companies' production. I don't remember you telling us that this response would be forthcoming."

Wei instantly knew what this meeting would be about and what his posture needed to be. "Good morning Min and my fellow members. To answer your question, I did foresee that there would be complaints from the American companies themselves regarding our factories not taking their production orders. It is natural to assume that their government leaders would be solicited by some of their bigger companies seeking help in the matter. Tao Hanwen, our good friend and loyal Communist, has a put a brilliant plan together that includes educating our factory managers and owners. His reasoning was very logical. Because of the current virus, factories have and continue to have natural trepidations regarding ramping up production as swiftly as we have in the past."

Wu Xin then added, "Yes, but at some point, they will question our ultimate motives. That point is fast approaching as their government now wants answers!"

Wei tried to calm them. "Colleagues, you are experiencing firsthand the impetuous nature of America. We have known about this behavior for decades. This is who they are. They want answers yesterday and they feel they are entitled to them. Our response is very logical and can actually be seen as a prudent business response."

"Wei, how do you believe we should now respond to the American government?"

"Shou, why do we have to respond at all? Why can't we just let our factories continue to put forth the message?" Huang Fu commented.

"Gentlemen. First, I do not believe this is as critical as you are making it out to be. Secondly, we should respond. We should let our Minister of Economics respond and simply put forth the logic of our factories' behavior. The U.S. may not like that reason but again, it makes good business sense on its own."

"Wei, I do not know if that tact and answer will appease them."

"It doesn't have to appease them Min; it just has to buy time. Phase Two will be beginning soon. Their government will have other pressing issues to think about other than why our factories aren't accepting more orders."

The members nodded and then they transitioned to other, noncritical business. After about forty-five minutes, the meeting ended and everyone prepared to have lunch together as was their custom following the meetings. Wei apologized that he had some pressing issues to take care of and left the room. He could tell that the members were becoming nervous. He was surprised that no one accused him of always having answers to their questions. Maybe it was his American background that allowed him to be bold with his answers. He knew his plan was well underway and this 'fear' of the American government would soon be stopped once and for all. He believed that his hand-holding of the Politburo would keep the members at bay for now.

———————————

Tim Chen had finally gotten the sleep he needed. He pulled into the building and went through the normal security checks and after dressing in the locker room, walked briskly into the secret lab. He went right to his station and discovered his lab partner wasn't there yet. Not thinking much about it, he began to work. He figured he needed to get some work done in the morning and then try at lunch to find out some more info on V2 and the vaccine candidate. After about forty-five minutes of continuous lab work, he looked up and stretched. He noticed again that his lab partner still wasn't there. It was a good time for a break anyway, so he walked to Dr. Ho's office, scanning the lab as he walked. It wasn't a long walk, maybe two minutes at the most if he walked slowly. Once he reached the office, Ho Min was inside at his desk and Tim knocked on the door which was partially cracked open.

"Come in."

"Good morning Sir. I have been at my station for about an hour and I have not seen my lab partner yet."

"Yes, I apologize. I should have come to your station and told you, but he called in sick this morning so you are on your own. Do you know what you need to do today?"

"Yes Sir. My lab-mate was very thorough yesterday and gave instructions for both days."

"Good, good. I have some off-site meetings, so I will be in and out of the lab all day. If you need further instructions please see my assistant, Li Na, or if I'm here, you can always ask me."

"I will be fine. Thank you." And with that, he walked back to his station. He wasn't one to ever look for a way to get out of work, but in this case, he needed non-work time to do more snooping around. He was so eager in his duties the day before that he finished about ninety percent of his work for both days. He knew he could probably finish the other ten percent in about an hour and then he'd have essentially nothing to do. He'd have to stretch this out a bit so at least he looked busy. Just then his eyes caught something on a workbench nearby. There it was, the vial with clear liquid that read '**vaccine candidate 3.**' He looked away and continued to his station. He needed to get that vial

or at least its contents. He didn't know the researcher
working at that station, but he certainly could introduce
himself if that might help his goal. Tim continued his work
while his brain was multi-tasking. The lab in general was
relatively quiet on Friday and this day was no exception. He
pondered an idea. He quietly prepared a label that read
'*vaccine candidate 3.*' Could he simply switch the vials?
What if he just switched vials with a different vaccine from
his lab on the third floor so at least if it was tested, it would
be a consistent vaccine type formula, but it simply wouldn't
work as an actual vaccine to whatever virus they were
working on in here, V2 or otherwise. He'd head down to the
third floor lab at lunch to say hi to his co-workers and
friends and grab a pesticide candidate that he'd worked on to
kill the 'armyworm,' the larva of the armyworm moth which
had infected nearly twenty-one provinces in China and
attacked China's farmlands. The invaders were attacking
corn, sugarcane, sorghum, and ginger crops and had cost
China millions of Yuan in fighting these little beasts.

Twenty minutes later he decided to go for a walk to
stretch his legs. The walk would serve several purposes.
He'd walk to Ho Min's office. If Dr. Ho was there, he'd
merely divert down a walkway before reaching his office so
that Dr. Ho didn't notice him. If Dr. Ho wasn't there, he'd
act as if he were there to see him. He'd knock, loiter a bit,
look confused, maybe even write a note and leave it on his
chair–anything to get a further look around his office. As
Tim proceeded, he again caught a glance of the vaccine
candidate 3 vial, but this time a researcher was working at
the station. He turned down the aisle way where Dr. Ho's

office was and immediately noticed he wasn't there. He proceeded with the plan. While feigning a need to see Dr. Ho, his eyes were lasers that scanned the office. Part of him, of course, hoped that Dr. Ho wasn't a part of this, but he had his doubts after seeing the 'V2 characteristics' binder. He needed to get a look at his desk. Tim Chen walked in, ready at any moment to get scolded by someone, but continued to Dr. Ho's desk and appeared to write him a note. As his hand was pretending to write a note, his eyes were glued to the five or six messages that were put on his desk by his assistant. When he got to the fourth one, he stopped. It read, *would prefer to release V2 between March 20 and April 20. Let me know if that will work–secure line. Li Wei.* He stood up and expected someone, Dr. Ho's assistant, to be standing there, but to his relief there was no one. He walked out wiping his brow from nervous sweat and proceeded back to his station. He decided to take a circuitous route back. If anyone was watching it would appear that he was taking the long way back to his station, simply killing time. What he didn't see was that Li Na, Dr. Ho's assistant, who was returning from the bathroom located at the opposite side of the lab from where Tim's lab station was, saw him exit her boss's office. She didn't think anything nefarious of Tim Chen so she just catalogued it away in her memory for future use if needed. Tim's new route took him right past the station where 'vaccine candidate 3' was located. He stopped to engage the researcher and instantly saw who it was.

"Hey Sam, what's up? They've got me assigned in here for a couple of days."

"Hey! Tim buddy. How's it going man? I haven't seen you since we tied one on."

"It's going well, but I've been super busy. This is a very cool lab."

"Yeah, it's the bomb. Dude, that was a fun night, we should do it again."

"For sure Sam. Hey, can I ask you a question? I'm running out of lunch places to go locally, know of anywhere good?"

"Try Weixin Noodle. It's just east of here about three kilometers. I go there at least twice a week. Really good. But you have to get there before noon because it gets packed after that and you won't get a seat."

"Perfect. I can't go there today, but I will try it on Monday."

"I'm going today. If you go another time just let me know and we can go together. You already have my mobile number. You'll have to take lunch a little earlier so we can get a seat, but I can't imagine your supervisor will mind."

"Thanks man, time to get back to work."

Sam gestured as if to acknowledge Tim's 'thank you' but he immediately returned to work. Tim walked to his station thinking that now he had a plan. He had about an hour before he would head down to the third floor lab and begin.

CHAPTER 17

The world was recovering. It had been almost a year
now since the world experienced its first worldwide
pandemic in over 100 years. President Hunter was re-elected
by a landslide, but it really felt to most like a non-event.
Recovery was proceeding slowly in most countries.
Countries had to balance public health with flat-out
capitalism and the U.S. was no different. Of course,
capitalism was alive and well in the media and had been
during the entire outbreak. Once infections and deaths
trailed off, the media began fueling the controversy of
whether shutting down the country was an over-reaction.
The media knew there could never be an answer but that
didn't matter. Just like Americans took sides politically,
Americans did the same thing with regards to public health
vs. freedom and lockdowns. The media had hoped this was
the case and they didn't miss a beat. Even after 9/11, as

Americans came together the media was cautious to pounce on any perceived divide. But as they say in business, time is money and the media were out to make a buck. Rather than come together over the shutdown and slow re-opening of business and life in America, Americans were divided and the media was there to make sure that they did their un-patriotic part in making this divide last as long as it could. Li Wei had been correct. Now that Americans were skeptical and at least half of them believed that the shutdown was indeed an over-reaction, he knew there was no way that Americans would listen to their government and quietly stay home the next time a 'so-called' pandemic struck.

———————————

Tim Chen was pretty sure that Sam Ji was not a part of the government's scheme. He was too junior on the totem pole and his complaints as to the lab and procedure further convinced Tim that Sam was an innocent bystander. Whether he could be trusted or not was a different story. Tim checked his watch, counting back from when he assumed Sam would be back from lunch. He had to get undressed in the locker room, redressed, and sterilized to go into the third floor lab, say hello, grab the pesticide, go back into the locker room, undress again, redress and re-sterilize again, and then beat Sam back to the secret lab and make the switch of the pesticide for vaccine candidate 3 all in about fifty minutes. That would give him about ten minutes to quietly have a panic attack and then resume work. This first part would be relatively easy, but he couldn't dawdle. He

entered the third floor lab and the few researchers who were
there smiled when they saw him. He'd given himself about
fifteen minutes to be in this lab. He couldn't seem eager, so
he took a breath, relaxed, and engaged two of his researcher
colleagues in talk. He glanced at his watch covertly, his
brain being one big countdown clock. After about eleven
minutes, he begged off saying he had to say hi to some
others and continued to his old lab station. He knew exactly
where the clear pesticide candidate would be. He went to a
cabinet next to his station, gave a quick glance over his
shoulder, and then grabbed the vial slipping it nonchalantly
into his lab coat. Now to head back to the locker room. As
he took a few steps toward the exit, another researcher
stopped him and engaged him. He didn't have time for this.
He was already at fourteen minutes. After about four
minutes of idle chit-chat, he excused himself and headed for
the locker room. He'd have to make up the time. By this
time, after all the undressing and re-dressing, he was ready
to enter back into the secret lab, but he'd lost some more
time in the process. He was at fifty-five minutes. He'd have
maybe five minutes before Sam came strolling in. He didn't
see him in the locker room, so he knew that meant one of
two things. Either Sam beat him back or he beat Sam back.

   As Tim entered the secret lab area, he was sweating
profusely. He had dressed and undressed faster than normal
and even though the lab had great temperature control and
was kept cool, he was under stress. Prior to him leaving the
secret lab, he'd prepared a label for the pesticide. The vial
had a slightly different color cork stopper, but there was no
time to replace it. While dressing in the locker room, he

removed the pesticide candidate label and replaced it with the 'vaccine candidate 3' label. As he walked the long way to Sam's station, he still didn't see him. 'Stay calm,' he insisted to himself. Every step felt like an eternity, but instinct kicked in and he readied for the switch by putting his hand in his lab coat and grabbing the vial, his James Bond moment quickly approaching. When he was about five steps away, he looked further down the aisle way. *Shit*, he exclaimed under his breath. Sam was already back and about twenty-five feet away, engaged in conversation with another researcher. *Dammit! I wasted too much time downstairs*, he thought to himself. No time to turn back now–he had to try. As he came up on Sam's station, he saw the vial right where it had been all morning. He briefly looked up to make sure Sam was still engaged. His hand was already coming out of his lab coat. He reached over to the vial and with one hand impressively made the quick switch. The 'vaccine candidate 3' vial he took was already back in his lab coat pocket. He had only stopped for maybe a second or two at the most, and once he continued walking it was then that Sam Ji finally caught a glance at him. Tim smiled at him and then made a right turn down another aisle toward his lab station.

Sam said loudly, "You should have come, it was very fresh today."

Tim did not stop, but he raised his free hand and waved an acknowledgement. He felt like he was going to puke at that very moment. It was over now and he needed to relax. *All was good*, he told himself. His heart was still pounding and he had to force himself to calm down. He sat down at his station and thanked God he had filled a glass of water prior to his departure an hour earlier thinking he might be thirsty after having executed the theft. He grabbed the glass, drinking it like he'd just returned from some intense hike or some similar thirst depriving exercise. He tilted the glass all the back to get every last drop, and as he put the glass down Dr. Ho Min was standing there at his station. Surprised, Tim said "OH! Hello Sir. You startled me for a second."

"Are you okay, Mr. Chen? You're sweating. Are you feeling ill?"

"No, no Sir. I was just so thirsty after my lunch that I guess I didn't realize it."

"My assistant said that you came to my office this morning while I was away. Did you need something?"

"No sir, I just wanted to say thank you again, for having me in the lab and allowing me to work under your supervision. It is a great honor."

"Mr. Chen, you have performed well and I'm sure it will be delightful to have you back someday."

"Thank you Sir."

As Dr. Ho left to go back to his office, Tim made a conscience effort to breathe again. He knew he couldn't show any emotion. He thought to himself, *I'm for sure going to puke now. I could never do this for a living.* With that thought he looked one last time at his watch. It was now past one o'clock. Five hours or so to go, of busy work, and then he could go home. The vial of vaccine candidate 3 stayed safely in his lab coat pocket. After his quick chat with Tim Chen, Dr. Ho strolled back to his office and sat down at his desk. He looked at his messages and saw that his fourth message was on top of the pile. That was odd, he thought. His assistant usually puts his messages in time order. Ho Min thought to himself that maybe his assistant saw it was from Li Wei and decided to put it on top as it was important. He didn't give it another thought and if he remembered, he would ask her about it later.

It was approaching five o'clock. Tim Chen and only a handful of researchers were left in the lab. Even Sam Ji had bugged out about twenty minutes earlier. He wanted to leave, but he certainly didn't want to raise suspicion or have Dr. Ho come by for another surprise visit. He usually worked till six, but he intended to send Parker the vial via FED EX and he had to prepare the shipment and get to the FED EX office before 7:00 pm. He decided enough was enough. It had been a harrowing day. Thank God the locker room was the opposite direction of Dr. Ho's office. He cleaned up his station and within ten minutes was unlocking his motorbike.

After another thirty minutes he was home, thankful and still eager to get into his apartment. Once inside he could truly relax and he immediately went to the fridge and cracked a beer. "Son of a bitch!" he said out loud. "There is no way in hell I could be a spy." He gave himself ten minutes to down his drink and relax. Then he'd get to work on the shipment and get to the FED EX office. He slipped the vial cleverly into the spine of a hardcover book he had. Even if the Chinese government scanned the package, the X-Ray machine wouldn't be able to distinguish the spine or its contents. The vial was secure, the book was secure, and he wrapped the book tightly in what looked like birthday wrapping paper. He put it in his backpack and bounded out to his motorbike. The FED EX office was only three blocks away so it would be a short ride. Normally he would walk, but he didn't need any additional close calls today. He addressed the package to Parker's home address, used a FED EX small box, and sent it priority express next day air. It cost over seven hundred Yuan, about 100 bucks U.S. He used his credit card and he'd make sure to send Ms. Hall the bill. Once back home, he could finally rest. He had to send Parker the email about the dates of V2 release and the tracking number to the package, but he was safe. Tomorrow was Saturday and he had this weekend off, returning to the regular fourth floor lab on Monday. He grabbed another Tsingtao from the fridge and sat on his couch. He'd grab his laptop in a minute. He finally had a moment to take in the day and the bigger picture. *Wow. A planned release of a virus*, he thought. *What is going on?* Just like the World War II movies he'd seen as a kid, he wanted to go to the window and see if formations of bombers were flying, preparing for attack somewhere. Maybe this is how war will be fought now and into the future, with microbes. He grabbed his laptop, logged-in, and began typing. He'd committed the message he saw on Dr. Ho Min's desk to memory and then grabbed the FED EX receipt and typed the tracking number. He'd wanted to tell the story as it was certainly harrowing, exciting, spy-like, and any other adjective he could think of, but he would tell her someday when they could talk in person and she could buy the drinks. He reread his email before sending it. He really hoped that she didn't need anything else. He didn't think he could go through another day like today. With that, he hit send and figured after one more beer he'd be ready to sleep well into the late morning.

Parker Hall was up at 6:00 am hoping for a response from Tim. She hated the fact that there was a 12-hour difference between Virginia and China. Email between the two was like a delayed ping-pong match, waiting twelve hours as the ball flew in slow-motion over the net and onto your side. Depending on when Tim decided to answer her email, it could be the difference of several hours after she woke up to start her day. On this day however, she saw the response email as soon as she logged in. Her immediate reaction was, *Wow, Timothy outdid himself.* She couldn't believe he found out more and had actually stolen a vial from the lab which was speeding on its way to her as she sat there. She leaned back in her chair, took a sip of her second cup of coffee, and tried to take it all in. She looked at the clock, too early to bother Mr. Myles. Even though she was a child of the digital age and had access to the proper time on her digital devices, she took after her parents and still had a clock on the wall in her kitchen. She texted Josh to get up, if he wasn't already, and come over which he almost immediately acknowledged. She decided to text Elliott Myles and give him a heads up that they needed to see him this morning. He responded a few minutes later saying that he was jumping in the shower and to come over at eight. *Perfect*, she thought. She'd just remembered that FED EX was coming. She tracked the package on their website and saw that it was 'out for delivery.' She'd write a note and put it on her door for the FED EX guy to go next door as she would be over there. Thirty minutes later the front door knob jiggled, then there was knock. She opened the door, "Did you think that you could just walk in?"

Josh laughed, "Nooo, I thought you might have unlocked the door for me."

"Yeah, well, think again. I could have been coming out of the shower!"

"Damn! That would have been fun."

"Oh my God! Is that all you think about?"

"What can I say? I'm a handsome man in my prime."

"I might give you cute, but handsome? Harrison Ford is handsome."

Josh thought for a second. "Han Solo? He's old."

"… and still handsome!" Parker then handed him the email printout from Tim Chen. "Here, do something useful and read." After thirty seconds Josh commented.

"Whooah. Did you get the FED EX?"

"No dummy, it's like 6:45 am! When have you ever received a FED EX shipment this early in the morning?"

"Never. Because I've never, ever, received a FED EX shipment."

"Oh my God, I'm not indulging you anymore. We're going over to see Elliott in about an hour. In the meantime, get online and I want to you start searching for China military mobilizations. I think it would be smart to see if any of this business coincides with movements by their military. Use the Homeland Security news and alert page and then use Google, never know what you might find."

"Yes, Ma'am! I'm on it."

It was 7:50 am and Parker could wait no longer. She tapped Josh on the shoulder, signaling for him to follow her. She had a couple copies of the 'Chen email' and the note she needed to tape on her front door for the FED EX man. They knocked on Elliott's door. Elliott, though he claimed to have just showered, was in robe, T-shirt, and slippers.

"Come in gang." Parker and Josh entered and before he shut the door, he instinctively looked outside. His 'spook' level training was still working. "How is everyone?"

As Parker handed him a copy of Tim's email, she simply said, "Email from Timothy." Elliott took it and as he read, he walked over to pour his coffee. He stopped reading as if to all of a sudden remember that he forgot to offer his guests anything to drink.

"Coffee?"

Parker and Josh responded in unison, "No thanks."

Elliott kept reading, stirring the sugar he just dumped in his coffee. "This is pretty much the proof we need. Did you track the FED EX package yet?"

"Coming this morning, I left a note on the door for the FED EX guy to come here."

"Geez, you didn't jump down his throat when he asked about the FED EX?" Josh said.

"He didn't ask if I received it, he asked if I *tracked* it! How did you ever get a job at Homeland Security??" Josh just smiled.

"This is it, nothing more?" Elliott asked.

Parker snarked back. "What did you want, an invite from Li Wei to the virus release party?" She realized that retort was a bit disrespectful. She instantly regretted her tone. This whole thing was starting to get to her.

Elliott overlooked the millennial disrespect. "Actually, yes. We need a certain date. In order to bring this to either the Homeland Security Director or anyone else higher up we need a specific date they will either release the virus or the vaccine. Then we'll have it."

"What if we can't get that?" asked Josh.

Parker answered for Elliott, "Then we simply have speculation which if not true, will get us both fired and blackballed from ever working again in DC."

"That would probably be more accurate than not."

"Suggestions Elliott?" asked Parker.

"So let's step back, sit down, and review what we have." Elliott grabbed the other email printouts and he and Parker went to the other room to sit down. Josh stayed in the kitchen to get some coffee and look around for some food before he would join them a minute or two later.

"We have three emails from Tim, correct?"

Parked responded, "No, that's incorrect, we have five."

Elliott got up abruptly and went over to a desk that had some papers on it. "Right ... I was looking at these two separately the other night. Okay, here we go, five."

Josh interrupted as he came back in the room with an open can of Spaghetti-O's, "... and let's not forget your Hong Kong spy pal that provided info of the Li Wei phone call."

"Very good Josh. What would we do without you?"

Josh smiled and Parker rolled her eyes. "Do you always have to be eating?"

Elliott got down to business. "Okay, let's review. Email one from Tim says he was asked to work on a vaccine in another lab. Email two says he saw a folder labeled 'V2– Human Vaccine Trials' and it was *not* for the current virus pandemic. Email three says the Chinese government is fast tracking the vaccine, skipping protocols, and going to the human trial stage. February or March deadline. Email four says he saw another folder which read 'V2 characteristics' and a vial labeled 'vaccine candidate'. Then I get a phone call from the NSA Hong Kong station where they overheard on an unsecure cell phone a conversation between Li Wei and a lab person named Min. Min says the vaccine will be done in early March and to pre-release the vaccine ten days prior to the release of … presumably V2. And lastly, email five says that Tim saw a message on Min's desk from Li Wei saying that Wei would prefer to release V2 between March 20 and April 20. Do I have all that correct?"

Josh nodded and Parker echoed the sentiment saying, "That's about it. Oh, and that Tim sent a vial of vaccine candidate 3, FED EX, arriving today."

"…and we learned that 'Min' is the famous Chinese infectious disease scientist, Dr. Ho Min."

"Right. And we've previously concluded that you'd only make a vaccine to a pre-determined schedule if you had the virus formula or characteristics, right?"

They both nodded in agreement.

"Sooo, it is a pretty good assumption that V2 is a

second virus. 'Vaccine candidate 3' is the third version of
their vaccine for V2, based allegedly on human trials.
Hopefully, candidate 3 *is* the actual vaccine."

"… and they need to release that vaccine into their
water supply ten days prior to releasing V2," Parker added.

Then Elliott added on to that, "… and they prefer to
release V2 sometime between March 20 and April 20."

"What good does it do China to release a virus they
already have a vaccine for?"

Elliott responded slowly to Josh. "Because the
world won't know they have a vaccine for that virus.
Remember, this second virus is completely different from
the first virus that we've all been dealing with. Even if the
world found a vaccine tomorrow for the first virus, that
wouldn't help anyone against the second virus."

"…and because the vaccine will be hidden in plain
sight in their water supply," Parker said.

As Josh tossed the empty can into the garbage, he
asked, "So like, is this a new way to wage war instead of
using tanks and planes and armies?"

"The quick answer," said Elliott, "is yes. Let's think
about the history of war. Thousands of years ago, war was
about land. Taking the land of your neighbor or enemy and
killing their armies as well, but it was mainly about taking
and possessing land. At that time that was the most valuable
thing your neighbor or enemy had. Then war became about
ideology and land. Hitler took land but he spewed an
ideology that most of the world didn't agree with. Then look
at the Gulf War in the 1990s. Saddam Hussein invaded
Kuwait. We're Kuwait's ally so we come in and beat back

Iraq. But why were we allies of Kuwait in the first place? Oil. Sure, we defended Kuwait and its people from the Iraqi aggressor, but what we really did was make sure a tyrant like Hussein didn't get those oil fields. Earthly power has changed from the land a country possesses to the economic power it has. Now, many factors go into a country's economic power. When you have economic power you have resources, you can dictate trade terms, you can dictate legal relationships with regards to Intellectual Property rights, you can dictate manufacturing relationships, and on and on. It has been long known that China has had their eyes set on being the world's only true superpower. One hundred years ago, I might have said military and economic superpower. But because the world is so intertwined economically, traditional war serves little purpose amongst big nations today. Sure, we still see the smaller countries get into skirmishes now and again, but as far as the biggies are concerned it would be a waste of resources and would probably lead to social issues, given social media, as well."

"So China wants to be the *only* superpower?"

"Maybe Parker. They certainly want to be the biggest. Again, remember that it does them no good to wipe out everyone else on the planet. They still want customers and business partners. They just want them on *their* terms and at *their* will. If they could seriously degrade everyone else's power, people, resources, economy, they could vault ahead for many decades to come."

"So I was right?"

"Pretty close Josh. Now, let me ask this. If you were China, and you ended up succeeding at this plan and the rest of the world's economies are downgraded significantly, especially the U.S., why wouldn't you think that the reduction of manufacturing will hurt you in the long run?"

Josh and Parker looked at each other and shrugged at Elliott.

"Because you've planned on diversification of your customers anyways. You don't want the U.S. to be your biggest customer. You don't put all your eggs in one basket. So, if say you're were a manufacturing giant, like China, you wouldn't want any of your factories to commit to producing a majority of goods for any one country or company. You'd spread out your customers and their orders so that no one country, no one superpower, was of such importance to any of your factories that they could dictate any terms or hold you hostage for their demands–economically speaking."

"That would be tough to do, for a factory to turn down orders."

"You're thinking like an American, Josh. Think like a Chinaman. Your country has been around for like four thousand years. For a country to survive that long, their culture has been bred to know suffering, strife, and struggle. The Chinese people certainly aren't like spoiled Americans who feel they're suffering when cable goes out or they have to wait twenty minutes at their favorite restaurant for a table."

"So in the diversification they would ask their people to suffer a little … for the good of the country?"

"For the good of the collectorate. A plan would have to be in place where all of their factories towed the party line–pun intended!"

"Right, because they're Communist."

Parker shook her head, "You don't miss a thing do you Josh?"

"I kept thinking about what my Hong Kong friend had said and I couldn't figure it out … until now–the Politburo has *ordered* their factories to *not* extend capacity to U.S. companies.

"Unbelievable," said Parker.

"You also want to make sure that no other countries could take your place or take up the slack. But you're both missing the big picture."

Josh and Parker looked at each other then looked at Elliott with puzzlement. Just then the doorbell rang. It was the FED EX guy. Parker sprang up to answer the door. She signed for the package, said thanks, and then proceeded to open it. All three looked confused as it was a book.

"I thought he sent a vial?"

"He did, he just forget to tell me that he obviously hid it in this book somewhere." As she turned the book all around, she could see the slight opening in the spine. She tried to reach it with her skinny fingers but it was too far down, near the middle of the book. She didn't want to shake it for fear of the damn thing spilling or breaking so she asked Elliott if he had some long tweezers or something like that. Elliott went to a kitchen drawer and produced a weird looking kitchen gadget.

"What? They're extra-long pick-up tongs. Twenty-four bucks at Walmart."

Josh laughed, "For what, pulling something out of your stomach?"

"So you don't have to bend over as much to pick up

things off the ground or in hard to reach spaces." He smiled
as if he were the cleverest person in the world to have these.
Parker didn't say anything and she was waiting for Josh to
make a dumb 'man' comment like, *how cool is that!* but
Josh remained silent. *Good for him*, she thought because she
might have smacked him had he said something. She
grabbed the tongs from Elliott and gently gripped the vial
extracting it ever so slowly.

"Just put it down over there, safely on the table for a
minute."

Parker complied with his instructions and then
Elliott resumed his thoughts, "Where did we leave off?"

"You said that we were missing the big picture."

"Right, Parker. So, if you really want to be the
world's only superpower, you wouldn't want to be hasty
with your plan. You'd craft a plan that had an out for you."

"What do you mean 'an out'?" asked Josh.

"You might try a first attack and see how it goes,
see what happens, see what the reaction of the world, their
governments, and their people were. You might sacrifice
some of your people as well, to show solidarity and
suffering right along with the rest of the world."

Josh asked, "Why not just hit hard with a first strike,
so to speak?"

"Ms. Hall?"

"Because if it didn't go well, you could stop after
the first attack and then do nothing more. You could just go
about your business and no one would be the wiser."

"…and how will you know if you should go forward
with the second attack?"

"If it generated the reaction you were hoping for," smiled Parker.

"Which would be.....what?"

"Fear, anger, controversy, confusion and most of all … and this is the key … an imposition by governments to impose restrictions on their own citizens which saves lives, but hurts their overall economy."

"That's exactly what has happened over the last year with this stupid overreaction to this virus!"

"Josh, you've just expressed the quintessential American response that China is depending on," Josh didn't realize that Elliott's comment wasn't really a compliment.

"Why, thank you."

"No, you idiot! Because most Americans probably *do* think like you," Parker said with frustration. *How and why I'll never know,* she thought to herself. "China will probably move forward. They're going to release a second virus on the world!"

"They will release Virus Two and their population will be vaccinated through their water supply, just like we have fluoridation in our water supply and have since the 1940s. The world will be weary of hearing from public health and medical experts about social distancing, additional lockdowns, and potential infections and deaths, especially since the original models the health experts gave us last year were wildly overestimated. Media around the world will love fueling the controversy. I can see the headlines, 'The World Cries Wolf–Again.'"

"So what do we do?"

Elliott looked at both of them. "It's time to seek a higher authority."

CHAPTER 18

P arker was able to make an appointment with the
Homeland Security Director for Monday at 2:00 pm.
She didn't explain that Elliott Myles was going to be there
as well, just her and Josh. She didn't know if Elliott and
Director Thomas had any history, but she'd hoped that
wasn't going to be an issue. *What a crazy day and what a
crazy world,* she thought. She had dreams of finding the
right guy someday, getting married, and having kids. *Is this
really where our world is headed? Microbe attacks that can
do more damage than nuclear war?* she thought to herself.
*What the world had gone through was bad enough. The
mass unemployment and crazy mask wearing and not
hugging or shaking hands. We're just beginning to get back
on our feet.* Parker was certainly driven, but she wanted that
slice of Americana just like all Americans did. Most world
citizens had the same thoughts. It was one thing to fight a

visible enemy that could be seen and destroyed. It was quite another to fight the invisible man. She wondered that even if they were somehow able to stop China and expose this terrible plot, were there other bad actors in the world that would see China as the great teacher of how to conquer the world in the future? She was tired. Her brain was tired. Before she crawled into bed and put the TV on for a bit, she'd send an email to Timothy. She hated the fact that she had to ask one more time for more information, more specific information, regarding China's plans. Even though Tim Chen didn't dramatize his emails, she knew there was always more to the story. She also knew that Timothy was kind and gentle and caring and that whatever he'd gone through to get that information, it must have been difficult for him or at the very least stressful. He was not a guy who liked to live on the edge where stress flourishes. She reflected on how close they had been in college. *Why hadn't they gotten together?* she wondered. I guess it was the old, *do we destroy our friendship by letting it go to the next level* philosophy. She crawled into bed and focused her thoughts on the positive and Monday's meeting.

The weekend came and went. Parker had worked all morning on trying to gather any more evidence of a sinister plot by the Chinese government to rule the world. Just thinking that sounded foolish to her, but she couldn't deny what they'd uncovered. She was confident in their conclusions, but then again, this was Washington. Sometimes this place didn't act from facts or logic. Most of the time the people that worked in Washington, DC made deals, self-interested political deals. She wondered when humans first made a 'political deal.' She thought to herself, *I*

can only imagine the conversation between Neanderthal–
Ok, if you endorse me as leader of the tribe, I'll make sure
you and your family live in the nicest cave. She shook her
head. It was almost time to round up the troops and head to
the meeting at Homeland Security. Elliott and Josh were
supposed to be over soon, by 1:00 pm, so that they could all
ride together. It was only noon, but Parker was ready. She
wasn't sure what to anticipate from the meeting. Certainly,
Elliott Myles had way more experience at such meetings
from his extensive years of government service. So did her
father, but she imagined this wouldn't be like any meeting
he ever had at State. Would the director get on a red 'Bat
Phone' and call the president? She knew she was being
ridiculous, but she was also really curious as to how this was
going to play out. She kept herself busy for the next hour
and before she knew it, Josh and Mr. Myles had shown up at
her door.

After Elliott received his visitors' badge, he
followed Parker and Josh through the halls of Homeland
Security and into a conference room on the fifth floor.

He commented quietly, "It looks different after all
these years."

Josh turned and looked at him, but didn't say
anything. Elliott had been there many years before, about a
year after 9/11. He had been assigned the task of researching
chemical and biological warfare after the Anthrax attacks
subsequent to 9/11. The NSA let him run with this task with
little oversight because, at the time, it was thought to
possibly be the next form of attack on the U.S. and the NSA,
CIA, and the newly formed Department of Homeland

Security had their hands full with the then current 9/11 investigation. Elliott spent nearly four years amassing data and analysis from different departments at NSA, Homeland Security, and the CIA. He had spent weeks at the government's biodefense lab at Fort Detrick in Frederick, Maryland. He wasn't a scientist, but he didn't need to be. His NSA training taught him how to be more of a 'detective' in everything he did. During that time, he learned more than he wanted to about Anthrax, spores, DNA sequencing, Ames strain, mutations, inhalational Anthrax, cutaneous Anthrax, and so on. Through all of this education, he learned one overriding fact–this was not science fiction, some kind of biological outbreak or attack could and would happen someday. That scared him. And because that scared him, he eventually put together a report warning that an attack was coming. Unfortunately, Elliott Myles had bad timing. It was nearly five years after 9/11 and the U.S. had moved on. The TSA, Transportation Security Agency, was put in place in 2003 and Americans were dealing with, and had adapted to, the new normal of flying. Some of the Anthrax attacks of 2001 were proven to be hoaxes perpetrated by copycats. Some of the conclusions by the FBI regarding the Anthrax attacks pointed to one bio-researcher who had a history of mental illness. Regardless, the American people had become weary and worn-out from 9/11 and all the emotions it had uncovered. Yes, Americans rallied as a result of 9/11, but Americans were more than ready to move on from the horror of the attacks. As such, Elliott's report came too late to be considered seriously. It wasn't that some officials didn't believe it, it was just, as they say, so 'yesterday.' He was shocked that his immediate higher-ups didn't take this as seriously as he did. Of course, he knew that without definitive proof, he was simply another soothsayer trying to predict the end of the world. Some even said that his report would make a great movie. He'd made over one hundred bound copies, at the taxpayer's expense, and sent them to all kinds of different officials in many different government departments. He'd hoped that at least one person would take his side and sound the alarm. He failed to understand that no one in this town went out on a limb, that's just not what people did. He kept pushing and told as many people in government as he could about his report. These actions were ultimately Elliott's undoing. Elliott knew his report was solid, his logic sound, and yet he just couldn't believe that he was getting the brush-off. Human behavior was a funny thing. The natural reaction to being disbelieved, especially when the facts were on your side, is too push back harder, believing that the louder you yell or the slower you talk, somehow the words now coming out will magically penetrate the non-believer. Of course, this has been time tested over human existence and rarely works. Unfortunately, Elliott fell prey to this instinctual human behavior. He eventually pushed too many people too hard. The NSA's response was to transfer him to an outpost far away and essentially let him rot there. He would not let them put him out to pasture, so he declined the transfer. Elliott Myles was eventually forced into accepting early retirement. He spent the next couple of years alone, isolated and miserable. He never married, didn't have a significant other, and had no children. At this point in his life, he'd regretted these facts. Work, at the NSA, had consumed his

life even though he knew he was very good at it. He
eventually made peace with the fact that no one really
listened to him regarding his cautionary tale. This 'peace'
would have to do and as life marched on, he moved on.
When the pandemic occurred a little over a year ago and
spread throughout the world, he felt slightly vindicated as he
watched the pundits night after night. Because he was out of
the loop as far as the NSA or other government information,
he couldn't trust most of what was being reported on TV. It
didn't matter to him at this point anyway. It was what it was.
He couldn't fight the 'man' and that was that. Then Parker
Hall showed up at his door. He'd reflected on the fact that
he hadn't been resistant to helping when she came to him
regarding her task of investigating the possibilities that
China perpetrated the pandemic. He wondered why he just
didn't pass, not wanting to be dragged into all this again. As
he thought about it, he reflected on what his father had told
him many years prior, that 'Time heals all wounds.' He
thought that maybe this was some kind of cruel second
chance. *Yeah*, he thought, *a second chance to be rebranded
a fool.* As he sat down in the conference room and they all
waited for Director Thomas to enter, he quite simply
decided, *what the hell, I am who I am and if someone is
willing to give me the time to spew my theories, then I'll be
a willing participant.*

Homeland Security Director Thomas entered the
room. He paused briefly once he saw Elliott Myles. He was
surprised that Elliott was there and was immediately suspect
as to why Parker Hall had dragged him along. Roger
Thomas was a mid-level analyst at the time of Elliot's

implosion years before, but he'd heard all kinds of rumors and stories and tended to go along with the crowd that branded Elliott Myles a nut. Like a good soldier, he kept his head down and went along to get along. He'd never read the actual report that Elliott produced, but from the water cooler talk at the time, he concluded that it was a huge dose of fear and worldwide calamity crap.

"Good morning director, do you know Elliott Myles?" Parker began. "I've been getting some advice from him regarding the assignment and we think we've found an important connection between the virus and China."

"Yes, Ms. Hall, we know each other," and with that, he gave a slow nod to Elliott, which wasn't exactly a 'Glad to see ya!' Director Thomas paused before continuing, saying, "More importantly, I hope you haven't divulged any confidential information?"

"Not that I'm aware of Sir," Parker of course was lying, but she had to and Josh and Elliott knew it but remained silent.

"Alright, I'll indulge you for a few minutes, but I have to say Ms. Hall, I'm disappointed that you've gotten into business with Mr. Myles here. Do you know of his reputation?"

"I do Sir, and I'm not sure what—"

"It doesn't matter right now, please proceed."

Elliott almost said something, but instead bit down on the inside of his cheek.

"The information we have gathered through a human source suggests that it's a real possibility that China was responsible for the current pandemic that we've all had to deal with for the last year. We believe the information also suggests that China has created a second, more deadly virus for which they are working on a vaccine. We believe that once the vaccine is finished, their plan is to release this second virus on the world and put the vaccine in their water supply prior to release."

"Those are pretty big claims," the director then looked at Elliott and addressed him directly. "Did you egg these two on toward that conclusion?"

"Roger–I'm a bystander here, there's no need to attack me. I looked at their information and made the same conclusions they did."

"Did you let them read your report from years ago? Sounds like they did. Must make you feel vindicated that we can finally pin a bio-attack on someone?"

"You know what Roger," Elliott said measuredly, "I can finally say this to your face—fuck you!"

Josh chimed in, "What report?"

"He didn't tell you guys?" Director Thomas smiled. "Well Elliott, you've left out the best part of your past. Maybe you should enlighten them?" Roger Thomas was being rude and he knew it.

"Sir, I don't know anything about any report and we did the work independently. I have a friend at a lab in China who—"

"A friend, Ms. Parker! Is he your human source? For Christ's, sake, Parker! How do you know him?"

"We attended Georgetown together and— "

"College pals? Drinking buddies? Maybe he's still trying to get into your pants. Great. Just great."

Elliott came to Parker's defense. "Listen Roger, you

can bash me all you want, but you have no fucking right to talk to her like that! She oughta sue your ass, she probably has a claim, too!"

Parker and Josh didn't dare look at each other or say anything else. This meeting wasn't going to go anywhere and probably would get them fired if not investigated. They knew the info they had gotten from Elliot's contact at NSA Hong Kong Station would be exposed and might jeopardize Elliott. They waited for his lead. He led alright.

"You know what Roger, you were always too stupid to see beyond your big ass nose!"

"That's it. Meeting over. And you two. I am seriously disappointed. This is a direct order, are you listening? Stop any further work on the China virus investigation. The damn thing emanated from a wet market! We will discuss this at a later date and hopefully my counseling can get you back on your feet onto the straight and narrow."

"Don't you mean get on your knees and— "

"Enough Elliott. This meeting is over."

All three were silent. The director stood and started to exit the conference room.

"Tell me Roger, did you ever actually read my report all those years ago or did you just adopt the herd's conclusions?" Elliott asked.

Director Thomas stopped, turned around, and said, "I didn't need to read it. I was informed."

"Maybe if you had, you'd realize that this shit is real. One last thing Roger," Elliott continued, "thanks for all your service as a steadfast, head-in-the-sand, fucking bureaucrat."

The director scowled. He wanted to flip him the bird, but he just decided to walk away.

Parker and Josh also stood and Parker was a bit shell shocked. She started to talk, "He didn't even look at our intel?"

"Parker, his mind was made up as soon as he saw me in the room. I'm sorry, you and Josh might have had an easier go if I hadn't been here."

Josh piped up, "That really sucked."

"So now what do we do?" Parker asked.

"Let's go to the press."

"Josh, we can't do that," Elliott cautioned. "We are all threading the needle with regards to National Security laws. This goes public right now and I'm afraid of what might happen to you guys. Let's just get out of here."

They exited the building and got into Parker's car with Josh in the back seat.

Parker started the car then turned it off. "Let me ask you both right now. Do you both still believe we are right and that something awful is going to happen soon?"

Elliott looked at Josh and they both answered, "Yes."

"However, next time we approach a government official, we need more proof. We need to know the exact

date of the V2 release."

"That's going to take a miracle, Mr. Myles."

"Maybe. Maybe not. Tim Chen has been quite resourceful."

Parker hesitated and was silent.

Josh looked at her. "What's wrong? Ask Tim to get us more. He hasn't complained yet."

"I will … I … I just want to make sure he stays safe. I know Timothy and I know that none of this is easy for him. Christ Josh, he's not a damn spy!"

"Geez. Seems like someone's got a bit of a crush going maybe? Poor little Timothy? Or is it *Timmy poo*?"

Elliott had to laugh a little, to lighten everything up.

Parker looked with disdain at Josh and said, "I pity the poor girl that ends up with you."

CHAPTER 19

Tim Chen was back on schedule working in the fourth floor lab. It was already Tuesday and he'd been playing a little catch-up. As he was finishing breakfast and getting ready to scoot off to work, he decided to check his email. He hadn't heard anything from Parker over the weekend about his last email or the sample. Not even a thank you. Guess we are *just* friends. He knew that was stupid talk since she was thousands of miles away. He logged into the secure site and there it was, right on que, an email from Parker Hall. He read it carefully, then breathed a sigh. *More? I'm not a damn spy!* he thought. He instinctively knew that she was right. Even though he had procured some amazing information, they needed a date certain for the release of the virus. He knew there was no way he would get back into the secret lab and besides, what's going to happen when Sam Ji runs a test on the liquid in the vial he'd switched out? He'd hoped what would happen would simply be a conclusion that the vial was tainted or otherwise compromised, and Sam would ask for another vial of 'vaccine candidate 3'. He's wasn't that worried because the lab was busy working toward their goal of completing the vaccine on time, not analyzing handling procedures or other processes. They would do that later, post mortem. He also thought that if he was able to find the date of release of Virus Two *and* if he didn't get caught in the process, his days at the Sunhexiang Bio Research lab were numbered. He'd worry about that later. Air travel still wasn't back to the levels it was before the pandemic, but today, over a year later, it was back to about 75% of where it had been. If he needed to hop on a plane and head back to the U.S. at a moment's notice, he could. Back to the issue at hand. He knew he'd been lucky so far by literally stumbling upon certain information. So now what? What was the plan? Dr. Ho Min was the key. Tim was back in the fourth floor lab with no access to Dr. Ho's office. He couldn't ask to work in the secret lab again because that might raise suspicion. The work he'd done for two days wasn't groundbreaking. He was testing amino acid solutions against a control specimen. He wasn't sure if those tests were directly related to the vaccine or not. He couldn't ask his supervisor; he'd have to contact Dr. Ho directly.

He parked his motorbike as usual and hustled into the building. As he walked in, he noticed Dr. Ho was a few steps ahead of him. This was his chance. He called out to him, "Dr. Ho, Sir, excuse me, sir."

"Hello Mr. Chen, how are you?"

"I'm very good Sir. I just wanted to thank you for

the opportunity to work in your lab last week."

"Mr. Chen it was my pleasure. I'm sorry I was absent most of the day on Friday. I came by your station at about 6 pm, but you were gone."

"Yes Sir, I finished my assigned work, so I left … but, I would welcome helping more if you'll have me."

"Yes, Mr. Chen, let's talk next month. We are finishing up a very important program and so my focus is on that. But next month, I will be able to give you more attention."

"I see. Yes, I will contact you then. Well thank you Sir … and if I can be of assistance in the meantime, please let me know."

"Yes, no problem, good to see you."

And with that Ho Min got into an elevator and left Tim Chen heading for the stairs. *Damn*, he thought, *he didn't take the bait*. He'd have to find another way. As he made his way to the locker room, he postulated an idea to himself. *What about Sam Ji?* He knew he stole the guy's vial and swapped it out for a dummy sample, but he had just rationalized, he hoped, that the 'bad sample' would be brushed away and Sam would simply move on requesting another sample. Sam did tell him to contact him about going to lunch. So how would that translate into getting in to Dr. Ho's office? He didn't know yet, but he had to try something. He sent Sam Ji a text asking about lunch tomorrow. Sam responded within a minute saying absolutely, they were 'on.'

Dr. Ho Min reached his office and started reflecting on Tim Chen. *What an industrious young man*, he thought.

Tim Chen reminded him of himself in younger days. Just then there was a knock on his door. "Come in," Dr. Ho said without looking up.

"Excuse me sir, you wanted a report on vaccine candidate 3?"

"Yes, yes, tell me good news Mr. Ji."

"Sir, if this were yesterday morning, I might have had bad news. I began testing the sample yesterday and it was not yielding positive results across any spectrum. It was very strange, as if the sample were something completely different or somehow corrupted."

"Oh, and so?"

"Sir, you were out in the morning so I took it upon myself to get another sample of vaccine candidate 3, assuming that the other lab working on it contaminated it somehow."

"… and?"

"And Sir, I'm happy to report, that the new sample has tested positive across all quadrants. We can confirm the outside lab human trials are now 100%. It is final."

"That is excellent Sam! So, the other sample must have been contaminated?"

"I can't absolutely confirm that, but it appears that way. We will run a trace and process review along with video review of all labs that had the sample, including ours, in a couple of weeks. We just have a few finishing items that need to be adhered to in order to send vaccine candidate 3 out for mass replication."

"That is wonderful. So how long in your estimate until vaccine candidate 3 will be ready for release?"

"Sir, it's about a week for the replication in mass,

and then to get it distributed to the hospitals and—"

"Once the replication is done, I will notify the production lab as to where to send it."

"Sir, I can do that, I've coordinated that many times before with various vaccines."

"Mr. Ji, you are a top notch lab researcher and I do not want to waste your time. Besides, this batch needs to be separated and shipped to roughly two thousand municipal wastewater treatment plants."

"Oh, I see … and can I ask—"

"Mr. Ji, I apologize, I'm very busy. Is there anything else you needed?"

"No sir, thank you Sir." And with that Sam walked out of his office to complete his tasks.

Ho Min walked over to the kitchen area which was only a short walk from his office. He poured some tea and headed back to his desk, shutting his office door once inside. He took a needed sip of the Ginseng Oolong concoction and settled into his work. First, he picked up the secure phone and dialed Li Wei's secure office line.

"Hello?"

"Wei my dear friend, how is life treating you, I hope you are well?" Min was scribbling on a piece of paper on his desk–just doodles for the most part.

"It is treating me very fairly Min, thank you my friend."

"I bring you more well wishes this morning. The vaccine is finished. We have another week to prepare it for replication at the production lab and then we can ship to the water treatment facilities."

"You are the bearer of great news! Very well Min, you have served China to the best of your ability, again."

"Thank you Wei. I would say that a safe estimate for actual integration into the water supply would be on March 22nd. We may be ready a day or two sooner, but definitely by March 22nd." Min kept scribbling…. and unconscientiously wrote "3-22 vax" in the midst of the other scribblings.

"No need to rush, March 22nd is fine and looking at my calendar … that means we can release virus two on April 1st."

"Yes, that would be an accurate calculation." Min continued to scribble but then again wrote "4-1 V2" without even realizing it.

"Min, do you know what significance that date has in America?"

"No Wei, I'm sorry I do not."

"That is what the Americans call 'April Fool's Day.' It originated in Europe in the 1300s and made its way to the U.S. It is a day where typically their citizens will play pranks or jokes on each other and then yell, April Fools!"

"I see. But V2 will be no joke, it is extremely deadly. In our secret human trials, we tried different methods of transmission on the subjects. It was lethal from most all methods and had a very high rate of human to human transmission through airborne particles. Once infected, most of the test subjects only lived about thirty-six hours until death."

"Very good Min. We plan to infect our agents prior to their various worldwide destinations. They will be contagious during *and* after they arrive. The vaccine you have created will be a fail-safe against any infections here in China."

"I understand and I will make the appropriate plans myself. Please know that this will be done unless I otherwise contact you. China will once again stand alone atop the world just like our half of Mount Everest."

"Thank you my dear friend," and with that Wei hung up. Ho Min heard the click on the line and hung up as well. He took another sip of his tea. Great achievement took great sacrifice. He was proud to play his part for China and the greater society. Min got busy doing other things and the white pad which essentially had top secret information on it was inadvertently shoved under some other papers and he really didn't give it another thought.

CHAPTER 20

P arker Hall woke early anticipating an email from
Timothy. She immediately logged in and checked.
Nothing. Well, nothing yet. Director Thomas had really
deflated her. She knew her logic was sound, but he didn't
even let them get out of the gate. She knew she'd have to go
around him. It would probably cost her her job, but unless
she alerted someone so they could take some kind of action,
there might not be a job to go back to anyway. She played
out the scenario in her mind. China would release their
vaccine into their water supply, then release V2 ten days
later. There's no way the citizens of the world would simply
believe the health officials again after going through what
the world had gone through over the last year. By now, the
extended shutdown of the economy was widely concluded
by many as an overreaction. If V2 was that deadly, by the
time government officials reacted the death toll would be

immense. China had devised the perfect storm. It was only perfect because they played on American sympathy and freedom. There was a saying that Parker's dad used to say to her and she was sure he didn't invent it. 'Fool me once, shame on you, fool me twice, shame on me.' America nearly revolted after this last so-called pandemic. There was no way they were going to accept the 'virus models' again. And because of that, millions would die before they even knew what was going on. The U.S. would be a shell of itself. Who knows how other countries would fare. but it would probably be equally as devastating. This is the end of the world scenario that only science fiction movies projected. She knew that until now, the U.S. and other countries were able to keep 'essential services' going. The media continually defined 'essential' as health care workers. She had another definition. People employed at the electric companies, water companies, Wi-Fi companies, cell phone companies, food processing plants, supermarkets, gas stations, police, fire, and other non-medical critical services. If these people were to not show up at work, due to fear, sickness, or death, that's when the real problems would start. Her father had played out this scenario with her one time and hearing it from him, Mr. Calm, Cool and Collected, made it even more scary.

At its basic level, human life demanded water, food and shelter and a way to defend those necessities. She remembered that 'doomsday prepper' TV show on one of the cable channels a few years back. Those people may have had it right, though they were laughed at by many. Her father had made her learn how to shoot a gun and he bought her one for her 21st birthday. She a had nice little Walther

PPS single-stack 9mm carry gun. It only carried eight rounds, but her dad knew she was more apt to practice with it and use it if it were light enough for her to handle. She hadn't been to the range in probably six months, but she made a point to now put it on her calendar. She wanted to stop thinking about the doomsday scenario but she couldn't shake it. Riots, lootings, shootings, barricading your space and defending it–she had to focus on a happier future. She remembered when she told Timothy that her dad had bought her a gun for self-protection. He had given her a look that questioned the decision but also shouted, 'Cool!' She laughed because his reaction came in class and it almost got them in trouble with… She suddenly stopped and said out loud to no one, "Professor Short!" She grabbed her phone and dialed.

"Professor Short? Hi, it's Parker Hall. How are you?"

"Parker, my ace student. How have you been? I've been wondering about whether you're making a difference over there at Homeland Security?"

"Oh, I'm trying. I need to meet with you and then ask you a huge favor."

"Sure, next week would be good."

"No, I need to meet with you soon. It's critical."

"Oh … okay. Sure. How about tomorrow morning, say 9:00 am, come over here. Margaret would love to see you again and she'll have a nice pot of coffee, the hazelnut kind you like."

"Okay professor that would be great. Text me your address again and I will see you in the morning."

"I'll do it now. See you then."

"Thanks professor. Bye."

She knew she was going to have to let him see the evidence. She had no choice. This was bigger than losing a job or possibly going to jail. He would have to conclude the same thing that she, Elliott, and Josh had concluded. If he didn't, it was over. That would be the only way that Professor Short would contact his old friend, the President.

Tim woke early. He was having lunch with Sam and he had to figure out how he could get back into the secret lab area. He really didn't have a plan. He thought out loud to himself while he was getting on his motorbike, *Jeez, I'm not some CIA agent, what does Parker want from me anyway?* A few seconds later he was off to work. Once he arrived at work, the process again took over. Security was as high as it had been in about a month and so it didn't alarm him, it just made getting in the lab take a little longer. He was always prompt to work but this caused him to leave even earlier and when 11:15 rolled around, he started to get ready to meet Sam for their lunch. By the time he was changed and outside at 11:30, Sam was waiting for him.

"It's about time dude. Let's go, I'll drive."

Tim hoped in on the passenger side and within a few minutes they were there. Tim simply made small talk while they ate, hoping that the conversation would somehow lead to an opening regarding the secret lab. Finally, it did.

"So you like the lab I work in, huh?"

"Yeah, I mean I was only there two days but it was very cool."

"It would be cool to have you up there permanently. I know they're always looking to move people up and into more responsibility."

"Yeah, that would be great. It would be nice to take another look around, without the pressure of a deadline or a project due."

"Dude, my shift ends at 6:00 pm, most people are out of there by 6:30, why don't you come up then and I'll give you another tour, especially of the stuff you didn't see."

"Very cool, you're on. How do I …" he showed Sam his badge.

"Oh, right, yeah. So, I'll just be on the other side of the locker room door and we'll go back in together."

"Don't I need a badge?"

"*No problemo* my friend," he said smiling. "I got you covered. We better get back."

They both went up to the counter and as Sam reached for his wallet, Tim put his arm out to stop him. "I got this man, no worries."

"Thanks pal!"

At 6:10 pm, Tim made his way to the locker room. He felt like he was moving deliberately in slow motion. He still did not have a plan, but for some reason he wasn't panicked. He would simply keep his eyes open as Sam showed him around though he had known for a few days where he'd need to go. He was sure a thorough inspection of Dr. Ho's office wasn't going to be on the agenda for tonight's tour. He went through the necessary change in the locker room, but exited out an unfamiliar door. Sure enough, Sam was there waiting.

"Hey Bro, how was your afternoon?"

"Just work, steady work."

"I know man, if you don't cut loose on your days off this job will kill you!"

"What do you mean?"

"I mean they work us to death, at least in my lab. Some stupid secret vaccine bullshit that we know nothing about, who it's for, what it's for, or anything!"

"That can be frustrating."

"Fuck. I never wanted to sign up for anything to do with military research and I thought when I took this job that it was agricultural stuff. But ever since we've had armed guards and all the security, I'm thinking we're working on something possibly for the Army, or worse."

Tim nodded and didn't say any more about it. He catalogued the conversation into his memory banks and thought that Sam Ji might be someone to confide in at some point if he needed to. He then followed Sam as they walked into the lab. Sam scanned his badge and then took another badge out of his pocket and scanned it for Tim's entrance.

"Ok, come in now."

Tim followed Sam's directions and they were in. Once inside, Tim felt much more relaxed. His pulse quickened for a moment, but Sam was a smooth operator. Tim asked him, "So do I dare ask what that other badge was?"

"Dude–it's a guest badge from Dr. Ho's office!" Sam laughed partly in amusement of himself and partly in relief.

"Are you shitting me? Dude (he liked mimicking his counterpart, sounded like something a spy would do, or so he thought), we could both get jammed up pretty bad if they check the log-in report."

"No worries Hernando, I swiped it from his desk after he left twenty minutes ago. Have you seen his assistant? Wow! I mean I've been trying to tap that for months. The ice queen is what we call her."

"Dude, no way, that would be incredible." *Okay, he thought to himself, I need to stop. I'm not cool, I'm an Asian-American nerd who couldn't even muster up the balls to kiss Parker Hall when we were in college!*

Sam proceeded to lead Tim through the lab. Tim, of course, already knew most of the lab from working there the other week, but he let Sam take the reins and lead. He needed a reason to get into Dr. Ho's office and returning the 'guest badge' was his opening. He quickly said, "Pal, give me the guest badge. If someone stops us at least I'll have it on me." The lab was mostly desolate. There was a worker here and there, but for the most part it was dead.

It was almost 7:00 pm and Sam stopped and turned, "Dude, I know which bar she goes to!"

Tim was caught a little off guard, "What bar *who* goes to?"

"Dr. Ho's assistant, Li Na! It's not far from here. I'll confirm where she is on WeChat and we can buzz over there–maybe one of us gets lucky!"

"Oh, right … sounds great, sure."

"Dude, let's get out of here, we've got more important things to do."

"Sure, after you."

Sam Ji was so excited about his upcoming potential conquest that he forgot all about the guest badge that needed to go back to Ho Min's office. Just before they left the secure area, Tim stopped him.

"Shit dude! I need to go put the badge back in Dr. Ho's office."

"I'll do it, you head into the locker room."

Tim was adamant. "No man, I'll do it. You need extra time to text our hottie. I'll see you in the locker room in a few minutes."

"Ok, you sure? You remember where it is? Just put it on his desk."

"Yep got it see you in a few." And with that Tim watched Sam head out of the lab past the secure area into the locker room. He turned and headed to Ho Min's office. *Was this easy or what?* he said to himself. He entered Min's office. It was dimly lit as only the emergency light that was always on shed light into the room. It was messy but he thought if he just snooped a bit he'd find something. He sat at the desk, slowly pushing papers aside, uncovering other piles of papers underneath and…*What is this*, he said to himself. A white pad with doodles but two dates. He read the pad, '3-22 vax … 4-1 V2. That's it.' Just then the other light flicked on. *SHIT!* he thought. He turned to look and it was Li Na.

"What are you doing here!" she demanded.

"I was … well …"

"Tell me right now or I call security!"

"I was putting back this guest badge."

"Why? Why do you have it?"

"I was up here visiting another colleague and I remembered that I forgot to turn it in from my time working here the other week."

"You should have called me. I could have taken care of that for you. You shouldn't be in here alone; we both could get in trouble."

"I'm so sorry, I didn't know the procedure. Next time I will call you, Na."

"I hope so, I was wondering anyway if you—" Just then her phone dinged. She had an incoming WeChat message. "OMG–that guy needs to stop."

"What guy?" Tim asked.

"There's a guy in this lab, Sam Ji, he keeps hitting on me and I have no desire to welcome his advances."

"I know Sam, he's not so bad. What does he want?" Tim knew exactly what Sam was up to.

"He wants to know what bar I'm at and if he can stop by to have a drink."

"I've got an idea. How about this. You tell him okay, and I will go with him and make sure he behaves and that way, maybe you and I can get to know each other as well."

"I would really like that. Are you sure, you don't mind?"

"I'm sure. Just give us thirty minutes and we'll be there. I'm looking forward to it."

"Well okay. But you better be there!"

"I will, I promise." And with that Tim left the badge on the desk and hustled to the locker room. He saw Na texting so he knew she went for it. *This spy shit has its perks, just like Bond.* He made it to the locker room and sure enough Sam was there already changed.

"Dude, she just responded! Hurry up man, she's waiting for us! This could be my lucky night."

Tim didn't even answer, but as he was changing, he snickered to himself. *No Dude, it could be my lucky night.* Five minutes later he was in his regular clothes and they were both heading out of the building. He knew he had to get Parker the information but he had to follow Sam to meet Na at her bar. He'd have to risk it–he'd text her a simple coded message the minute he got to the bar. *What the fuck, he thought–he was Bond, James Bond.*

CHAPTER 21

P arker couldn't sleep. She tossed and turned all night.
She had woken up at 5:00 am to check her email but
nothing. After she fell back asleep, she awoke again at 8:00
am. *Crap!* She thought and jumped out of bed. She checked
her secure email again, still nothing. She was starting to get
pissed. *I asked him to do something simple and he needs to
respond to me, how hard is that?* She was actually feeling a
little afraid for him. She realized she was being stupid, but
things were getting crazy and this wasn't a game. This was
real, though it didn't seem real. The whole last year didn't
seem real. People had simply accepted the alleged horrible
killing machine virus willingly and shut down their
businesses and their lives. Yes, she knew it was deadly, but
only seemingly for a distinct part of the world demographic.
Anyway, the situation *now* was deadly and she knew it. She
got in and out of the shower in record time and as she was

getting dressed, she was compiling the emails and her notes of phone calls into a folder to bring to the professor's home. *Where was Timothy? Damn.* She checked one last time before heading out to her car. It was a twenty-five-minute drive to Professor Jared Short's home and she needed to calm herself and present the evidence methodically, as Elliott Myles would have wanted her to.

She rounded a corner and saw the professor's house. As she slowed to hug the curb, her phone beeped. *What the hell?* the sound was not a normal text or email. It was a WeChat text which she had initially used when Tim Chen left to go to China. She tried to find the app, but it was in a folder somewhere. *Dammit!* she said out loud. The car was still running and she knew that the professor was probably wondering what she was doing in the car. She finally found the damn app, tapped it, and read the message. It had only two strings of numbers separated by a period. 322.22124 and 41.22.2. *Holy shit, now I need time to figure this out!* she thought. She finally turned the car off and saw the professor standing at his front door. She'd deal with code in a bit.

"Hi Professor, just gathering my things," she yelled politely. With that, she shut her car door and proceeded up the steps to his front door. It was a classic New England Tudor he and his wife had built. It was slightly out of place in the DC suburbs, but not that much. It was a gorgeous home and when you had money, and Jared Short did, then you could do whatever you wanted to do.

"Welcome Parker, great to see you." He normally would have given her a big hug but in this new post-virus world, no one hugged or shook hands, at least not yet.

"Hi professor, I hope I didn't alarm you yesterday."

"Honestly, you did. But that's okay. I'm a big boy so how can I help?"

Just then Margaret Short entered. "Hi Parker, how are you? It's been so long."

"Hi Mrs. Short, I know, I'm sorry. I've been so busy at Homeland Security."

"Please, call me Margaret. Well, here's some coffee, let me know if you need anything. I'll leave you two alone."

"Thank you Margaret."

Margaret shut the door to the study and Parker and the professor now had the privacy that Parker needed to divulge her thoughts. "Professor Short, I need to layout a hypothesis for you. If after you've seen the evidence, you conclude I'm more right than wrong, I'm going to need you to call the president."

"Whoa Nellie! I haven't talked to him for over a year and Parker, well ... Let's just see what you have."

Over the next forty-five minutes, Parker methodically laid out the theory, the communications, and the phone calls that she hoped added up to rational analysis. There was a point in the presentation where Professor Short asked her if he could have a moment to reread some of the emails. She acknowledged and took that opportunity to work on the code from Timothy. It was a code and she knew it. Tim must have been rushed for time and decided to code her a message. She needed to decode that message before the end of this meeting. It was that important. She asked Professor Short for a pen and paper. Without really looking up, he reached over to a side table and grabbed a notepad and a pen and handed them to her. She started scribbling. 322.22124 and 41.22.2. *Could be longitude and latitude numbers?* she thought. *Damn*, she needed Josh and Mr. Myles here. She started to write some more. *Maybe the period is a separator rather than a decimal point. '322, 32-2, 3-22....3-22 – MARCH 22nd? Maybe*, she thought. What was it that Timothy had said when they were in college, 'codes followed rules and different strings followed those rules as well.' *Okay*, she thought, so *41 would be 4-1, April 1st*. Just then, Professor Short started to talk.

"Parker, first off, I'm incredibly proud of you for the research you've done and secondly, this is amazing. If this is true, the world has a serious problem on its hands."

"I know professor, I know."

"Who else knows about this?"

"My colleague Josh, that has been working with me at Homeland Security, and my neighbor Elliott Myles."

"Elliott Myles, the ex-NSA—"

"Yes, that's the one. And before you say anything, my Dad trusts him and his analysis."

"I was one of the few who believed him. Okay, enough said on that. What about your China contact?"

"That's Timothy Chen, Professor – remember him from class?"

"No kidding! Really? He was always so quiet. *You* were the talkative one."

"Speaking of Timothy, as I pulled up to your house, I got a text from him that we've been waiting for."

"We'll get to that in a minute. I want to make sure I have it all so far but … before I do, you understand you've probably broken the law?"

"I guess so, yes, but this is life or death, professor."

"I know that. And I'm not saying that it's not warranted, but by telling me, probably telling and involving Elliott Myles, you've broken the law. You could go to jail."

"Professor, I get it. I know that I'm still young, but I've done the work and China is about to attack us and we need to alert the president. Elliott and Josh and I met with Director Thomas and tried to tell him, but before we even got to the evidence, he took one look at Elliott and laughed us out of the room. I'm surprised I still have a job and top-secret clearance."

"I can only imagine how that drama played out. Let's keep pressing onward. You made a statement at the beginning of your presentation and I was incredibly skeptical. However, now I believe you have presented the evidence necessary to conclude that China will be releasing another, more deadly virus. Of course, I have so many more questions and I want to talk to your co-worker Josh, and especially Elliott. Can we talk to Tim? Oh, and Miss Hall ... you've earned this. I will make the call to President Hunter on your behalf and get you a meeting ASAP."

Parker fell back in her chair. She *knew* she was right, but being right means nothing if no one agrees with you–even if they are wrong. *Thank God*, she thought to herself. She almost started crying.

"Thank you for the vote of confidence professor. What do we need to do next?"

"Before I make that call to the president, I want to meet with Elliott Myles and Josh and then ... didn't you say you just got a text from Tim Chen–what did that say?"

"Yes, it's a coded message that I've been trying to decode. I have part of it. Do you want me to text Mr. Myles and Josh to come over now?"

"Yes, text them now please. Show me the coded message."

Parker shared the coded message and what she had thus far concluded. While the professor looked at her notes for a minute, she texted Josh and Elliott. They both responded and said they'd be there in 30 minutes. Professor Short then got up and went to a bookshelf to grab a book.

"*Code Making for Dummies*? Kind of simplistic, professor, no?"

"Some of the most complicated codes in history have been the simplest. You said Tim usually sent you emails over the secure Homeland Security portal?"

"That's correct. He's never sent me a text on WeChat during this time."

"Hmm. I'm going to conclude that he was rushed or under duress after discovering whatever it was that he discovered. I agree with your initial decoding. So, let's recap. 322.22124 and 41.22.2 can be interpreted as March 22 then 5 numbers, 22124 and the second string are April 1 then 3 numbers separated by a decimal."

"I was thinking longitude/latitude? Some kind of internet address?"

Professor Short opened the *Dummies* book. "Let's just take a quick look." Parker couldn't sit still. She looked at her watch. She was one of the few people her age that even wore a watch. Usually her age group looked at their

cell phones. Her dad had bought her a gorgeous Tag Heuer
for her graduation from college. It was still a little geeky,
but it worked and she loved it because she knew her dad was
with her all the time when she wore it–at least that's how
she felt.

"Assume Tim was trying to tell us a date and an
occurrence."

"I'm confused Professor, what do you mean?"

"I mean, assume Tim wouldn't tell us two dates in
one string–there'd be no logical reason to do so. So that
second string of numbers would not be another date."

"Great, so we can eliminate the second string as a
date–at this rate, it's going to take us forever."

"Now, now, patience my dear. This is how it works.
I'm sure that Elliott will be able to help, when are they due
to arrive?"

"Probably another five to ten minutes or so."

"Good. I've got some other ideas, but before I go
there, I think it prudent to ask the NSA man."

Parker excused herself to take a bathroom break and
make some small talk with Margaret in the kitchen. When
she emerged, Elliott and Josh were sitting in the professor's
study.

"Hi guys," she said when she entered the room.
Elliott and Josh both acknowledged her, and then Professor
Short spoke. He proceeded to bring Elliott and Josh up to
speed on where he was with the whole thing. Then he
focused on the coded message and asked Elliott to take a
look.

"Okay, so I also agree with Parker's deduction of

the first part of the codes or both strings," Elliott said after quickly studying the codes. "I also agree that the second part of the code for both strings wouldn't be another date. My experience at the NSA is to start with basic coding objectives first, before moving to more complicated schemes."

"So any thoughts?" Josh asked.

Elliott bounced the question over to Jarod. "Professor, your thoughts?"

"My instinct tells me that if Timmy boy was indeed rushed, he would have made a simple code. The simplest code I know attaches numbers to letters. Elliott?"

"I agree. Let's start there."

Jarod handed all of them a pad of paper and they all started to write. After about fifteen minutes, it was apparent that Parker and Josh were not making any progress. Elliott leaned over to Jared and showed him something on his paper. Jarod then went back to his paper, crossing something out and writing some more. This kept going for about another ten minutes. Parker looked over at Josh, shrugging her shoulders. Josh decided he'd be the one to break the silence.

"So … how long do we keep this up?" No one responded for another minute.

Elliott spoke, saying, "We may have it. One minute." Parker sat back up and leaned in.

"That's it. Elliott, do the honors."

"Thank you Jarod. Okay. If Tim simply associated the alphabet with the numbers, then let's start with the second part of the first string. 22124 breaks down as 22, then 1, then 24."

"How'd did you decide to break down the string like that?"

"Just trial and error, Josh ... and experience," Elliott continued, "22 is V, 1 is A and 24 is X. VAX would stand for 'vaccine'."

"What about the second string, second part?" Parker asked.

"That was little harder, but not much. If you go by what we just did, 22.2 would mean 22 is again V. Then the decimal point is a separator telling the reader that this is not equivalent to a letter. The only other thing it could be equivalent to is—"

Parker interjected, "A number!"

"Right. So, 22.2 is V2."

"Timothy is telling us when the vaccine is going to be released and when Virus Two will be released. That's about six weeks from now for the vaccine release," Parker summarized.

"Yes, and a little more than seven weeks for the virus release," Jarod added.

Josh blurted, "Holy crap! This is crazy."

"No, this is real and it's happening soon," Elliott grimly added.

"Yes, it is Elliott," Professor Short stood. "I need some privacy, gang. Let me go make the call to the president. I'm not sure if he'll take my call directly, but my message will get to him pretty quickly and he knows that if I say it's critical to see us, he'll make the time."

Two days later, all of them were passing through White House security receiving their temporary badges and being shown to the Oval Office. Already present was the director of the CIA, the NSA director, and the Chief of Staff. Quick introductions were made and then the president entered the Oval Office from an alcove off the president's private dining room and study. All stood and the president immediately shook hands with his long-time friend Jarod Short and then was introduced to the others. Just then, another door to the Oval Office opened and the Director of Homeland Security, Roger Thomas, entered. He only knew that the meeting involved Professor Jarod Short, the president's long-time friend, and he was prepared to quickly apologize for being late, but then he saw Elliott Myles, Parker Hall, and Josh Bennett and his apology quickly turned into a different kind of apology.

"I'm sorry Mr. President I … Mr. President, please forgive these three (pointing at Elliott, Parker and Josh). I've already met with them and there's nothing more to discuss or alert you to. I will see that they are escorted out of the building immediately."

"Now hold on, Roger. Jarod has looked at what they have and used a pretty big favor to get this meeting. I want to hear what they have to say."

"But Mr. President, I already—"

The Chief of Staff, Alden Scott, interrupted, "Mr. Director, that's enough. If you've got a problem, *you* can

leave and you'll be briefed later." Roger Thomas sat down, but was visibly pissed.

"Now Jarod, why don't you tell us what all this is about? Just to let you know, I only have about thirty minutes for this meeting so make it good."

Professor Short then proceeded to explain and lay out the case that China performed a trial run with a bio-weapon, which was the pandemic the world had just gone through, and was now preparing for a second, more deadly virus to be released. They all listened intently. As Jarod outlined what Parker, Elliott, and Josh had found, the president would occasionally glance over at the Homeland Security director with a disapproving look. On one of the looks, he felt compelled to speak.

"Roger, they told you all this and you ignored it?"

"Sir, I did not, I can explain—"

"No, I don't think you can. What else have you ignored over there at Homeland Security?" It was a redundant question as the president turned immediately toward Jarod Short and asked him to continue. The professor wrapped up the briefing with the final coded message from Tim Chen. They all sat quietly for a moment before the president spoke. "What do you think Alden?"

"I think that I've seen enough proof, Sir. That said, Ms. Hall, where is the sample vaccine that Tim Chen sent you?"

"I have it at my home. I can go get it and bring it back?"

"You don't have to do that Ms. Hall. We'll have two Secret Service agents meet you at your home right after this meeting." Alden Scott then turned to the president. "Sir, at this point, I think the discussion needs to move to the Situation Room."

"Agreed, but I want Parker and her cohorts kept in

the loop and if that means that need greater security clearances, get them for them immediately."

"Yessir, right away."

"Parker Hall, you are quite a resourceful young women and under any other circumstance I would ask you to come work in my White House, but because there has been a lack of understanding over at Homeland Security, I need you there, helping with our response."

Director Thomas spoke up, "Mr. President, I don't appreciate the innuendo. I've been Homeland Security Director for—"

"Roger, you're damn lucky I don't summarily remove you from your post. Why don't you take a nice vacation for the next seven weeks? That's not a suggestion. After this is over, you and will discuss any future you may have at Homeland Security. If you can't do that, then I'll have security escort you back to your office so you can pack your things."

"Sir, with all due respect, I'm not sold on any perceived attack and so I think it best if I resign immediately."

Alden Scott picked up the phone and paused a second, "Get me Robertson over here from security and get the White House counsel here now."

"Your resignation is accepted. Security will escort you out, I expect to have your letter on my desk within the hour."

Security entered the Oval Office at that moment with the White House counsel. They proceeded to walk Roger Thomas out of the Oval and Alden Scott followed.

Elliott just had to hit him with a parting shot. "Bye Roger! Nice knowing you." He couldn't even begin to describe how good that dig felt.

Before Alden Scott left the Oval, he turned and addressed the President. "Mr. President, I'll see you down in the Situation Room in fifteen minutes?"

The President nodded to his Chief of Staff. At that time, the CIA Director and the NSA Director both exited heading down to the Situation Room as well. The President then addressed the four people remaining in the room.

"As you can see, I need to get to the Situation Room and make plans for stopping this. You have all done your country a great service. When this is all over, I will properly–the country will properly–thank you for your effort. We'll keep you in the loop as best we can. Thank you."

The president and the other four stood. This time the president shook all their hands and a secretary came in, somehow on cue, to escort them out of the Oval Office. When they were clear of the Oval and walking down the hall to the foyer and exit, Josh finally blurted out, "Mother of God, I'm writing a book!"

Parker elbowed him in the side. "Shut up Josh."

Jarod smiled, "He gets it. You won. Let's just hope for all our sakes he can find a way to stop this."

CHAPTER 22

C hief of Staff to the President of the United States, Alden Scott, had briefed the other players in the Situation Room so that they would be prepared to analyze and consider solutions. As the president entered, everyone stood.

The president waved for them to sit and began. "Okay, you all know the situation. I want your thoughts for ten minutes, then I want to turn to solutions. Go."

It was clear that the intelligence community of the United States had failed this president big time. An intern, a first-year employee at Homeland Security, a washed-up NSA agent, a Professor at Georgetown, and an Asian-American recent college graduate working in China at a research lab had uncovered possibly the biggest attack the world has ever seen in the history of humanity. The President realized this, but had to deal with the immediate problem. As they went around the room, they all drew the same conclusions: the evidence was clear and that the United States was lucky to have found this out. The president certainly noticed that none of them said *they* failed; it was that *we* got lucky. Whatever. He had to focus on the pending attack and would deal with all the B.S. politics later.

"Alright ladies and gentlemen, onto possible solutions."

The people in the room suggested everything from 'leak it to the press' to 'all-out war and attack China.' This President was no war monger. He used the military during his tenure as a sword to achieve outcomes the U.S. desired. He would take that same approach in this situation. He suggested his plan to the room. They all nodded that his way was the best course of action.

"Okay. I want this plan in motion within twenty-four hours. I will contact the heads of state of the other relevant countries. Thank you all and Godspeed to all of you."

With that, the President stood and so did the rest of the room. He and Alden walked out and back into the Oval Office.

"Alden, do you think we can stop this?"

"Sir, your plan makes sense, I know we'll give it our best. I will start setting up the phone calls for you. Give me thirty minutes?"

"Yep, I'll be ready."

The Chief of Staff went back to his office to prepare. The president sat down at the Resolute desk. He looked at it for a second, wondering what other Presidents were thinking in times of crisis when they sat down at the same desk. It didn't matter. This crisis was like no other. He reviewed his plan and wrote some notes as he'd have to not only brief the other Heads of State, but propose they participate in the solution. Before he knew it, he was on his first call to the Prime Minister of the UK. After explaining the situation, he was ready to suggest his plan for a solution.

"Mr. Prime Minister, I will now tell you the basics of my plan for how we, the world, need to respond to China. I suggest that we form a coalition force amongst the greater Western countries. We know the date of the release of the second virus. I suggest we actually do a reverse-lockdown. Instead of all of us locking ourselves down against the virus, we lockdown China so the virus doesn't escape. We will do this in several ways. First, our coalition military will be posted around their entire border and no one will be allowed to exit their country. Secondly, we will lock down their air travel and announce ahead of time that their aircraft will not be allowed to land anywhere outside of China. Third, we will lock down their ports and marinas and not allow any travel by sea. Their military ships will be allowed to sail, but not dock anywhere except for a Chinese military port located on the coast of the Chinese mainland. If China allows, citizens of China will be allowed to return to China, but once they return, they cannot leave again. Basically, Mr. Prime Minister, we will isolate China from the rest of the world until such time as the virus is not a threat to the world or the world is vaccinated. We are starting efforts to quietly prepare the vaccination from the sample that was secretly obtained from a Chinese lab. There are many more details that need to be worked out, but that is the gist of it and we have about six weeks to make all this happen."

The Prime Minister asked a couple more questions before saying goodbye. The President continued to call all of the other Western powers and essentially have the same conversation. After a quick bite to eat for dinner, he was back in the Situation Room where he and his team outlined the plan and timeline. Six weeks was not a long time when planning to surround a country and lock them down. He knew this plan might also lead to the death of innocent civilians or a world war. What if a commercial jet didn't turn around and landed anyway? He would use the military to try to effectuate a positive response from a jetliner full of innocent passengers, but either way, he and the rest of the world couldn't allow anyone to get off a plane from China and just walk into the rest of society. All of these type contingencies had to be taken into account. He and others in the government wouldn't get much sleep during the next forty-two days, but it had to be done.

As the president worked with his team and the leaders of other countries, they made great progress over the next couple of weeks. The president's leadership was perfect for this effort. The other person that the president relied upon greatly was the White House spokesperson, Jordon McKenna. She was a deft speaker, attorney, and bulldog. She focused her briefings on current happenings with Americans and the continued recovery of businesses and the good progress of the research labs toward a vaccine (for the first virus). Alden Scott had dramatically reduced the President's travel and outside event schedule so he could focus from the Oval Office and Situation Room. If Jordon got a question during a briefing about where the president was or why he cancelled a certain event, she would give it right back to the media, "The president is very aware that his travel involves hundreds of people and causes major disruptions, neither of which are needed right now in any American town or city for business or health reasons." The media bought the double-talk, for now, but she didn't really care what they bought. That was the party line and would be for the next four weeks. During the initial two weeks of planning, the President focused on two fronts. Lockdown by land and lockdown by air. Lockdown by land was a vast exercise as China had over 13,700 miles of land border, the longest land border of any country on earth, as well as many miles of ocean border. The key here was to at least get the countries who shared existing borders with China to make a 100% effort with their military first and then use the coalition forces as a gap filler. This included Mongolia, Russia, Hong Kong (even though it was a Special Administration Region and technically under Chinese jurisdiction), Vietnam, Laos, Middle East countries, and others. It was nearly an impossible undertaking, but President Hunter had to make every country understand that death of the citizenry was the alternative. The U.S. and its coalition forces would be offered to the border countries to bolster their effort. The president knew that this was akin to an occupation, but these were different and somewhat desperate times. Of course, the various leaders asked him the one big question he couldn't really answer. 'If we are successful at locking down China, then how long will the lockdown measure have to remain in place?' That was the million-dollar question. That had been a huge question a year earlier when the first virus hit. Every pundit, medical doctor, nurse, scientist, researcher, news host, journalist, government official including congresspersons and senators down to the ordinary citizen, was calling into a radio show with an opinion. It was all guesswork. No one actually knew; it was like asking ten people around a craps table to predict the next roll of the dice. You would get ten different answers. They weren't just opinions either, no, these were so-called experts on viruses. Some actually were experts and many just anointed themselves experts. Some brought rational logic and their scenarios were more plausible than others. Most just resorted to an opinion which was clothed in political bias. If one political side wanted to open, then the other political side said stay closed. If the other political side said wear a mask, the other said don't. Li Wei was correct in his assessment of America and its citizenry. The U.S. was divided, even when trying to fight a damn virus.

The President knew that he couldn't tell world leaders that the engagement would be open-ended, no one would go for that. His ace-in-the-hole was the vaccine or the vile of liquid that was sent to Parker Hall that *represented* a vaccine. He contacted the major pharmaceutical companies early on after his meeting with Jarod Short and put the CEO's on a secure video call. He didn't just ask for help, he demanded it. And he also made it clear there would be no turf wars, there would be no IP grabbing and filing patents or trademarks around the vaccine, and they would all participate in the making and selling of the vaccine. In fact, the president made them all agree that no matter what quantity of the vaccine they each made, within reason, they would all revenue share. The CEO's didn't exactly capitulate willingly. There was some pushback, but the president said it was life and death and that if they didn't go along, he would use his bully pulpit to ruin them. Of course, he said this 'off the record.' One CEO went so far as to say that it was blackmail and the president nodded and said, "Yep, it is. And if you were in this room, I'd grab you by the neck and push you against the wall and use physical intimidation as well. Any questions gentlemen?" No one responded. The president knew this could come back to bite him politically, but he didn't care. He had one job to do which was to save the U.S. and by extension, save humanity.

CHAPTER 23

It had been a couple of weeks since Tim sent his coded text. Parker sent a very short secure email two days after he sent the WeChat which read, '*Got it. Understood.*' He assumed that she had decoded it because she hadn't sent another email since that time. He knew what this meant, and he was a bit perplexed as to what to do next. After that crazy night with Li Na and Sam Ji, he kept going to work as if nothing happened. Na must have been satisfied because she obviously didn't report him to her superiors. She did send him a text a couple days after their night out, asking if he wanted to have a drink after work, but Tim was so nervous at that point of being arrested or something else bad happening, that he sent her a reply saying, '*Maybe next week, really busy right now.*' He knew that sounded like he was blowing her off, but he really wasn't. He liked her and they had spent the night together, but he wasn't sure that he wanted a relationship. In the midst of all that was happening he would have thought that some steady physical companionship would be a welcome diversion. *What was wrong with him*, he wondered? She was very nice, educated, and had a great body. *No, c'mon*, he thought, *that's ridiculous. She's not even interested in me that way.*

Tim forgot how smitten he was in college with Parker and because their friendship developed so rapidly, he never questioned, or frankly wanted, to ruin that. He had a baseball analogy for it that he reminded himself of often, *He'd rather be on the field versus sitting in the dugout.* It wasn't like they were two-peas-in-a-pod perfect for each other anyway. They were different, but there was some sort of weird chemistry and appreciation of the other that any differences they had brought them closer as friends.

He hadn't talked to Sam since that night. Tim wondered if Sam knew that he stayed at the bar and eventually went home with Li Na. He hoped not; no need for loose talk around the lab at this point. No, Sam had been totally embarrassed that night and so Tim thought he was probably off licking his wounds to some degree and laying low. Back to the business at hand. Tim hopped on his motorbike and headed to work. He knew full well what those dates meant on the paper in Dr. Ho's office. Was he supposed to just keep working and watch this thing unfold like a car crash that was about to happen? Or was he supposed to revolt somehow or simply quit and fly home? At that moment, he wished he could actually talk to Parker. She would definitely have an opinion or suggestion and she was good at boiling down problems or challenges to action items. He would email her tonight.

As Parker Hall drove home from a grueling 12-hour day, she reflected on how busy she and Josh had been over the last weeks with preparations regarding the potential Virus Two attack. With Roger Thomas gone, the interim Homeland Security Director was Frank Stackhouse. He came in from the CIA and was hired at under the current presidential administration. He directed Parker and Josh's activities, but he certainly understood their relationship to the president and he didn't get in their way. Of course, when the president said to them in their meeting that he'd keep them in the loop, he meant that someone down the chain of command would keep them appraised of what was happening. At this point, Parker and Josh, and even Elliott, had done all they could to uncover the plot by China. Now, they needed to do what they could to support the president's plan. She exited the freeway and was almost home. She was well aware that she had neglected communicating with Timothy. In fact, she owed him an email and she would make a point to do that as soon as she got home. She pulled up to her house and Mr. Myles was outside waiting for her.

"I see you made it home in one piece again."

"Tired and beat but yes, in one piece."

"What's the latest?"

"Would it be okay if I decompressed for forty-five minutes and then came over and updated you?"

"Sure. I'll have a cold one ready."

"Thanks."

She opened her front door, dropped her computer bag, and sat down in the comfiest chair she could find. She'd allow herself to close her eyes for ten minutes, then she'd answer Timothy's email, and then she'd go over to Mr. Myles' house. *How crazy,* she thought. *Oh, and I've got to call dad in the next couple of days.* As she let herself sink further into her chair, she wondered about Timothy's email. Why had he said what he said? Their friendship was solid. Did he want more? How was that possible with him thousands of miles away in what now could only be described as a hostile country? She thought about it for a few more minutes and then turned her thoughts inward. What did she feel? Did she want something more in the middle of getting out of one pandemic and into World War III? Were those situations supposed to have a bearing on feelings? She was confused, frustrated, over-worked, and just wanted to be back in college, laughing with him. That was easy. That life was sheltered and she never realized how much until now. She opened her eyes. *Damn, thirty minutes. Got to get up.* She hadn't even kicked off her shoes yet, which she then did with a resounding *ahhh*. She got herself a tall glass of ice water and opened her computer laptop. She'd reread Timothy's email one more time.

> *I hope you are well. I'm pretty sure you decoded the message I sent or I assume you'd have said something. You never were shy to speak your mind. Anyway, I'm wondering what happened with all that and what I should do at this point? Do you have any thoughts or suggestions? I really wish we could talk on the phone and I really hope that there's a way for your government to stop this madness. Okay, this may sound weird, but I've been thinking a lot about you, not just about the virus stuff, but about*

how we used to laugh a ton in school. I miss that.
I'm wondering if you feel the same way? Anyway,
please write when you can and let me know your
thoughts.

    – frankie

Parker thought about his email for a second, *...let me know*
your thoughts on the situation, our friendship, more, what?
This was exactly why long-distance relationships don't
work. Ambiguity. She hated trying to interpret and attribute
someone's feelings in their emails. *Well*, she thought, *here*
goes. She said her introduction, apologized for the tardy
email response, and then updated him as to her meeting with
the president. So far, pretty much all business. Then she
decided to float a balloon and started a new paragraph.

    I miss laughing with you, too! I can only imagine
    that besides playing James Bond a little you have all
    the girls eating out of your hand. Have you been
    dating anyone? If not, why? You're an attractive,
    smart guy and you deserve to be happy. I do also
    think about you and hope that I haven't asked too
    much of you and that you are safe. I look forward to
    the day we can laugh together in the same room.
    You asked me what I thought you should do. I think
    the world is going to get rather crazy in about four
    weeks so if I were you, I'd go somewhere safe or
    come home. Just a suggestion. Hugs!

    – PJ

She hit send and that was that. She went to the fridge and found a leftover rice concoction she'd made two-days earlier. She popped it in the microwave and forty-five seconds later she was picking at it with her fork. Ten minutes later she was upstairs and in bed. *Damn, Elliott.* She texted him before turning out the light.

Exhausted, can we talk tomorrow morning? Sorry.

Two minutes later she was sound asleep.

With two weeks to go until the vaccine release and then another ten days until the Virus Two release, the president was growing more worried about the coalition and whether the world could really pull this off. Secrecy was ultra-high but as every government knows, there are spies everywhere. It was time for the president to begin the border operation. They needed not only troops, but supplies, armor, planes, ships—it was the largest effort the world had ever seen next to the D-Day invasion. Fortunately, the coalition troops would be primarily a backstop to the border country troops. Russia was the most difficult to deal with as they resisted any coalition forces on their soil. The president had the assurance of the Russia's president that they would secure their border with China themselves and didn't need coalition help. President Hunter knew they could, but he ultimately didn't trust Russia to not gain some kind of advantage out of this situation. He agreed with the President of Russia, but said that the U.S. would be monitoring the entire situation from the air and that the coalition and the plan called for a 20-mile 'green fly zone' into each country from the China border where U.S. aircraft could patrol and fly without retribution from the overflown country. The President of Russia refused at first, and then President Hunter reminded him that it was a matter of life and death and if he didn't agree, the U.S. would blame Russia and take its own action against the communist country. The U.S. President basically said, *you allow this or we will happily kick the shit out of you once and for all*. Besides being a good leader, he was a great poker player. The President of Russia reluctantly agreed.

Though the President was happy with his plan, as happy as a leader could be when facing worldwide death beyond imagination, he wished he had more of an ability to curtail this in the future. For that, he knew that China had to change and that would be impossible without their own people rising up against their government and military. There was nothing he could do at this moment to aid an internal revolt and even if he could, it *had* to come from the people. That's the only way democracy works. The president knew that there were about two million police in China which equated to about 143 police officers to every 100,000 citizens. The real problem was China's military. They acted at the behest of the Politburo and in China, there was no *Posse Comitatus* law like in the U.S. that effectively restricted the U.S. military from acting against U.S. citizens on U.S. soil. He instantly thought of the Tiananmen Square incident he remembered vividly, in which Chinese citizens were killed by their military. If revolt were to happen in China, the odds were against the people, even though there were about 1.5 billion of them. Just then his phone buzzed and he stood from behind his Oval Office desk and pressed a button.

"Send them in, Jane."

With that command, the Chairman of the Joint Chiefs of Staff, the CIA Director, the NSA Director, and the Chief of Staff to the President entered. When they were all in the Oval and the door was closed, the president announced to the room, "You may begin Operation Border Patrol."

As quickly as the men had entered the room, they exited. The Chief of Staff remained behind.

"You think we'll have enough time to get everyone in place?"

"I think that we've done the best we can, with the time allotted, and history will determine the rest."

CHAPTER 24

Heads of State were alerted as to the president's order and troops and machines started moving. The president was clear that this wasn't an occupation, but rather an operation and did not want anyone settling in for the long haul–there was to be no long haul. Once China was alerted as to the situation and that essentially the 'gig was up,' the president would demand an ultimatum from the Chinese president. Only the president and a few heads of state knew what this was going to ultimately be, but it was akin to surrender and the ensuing Potsdam Conference after World War II where the leaders of Britain, the Soviet Union, and the United States established a Council of Foreign Ministers and a central Allied Control Council for the administration of Germany. President Hunter knew this arrangement would be slightly different because, unlike Germany in 1945 when Germany had no leader as the war ended (Hitler committed suicide), it was unclear what leadership would be, or remain, in power after the world lockdown.

His phone buzzed again and he answered, "Great, show them in." The door to the Oval opened and three men entered along with an Army General. Introductions were made around the room.

"Gentlemen, please, tell me some good news."

"Good morning Sir. We have been able to take the sample you gave us and replicate it in significant amounts over the last four weeks. However, Sir, without having the actual virus, we have no idea if this will work."

"I understand, Dr. Schaul. We need some luck to break our way and I'm rolling the dice. I assume you've at least understood the characteristics of the liquid in the vial? It wasn't vodka or something, right?"

"No Sir, correct. The liquid in the vial is absolutely a vaccine to *something*. If we had another few months, we might be able to reverse engineer the virus itself."

"I suspect you'll have a sample of the virus soon enough, Dr. Ricci, one way or another. Hap, talk to me about logistics."

Brigadier General Forrest 'Hap' Wilson was an icon in military logistics. He was named after the famous Civil War commander Nathan Bedford Forrest, who was regarded as the greatest military genius of all the Civil War commanders. The president had known Hap Wilson since his days in the military and trusted and respected Hap to get things done. "Sir, we currently have fifty million doses stockpiled at ten Army bases across the U.S."

"I'm confused. The task was to figure out a way to get it distributed *en masse*, like the Chinese are going to be doing in about nine days?"

Dr. Kabir Anand spoke up before the general could answer. "Sir, I can discuss that aspect of things. We took a two-fold approach. One, where we replicated the serum and stockpiled it for conventional distribution. This was done as a backup and didn't hamper any other efforts of mass distribution."

"Go on Doctor."

"When we took the approach of putting it in the water supply and ran initial tests, we were seeing that some of the elements in the serum were breaking down."

"Hold on. Here's my understanding of a vaccine. You take some of the virus, somehow weaken it, and then inject it into a human in a portion that is small enough to trigger a reaction from the body to essentially start building anti-bodies to fight it. Correct?"

Dr. Schaul then spoke, "Yes Mr. President, that is basically the idea of a vaccine. In this case we don't have the virus to work from, we just have the *actual* supposed vaccine. We're not sure what elements are crucial to developing anti-bodies and which elements are not."

"So either the Chinese know what they are doing or they don't?" the president questioned. "We can only assume that the serum procured from the Chinese lab is indeed the vaccine. If the Chinese scientists blew it or missed something, then all of this is irrelevant because we all may be dead very soon."

"Sir, yes, that is understood. I had said our initial tests. When we looked deeper into the Chinese water system, which the vaccine was developed for, we realized that they don't provide fluoride in their water system. In fact, their water system has *excess* fluoride for which, in many instances, they use defluorination techniques to reduce fluoride." Dr. Anand paused so the President could catch up. "When we ran our initial tests, we did so with our water system which has a *normal* amount of fluoridation."

"I think I'm following, so cut to the chase."

Dr. Anand finished his thoughts, "Subsequent tests run on a de-fluorinated water supply didn't show any breakdown of the serum provided."

"So we *can* vaccinate through the water supply, but we have to remove the fluoride? Dentists are going to love me."

Dr. Ricci then responded, "Sort of Sir. We can add an enzyme to the serum to counter-act the fluoridation and in those areas that may not fluoridate, it won't affect the serum or the end result at all."

"Great, so I guess that's it right, we're good to go?"

"Sir, there's another issue."

"You guys are killing me, what General?" When the president reverted to titles versus first names, all could tell he was getting frustrated.

Dr. Schaul illuminated the issue. "Sir, we can put it in the water supply, but many citizens don't drink from the water supply, they drink bottled water."

"So we give it to the bottled water companies to put in their water."

"Sir, the way those companies work with manufacturing, warehousing, and distribution, there isn't enough time."

"General … gentlemen … we can only do what we can do. Give it to them anyway, tell them that the Federal Government will pay to pull their existing water off the shelves immediately and get them moving on replenishing their distributors or retailers with bottled water that includes the vaccine. They can tell their customers it's a recall or something. Just to make sure, I assume, General, that you've made plans to also put it in the water supply with the additive just discussed?"

"Yes Sir, it's all in motion."

"Good General, that's all we can do. Good work all. General, please keep me up-to-date on these efforts."

"Yes Sir, thank you."

With that all four men left the Oval and the president was left looking at his Chief of Staff. The president leaned back in his chair, "Jesus, that was like pulling teeth. Why the hell couldn't they just say they made it work for the water supply?"

"Everyone wants to look good in your eyes. They want to let you know they are solving problems."

"I guess. There's a reason every four years only a handful of the 330 million Americans decide to run for the presidency."

"It's called money."

"No, it's called lunacy. The more I do this job, the more I wished I just lived a quiet life."

"That's not true, you were born for this Sir."

"Time will tell on that."

Li Wei had been thinking about the future the last few days. His place in Chinese lore would be ensconced forever. This time in history would attribute his name to the defeat of the great Satan America. To the vile culture of the West, to its 'freedoms.' He knew he was a being a bit of a hypocrite. He certainly had enjoyed the West's culture when he lived and attended school there. He brushed the thought aside for now and focused on what was to be. China would dominate the world and, though they would still have to deal with an 'America,' it would be greatly diminished in power. Its people would be in disarray, maybe even in revolt. *Who knows*, he thought, *maybe America will split into two or more countries. Maybe it will go by way of the old Soviet Union?* He smiled as he looked outside at the beautiful Spring day. He knew this day was the start of a new China, a new bolder vision for its people and the planet. As he picked up the phone and dialed China's Head of Infrastructure, he glanced at his computer screen date which read March 20.

"Qiang, good morning. Are we ready?"

"Yes your excellency. All preparations have been made and waiting for your word."

"Very well, release the vaccine into the water supply country wide. Please update me on any progress or irregularities."

Mao Qiang responded without hesitation. "Yes Sir, absolutely. It is done."

And with that Wei hung up the phone and turned his attention to lunch.

Tim Chen read the email and shook his head. *Did she not get what I was saying? Do I have a girlfriend?? Talk about cutting a guy off at the knees–jeez! Well, she obviously doesn't feel the same way if she's asking about my dating habits. I should have left well enough alone.* He popped the cap of another Tsing Tao. He put aside any possible feelings he had for Parker Hall and thought about the last part of her email. She had written, *'Go somewhere safe or come home.'* Tim was resigned to the fact that he probably couldn't go back to work at the lab after this all went down. So what was he supposed to do? He wasn't ready to go back the U.S. He really liked discovering his homeland and if it weren't for the fucked-up government, China would be a great place to hang out for a while. He'd met some great people and for the most part, really liked his life. The Chinese people certainly didn't deserve the crap the government was about to do. He knew there was a chance that the rest of the world would take it out on the people rather than the damn Politburo members. This is what happened to the German people after World War II. They were blamed for essentially capitulating and not revolting. It would be no different for the Chinese people. *Why did the Chinese people accept this style of governance and why hadn't they revolted?* Tim thought to himself. He wondered if it was a case of what people knew for their lives. He knew capitalism and freedom all of his life. But maybe, if all someone ever knew was communism which included less freedoms, then they really wouldn't know what you were missing.

Tim remembered reading about the Tiananmen Square incident. Chinese students tried to push for democratic reforms and after a few weeks of protests, the Chinese government didn't think twice about bringing in the military and opening fire on the protestors. Thousands died and that was that. Tim opined to himself, *that's not the way to reform here–this wasn't the U.S.* He instinctively knew reform in China had to come from the top officials, or a replacement of the top officials. Then the military would have nowhere to turn, new top officials would give new directives. After all, the military is simply a tool of government. He reflected on the U.S. style of governance, its democracy versus China's Communism. America's democracy was by no means perfect and certainly needed reform in many areas as well, but he couldn't help but think that the people had the ultimate power. Even when thinking about the recent lockdown due to the (first) virus, as U.S. citizens felt their civil liberties slipping away, they took to the streets with arms in protest. Unlike China, U.S. state governors didn't roll in tanks and massacre its citizens. They relented in many cases. China needed new leadership and he knew that was easier said than done. However, if the U.S. was successful in stopping China and its second virus, the Chinese people, with the support of the entire world, might just be able to oust the Politburo and other government leaders. He tilted his beer bottle up and drank the last sip. *Hell, something has to be done. The world, and especially the Chinese people, can't let the government get away with this atrocity.* He felt a bit of resolve like he hadn't felt before. He also felt a little pissed at Parker. He was just frustrated. He opened his laptop and sent an email to Parker.

> *I appreciate your suggestion but I feel a need to stay here and help the Chinese people. I don't know how yet, but I'll figure it out, I always do. Oh, and yeah, dating a few women, too many to keep straight. Take care and good luck.*
>
> *– Mr. Frank*

CHAPTER 25

The world was ready. With only a few days to go before it was assumed that China would release the second virus, it was time to complete the lockdown. Coalition troops were in place around China, mainly where there weren't any actual border crossings. Security was beefed up at border crossings into the border countries. U.S. and coalition ships were close to the line where China waters crossed into international waters. They announced they were running joint war game exercises thirty days prior. That always alerted the Chinese, but not to the point where they would have suspected anything out of the ordinary. It was standard practice amongst the various navies, especially in international waters. The entire plan was a massive undertaking. The world's airlines had begun to pull their airliners back from Chinese routes a couple of days prior. Flights into China were canceled or rescheduled. The Civil

Aviation Administration of China (CAAC) wasn't
necessarily monitoring the situation as a whole, so by the
time any of this was brought to the attention of any CAAC
official, it would be too late. China was effectively locked in
and they didn't even realize it.

If China didn't release Virus Two per the
intercepted schedule, then the gig would be up. This
'lockdown' could only be secretive for a couple of days.
One wildcard was the press, of all nations. The press loved a
good story no matter the cost. They didn't see life and death
or 'national interest.' Those days were well behind the
world. If the press had 'breaking news' (as the banners on
all of their news stations continuously indicated), they felt it
was their duty to release it. The president of the U.S. took a
different approach and he recommended other world leaders
do the same. He basically used the press's insatiable appetite
for all things political to keep them busy. He created
controversies over the past six weeks, stories about
administration officials, hints at alleged wrongdoing, affairs,
new bills being floated, and more. Everything and anything
to keep them preoccupied while world leaders, their
militaries, and those in the aviation industry embarked upon
saving the world.

The U.S. president had had enough of the so-called
free press. They had become a sleazy arm of propaganda for
one political cause or another. They continually argued that
they were doing the 'people's work' under the First
Amendment of the Constitution, but everyone knew they
were just out for a story which meant viewers which in turn
meant they could charge higher rates to advertisers. Period.
It was one of the terrible sides of capitalism. Over the course

of the preparations, there were a few small leaks and
suggestions by rogue reporters that this or that was
happening, but nothing hit the mainstream airwaves. World
leaders, including the president of the United States, knew
they had to do everything they could to try to stop this
planetary disaster. The vaccine, or what they all hoped was
the vaccine, was running through most of the world's water
supply by now, unbeknownst to the public at large. He and
all the other leaders would either be tarred and feathered or
go down in history as heroes.

Li Wei woke up early. Things appeared normal to most, but
he knew today was a special day. It was April Fool's Day in
the West. He'd actually gave the 'go order' the previous
night so that by the time he woke up, Virus Two would be
well on its way throughout China and the world. The plan
was for fifty agents from the Ministry of State Security to
get on international flights or cross over borders starting
today. These agents had been infected early this morning
with Virus Two and had about thirty-six hours to get to their
destinations before they would succumb to the virus. It was
a suicide mission for which the Chinese government paid
each agent and their family about seven million Yuan–about
a million U.S. dollars. Their families only knew it was
dangerous, but the agents themselves knew it was a death
sentence.

     As Wei poured his morning tea, he also knew that

the virus had already been released several hours earlier into the streets of China. He and the other Politburo members received direct injection vaccinations, but he knew that there would be some Chinese population deaths even though the vaccine had been released into their water system ten days earlier. Some deaths were acceptable as a part of the plan. Wei thought, *even if one-million Chinese die, it will be worth it. We have the population and the more that die, the more empathy we will receive from the world.* All he had to do now was wait. He knew it might take a full day for the agents to get to their destinations, infect local citizens, and those citizens become sick and report to a hospital. He started to reach for his cell phone when he decided that he would savor this moment. He would shower and take his time getting into the office, there might be some news by then. He then grabbed his cell phone, but only to silence the ringer.

Parker Hall, Josh Bennett, and others were in their respective organization's situation rooms. No one really knew if China, through its high-ranking officials, had put into motion the release of Virus Two. They all had to act as if China did. At 12:01 am on April 1, all countries bordering China closed their borders to people trying to enter from China. Coalition forces which had aircraft carriers on the seas near China began flying sorites to turn back airliners flying out of China. They remained outside Chinese airspace, so these engagements were happening at cruising altitudes of 30,000 feet and higher. Fighter jets used intimidation and the threat of being shot down to get most all Chinese pilots to comply and head back into Chinese airspace. The cargo ships and fishing trawlers that were headed out of Chinese ports for open water were intercepted by smaller vessels such as frigates and destroyers which were nimble enough to maneuver into a blocking position so as to stop the vessels and get them to turn around. Most troops not at regular border crossings didn't see much activity. The Chinese government, knowing nothing of the 'lockdown,' would not have planned to send anyone through irregular crossings. By the time the Chinese agents were prohibited from crossing, all they could do was call their superiors because there was no plan for a closed border.

The U.S. Intelligence agencies as well as other coalition intelligence agencies were all getting reports of these initial intercepts and closings. So far so good. World leaders knew that somehow, someway, Virus Two would get out beyond China's borders and so they still were trepidatious as to any celebration of early good reports. It was decided that the president would appear on all the networks in a few hours, along with other world leaders in 'Zoom squares' on the screen, as he told the world about China's devious plot regarding both viruses and the world's response. This was a calculated first 'media' strike so that the Chinese government didn't have time to adapt to the lockdown and make other plans or respond with propaganda.

It was nearly noon by the time Li Wei got to his office. As he walked in, his assistant had a stack of telephone messages in his hand and he looked concerned. Wei looked at him and said, "What is wrong Xiang? Okay, yes, everyone wants me today. Put them on my desk and I will address them one by one."

"But sir, there are some pressing messages—"

"Please Xiang, relax and get me a cup of tea, and I will get to them soon enough." Wei put down his briefcase and sat down at his desk. Before he could even address the first message, his desk phone buzzed. "Yes Xiang, what now?"

"Sir, it is Mr. Wang Lei, the Head of the CAAC, he says it is urgent."

"Fine, put him through."

"Sir, something is happening to our commercial flights leaving China for destinations around the world. They are being intercepted by the U.S. and other foreign military planes in international airspace and being told to turn around and land back in China."

"What? What are you talking about? What airlines? What flights?"

"Sir, it is only happening to Air China flights. There are no other flights internationally."

"You're not making sense. What do you mean 'there are no other flights'?"

Wang Lei sounded apologetic. "Sir, I'm sorry we didn't notice this a couple of days ago, but all of the other airlines haven't flown any of their flights into China for about two days now, and any planes they had been in China all left yesterday."

"What is going on? Why? Have you contacted any of the other airlines?"

"No sir, not yet. Like I said, we just figured this out about an hour ago."

"Why didn't you call me immediately!?"

"I did sir, your assistant said you were not there and when he tried your cell phone there was no answer."

Wei grabbed his cell phone out of his pocket. "Dammit!" he said out loud. He'd forgotten to turn his phone ringer back on–the screen said 12 messages. "Call the other airlines and find out what is going on. Call me back in one hour." No sooner did Wei hang up with that call than his phone buzzed again with his assistant telling him it was Gao Tang with an urgent message. "Very well, put him through."

"Sir, we've been trying to reach you for hours. There's a problem at several of the border crossings."

"What is it?"

"Sir, it appears that these border crossings are closed for Chinese nationals....well, *anyone* leaving China."

"What do you mean closed?"

"No Chinese citizen, or anyone else for that matter, is allowed to leave China and cross into … wait one second, Sir … yes, that's twenty-five more crossings closed, making a total of forty of our ninety-one border crossings closed by the bordering country."

"What is going on? Are the other crossings closed?"

"No reports yet sir."

"Well find out, NOW!" Wei slammed the phone down and grabbed his messages. His first thought was that they were under attack. He knew that wasn't the case though. There were no military engagements along the border, no missile launches by any other country, no bombing raids–so just what the hell was going on? He briefly looked at his paper messages and then stuffed them into his pocket and headed out of his office. As he passed his assistant, he told him to contact the other Politburo members and tell them they need an emergency meeting in one hour and that he was heading over to the operations center in the basement of the Politburo building. The walk, which normally took him fifteen minutes, only took him ten today. One of the messages was from Dr. Ho Min. As he walked, he dialed his longtime friend.

Ho Min answered on the first ring. "Hello?"

"Min, I am very busy so please make it brief."

"Yes, Wei, of course. I just wanted to let you know we may have had a security breach."

"When?"

"We just went over some video tape of the lab and it appears that a young researcher in another lab gained access to my lab and stole a vial of the vaccine about a month ago."

"And you're just now finding out?"

"It was an odd situation that didn't really ring any alarm bells until the other day when my assistant confessed that the same researcher was in my office and saw my notes on our last conversation."

"What did your notes reflect?"

"I wrote down the vaccine date and the Virus Two

release date."

"Dammit, Min! Send me an email with this researcher's name, phone number, and home address. Right NOW, please!"

"Yes, Wei, okay. I am sorry my friend."

Wei hung up the call and started thinking. *A spy? How could a spy possibly know of our plans?* He entered the Politburo building and headed to the operations center. As soon as he entered the secure room, Gao Tang gave him an update.

"Sir, the remaining border crossings all report that they are closed to anyone trying to leave China."

"What other information is coming in?"

"Several fishing trawlers and one cargo ship report that when they got into international waters, they were met by military ships telling them to turn around."

Wei studied the map and then a call came in for him from his office. Tang handed Wei the phone.

"Sir, the Minister of State Security, Zau Fang is on the line, says its urgent, shall I—"

"Yes, dammit, put him through!"

"Sir, I've been trying to reach you for several hours now—"

Wei cut him off. "Yes, I know–what is it?"

"Sir, most of the agents we had traveling today by air or land have been stopped from leaving China or turned back if on an airplane."

"Have you re-routed them Fang?"

"Rerouted how, Sir? All the border crossings are closed and every airliner is being turned around."

"Get them across the border somehow–have them cross illegally, give the order now!"

"Sir, one of our agents, who left last night on a flight to San Francisco, has called on his satellite phone. He saw two military jets outside the plane and so he went to the cockpit. The captain agrees that they cannot turn around, they are passed the halfway point."

"Fang, you tell him that plane must reach its destination, whatever he has to do."

"What about the agents traveling by air that have returned to China?"

"Have them use private jets. Tell them to tell the pilots to avoid radar and fly low. Focus on destinations that will get them to an international airport in any other country as quickly as possible. Go!"

Gao Tang then spoke, "Sir, there has just been an announcement by the American press that their President is speaking on TV in fifteen minutes."

"I need to get upstairs; the Politburo members and I will watch from there." Wei started to walk out when his phone chirped indicating an email. He stopped, read it, and forwarded it to Gao Tang. "Also, I just forwarded an email to you. Send the police to arrest this man and trace his phone for any messages he might have sent in the last three months."

"Yes sir, right away."

With that Wei headed up to the Politburo Chamber. When he opened the huge doors to walk into the cavernous room, the other members were already there and began to pepper him with questions all at once.

CHAPTER 26

The U.S. president was getting ready to address the world. This might be the single-most important address in the history of the world. He had about twenty minutes before he would walk into the press room. At that moment, his Chief of Staff walked in and said he needed him in the Situation Room ASAP. That's all he needed–another crisis to derail his thoughts. This president wasn't one for a teleprompter. He liked good old-fashioned note cards with typed bullet points. Once he was in the Situation Room with all around, the Chairman of the Joint Chiefs of Staff was on his right. He spoke first.

"Sir, there's a commercial flight bound for San Francisco out of Beijing. It's Air China flight 983, a Boeing 777, and it left last night before we activated our Combat Air Patrols. It's now over the Pacific past the halfway point. All of the other flights we turned around had plenty of fuel to reverse course. The pilot is saying that they are committed and will not turn around. What do you want to do sir?"

The president looked at Alden Scott as if wanting his opinion.

Alden gave it to him. "Sir, it would be really bad to shoot this plane down. We have done very well so far in turning around these flights. This one slipped through."

"Why did this one slip through Admiral?"

"Mr. President, when our patrols started, we weren't looking that far out. We were focused on flights leaving mainland China and just heading out over the ocean. Our boys in the E3 thought this was a plane returning home. They didn't alert anyone until a supervisor inquired hours later about the flight."

"Jesus. Okay, options?" No one else spoke. The president piped up again, "No one has any options for me?"

"Sir, there are two F/A 18s alongside, ready to fire. What are your orders?"

"Admiral Reed, we're not going to shoot the damn thing down–just yet. He can't turn back, right? Can we force him to land in Alaska or something?"

"I'm not sure he will listen. This pilot, if it is the pilot we're talking to, is pretty adamant about continuing to San Francisco."

"How long before it gets to San Fran?"

Alden interjected before the Admiral could answer. "About another five hours, Sir."

"Alright, have the fighters escort him to San Francisco. If there is any deviation in his flight plan, I want to know about it ASAP–we may have to use the military option at that point, but only on my command, understood?

Otherwise, prepare SFO for an incoming plane that must be quarantined on the tarmac. It is not to park at any gate. No one gets off. We refuel her, we get the passengers food and water, but I want the military to surround the plane. I want two … the plane has two pilots, right? I want two military pilots qualified to fly that plane, in hazmat suits, to replace the two pilots on board and I want it flown the hell out of the continental U.S. Fly it to Alaska or another U.S. military base in a friendly nation or even back to China for that matter."

"Four Sir."

"Four what?"

"Four pilots, they switched crews at the halfway point."

"Fine, Admiral, four. And you better give those pilots some security up there in case one of the persons on board is a Chinese agent or something."

"Yes Sir. Thank you, Sir."

Li Wei tried to walk calmly to his seat and then spoke. "Please, one at a time."

Shou spoke first. "What the hell is going on?"

Wu Xin followed with another question, "I'm hearing about airliners and border crossings–are we at war Wei?"

"Gentlemen, I do not know exactly what is going on. As you are aware, we released the vaccine into our water supply ten days ago. I then ordered the release of Virus Two last night."

"Wei, it appears that your plan is having some problems."

"Fu, may I remind you all that it is *our* plan. You all adopted it and gave me your consent to move forward."

Fu sidestepped the response, "I understand the U.S. president will be speaking in a few minutes on TV."

"Yes, that is my understanding as well. I assumed we would all watch it together."

Wei was going to tell them about the spy at Ho Min's lab, but he thought that would only add fuel to the fire of blaming Dr. Ho for the plan not working. Wei still needed more intel to fully understand what was happening, but he had a rough idea. Somehow, America found out about the release, possibly from a spy at the lab, and they had taken measures to prevent the virus from escaping China.

Shou spoke to the room, "Someone please turn up the sound, the U.S. president is about to speak."

––––––––––––––––––––

The president went directly from the Situation Room to the press room. His note cards were in his pocket and as he entered the room, he took them out and placed them on the podium.

"My fellow Americans and citizens of the world, we've all gone through what can only be described as a life-changing event beginning with the with the virus over a year ago, the lockdown, the re-opening and everything in-between. We are all still getting used to a new normal. At first, we understood this virus to be a natural event, but I am here to tell you, and to provide proof, that the virus was a devious plot by the Chinese government to ensconce their country as the one and only superpower on the planet. The virus we just went through was only half of their plan. The other part of their plan is even more sinister, and I and other leaders around the world have put our own plans in place to stop the second half of China's plan. I will now tell you about their plan and I will show you the evidence. I will also tell you what I and the other leaders have put in place to stop China from destroying the world. Before I continue, I want to emphasize one thing. The Chinese government and its Politburo members are the bad actors and it is incredibly unfortunate that their actions represent an entire country. The Chinese people had nothing to do with these actions. I have faith that the Chinese people will finally take control of their lives and demand freedom from their government, whatever that may look like In the future."

With that, the president went on for another forty-five minutes explaining Virus Two, the evidence, the vaccinated water supply worldwide, and the coalition's 'Lockdown of China' response. Most people in the press room and those watching around the world were shocked. The president didn't take any questions from reporters. He ended by saying that Communism had no place in the 21st century. In under an hour, the president gave the press and all media outlets worldwide fodder for months, if not years. Oh, they would not simply just report this news, they would take sides and hash out possibilities and second-guess actions by all. They would fabricate and create content that all would consume. The president knew this, but he had more important things to be concerned about at the moment. He knew the world wasn't home free yet. There was a deadly virus trying to escape China and he knew that his appearance was seen by the world. The big question for him now was how would China, and he meant China's Politburo members, respond?

The Politburo members were silent as the big screen TV was switched off after the president's address. Li Wei was truly shocked that his wonderful plan had been uncovered because some researcher, who apparently happened to be snooping around, and completely by chance stumbled upon a scrap piece of paper. The kid apparently wasn't even a spy, but basically a friend of an American that worked in the U.S. government. While Wei was lamenting his bad luck, the other Politburo members were reflecting on how this would affect China.

Shou spoke first again. "Colleagues. The situation is not good. We must discuss options."

"One option is to do nothing," said Fu. "We deny everything. The evidence that the U.S. president cited is not that strong; it is coincidental and circumstantial."

Xin then spoke, "That is one option Fu. Another option is to take the offensive and not only deny the allegations, but blame the U.S. for manufacturing this alleged new crisis?"

Zhang Min switched topics. "Wei, what is the current situation of Virus Two and our own people?"

"I … I do not know. No one knows yet. It is too early. We won't know the effect of the vaccinated water on Virus Two for a few days."

"And what of the agents that were deliberately infected? It would appear they didn't make their destinations."

"Most did not, but they are trying to find alternative paths. I am hopeful, Min."

"But didn't the American president say they had the vaccine?" inserted Xin. "What is the point of continuing with the plan?"

"I ordered the alternative paths before I heard the president's address," answered Wei. "I'm not sure what the next course of action is. I am truly shocked, my friends. I still believe our plan was solid. I can only believe that a higher power intervened to change our destiny."

Shou's tone was much harsher. "Higher power? This was our responsibility and I admit, when you laid out the plan it was solid, but I believe there was also discussion that we should simply do no more. We had degraded the world with Virus One and we could have lived with that and been proud of our service to China."

"Shou, hindsight is always 20/20. You cannot second-guess a decision we all made. Yes, there was discussion, but our decision was still solid."

"Listen to us," Xin shook his head. "We are justifying a decision that didn't work out. Is this justification for us, our people, or the world?"

"We have a problem now. Forget justification," Fu said. "We need to figure out how China comes out of this in one piece and is not thought of or treated as the pariah of the world."

"That is a good point, Fu." Shou said. "Is there a military option? If we take the offensive position is there a use for our military to take a posture which might be seen as a genuine response to an unbelievable fabricated story."

"I do not recommend the military option," Wei said. "There is too much opposition in place to anything we might do at the present time. We risk being invaded, bombed, or further destroyed in the eyes of the world."

"Wei, are you advocating we surrender to world opinion?" asked Fu incredulously. "We have never done that! Even when we have told half-truths to the world, we never have relented."

"I think this is different. Whether you want to believe it or not, we have been exposed. The backlash will be harsh and could range from companies pulling their manufacturing altogether, to economic sanctions, to full blown reparations."

Shou spoke out. "Wei, I cannot and I will not disrespect my name and my family by capitulating to the West. I would rather go down fighting. At least my family would respect me."

Min echoed the sentiment, "I am in agreement with Shou. I would rather die with respect than live through anything the West may subject us too."

Wei tried to interject some calm. "May I suggest that we all retire to our homes and do some serious thinking about our next course of action. If death is preferential, in order to respect our names, then we may be able to craft a course of action that at least inflicts some kind of pain on the West."

Xin seemed to speak for the group when he said, "We can all agree with that and I suggest we meet again in two days. I suggest you all see your families as well."

They all got up slowly from their heavily cushioned chairs and headed for the door. They were somber and didn't speak as they left. Wei knew he had failed. He had lost. It was 'game over' as his friends in the West would put it.

Wei didn't have family per se. He never married and always did whatever he wanted to do in order to fulfill his happiness. He liked that because he was never responsible to anyone nor would he ever disappoint anyone. He knew what was coming. The members would vote to fight and that meant war and that also meant destruction. He contemplated his own course of action. He may not have brought disgrace on a family, but he certainly brought disgrace upon himself and his country. He had a good life. He had risen to a very high level in the Chinese government. He'd led a comfortable life; he'd had fun as a kid and enjoyed some of the West's devilish pleasures. He couldn't help but think, as he walked across the quad to his office, that his plan was solid. How had such a random person extinguished such a perfectly conceived plan? Was it luck? He was not sure he believed in luck. He believed in planning and thoughtfulness. Back at his office he gathered his things without saying much to his assistant and headed home. He would enjoy a libation or two tonight. He would reflect on his life and whatever tomorrow needed to bring, it would bring.

———————————————

The Chinese people had listened to the U.S. president's address country wide. The announcement and subsequent broadcast were pronounced too quickly for the government to censor either the TV or the radio broadcast. Not only did the major networks worldwide carry the president's address, but all of the digital entities did as well. YouTube, Twitter, Hulu, Amazon, Showtime, Starz, HBO, and others interrupted their regular programming. Even the Playboy Channel broadcast the address. Twitter and WeChat were abuzz. History would show that it was a breaking point for the citizens of China. If Tiananmen Square was a pre-cursor, today and the next few days would be the main act.

Tim Chen had no idea how he'd fit into all of this, but he felt as though his purpose was clear, at least for the next few days. He did not go to work that day and would never return to the lab. Once he heard the president refer to him as a 'clandestine researcher at a Chinese lab,' he knew the Chinese government would immediately put two and two together and be looking for him. He was listening to the broadcast in a local bar a couple of miles from his apartment. He immediately got on his motorbike and went home to pack some things and leave. If he was found by the Chinese police, he would be arrested and tortured for the rest of his life if not outright killed. As he ran upstairs to his apartment, he called Sam Ji and told him he needed to see him ASAP. Sam reminded him he was currently at work. Tim told him to leave immediately, he was in danger, and he needed to go to his apartment immediately. Sam knew that Tim was not really a bullshitter, so he did as Tim said. Forty-five minutes later both were at Sam's apartment and Tim was anxious to get inside. He took the next thirty minutes and explained everything to Sam. Sam interrupted and said, "I knew it! I knew they had us doing some dirty shit."

"Yep. Dirty shit alright. Planetary death is more accurate."

"I know this group of people who are into democratic reform. They've been really into trying to trying to push for a 'new China.' Let me reach out to them right now and see what they think."

"Ok, sure," Tim agreed. "Hey, I'm not sure the government won't look for us here either. I think we bought a few hours, but they'll find out that you and I are friends. It was your sample that went missing, and they will come here looking for you, also."

"First off dude, *you* stole the sample and I had nothing to do with that."

"DUDE! Don't you get it? It doesn't matter. You're now guilty by association. Ask your friends if we can crash with them."

Ten minutes later Sam packed some things and they both got in Sam's car and headed out. Sam was more into the social media and the pulse of the young revolutionists than Tim. Sam commented during the thirty-minute drive that his 'friends' had told him that the U.S. president's speech was damning to the Chinese Politburo and that many people, young and old, were ready to finally do whatever was needed to change their government. Mass protests country wide had already begun, but as Tim knew, that would simply be met with tanks and bullets. It was the Politburo members who needed to be removed, peacefully or by force. That was the only way. When they got to their destination, they were welcomed and shown a spare room. Once they tossed their things in the room, they joined a discussion of ten or so other 'reformists.' There was talk of getting guns and going to war with the police or military.

Tim shook his head and spoke up, "My name is Tim Chen. I am a Chinese American. I have studied the situation and the only way to resolve this is to march on the Politburo and remove the members themselves. We will not win against tanks or machine guns, that's what happened in 1989 at Tiananmen Square. We don't want to repeat history."

Others perked up and the discussion got rowdy again. Sam then whistled and asked for quiet.

Tim spoke up while it was still silent, "If we spend the night planning, we might be able to forcibly remove the Politburo members tomorrow or the next day. But we need to hurry. If we do not act before the military is summoned to protect the Politburo, then we lose our chance."

The group started texting and discussing a plan. Tim's head was spinning, there were so many comments. Two things happened that night. By about 2:00 am, they had gathered the support of at least a hundred thousand people who were willing to show up whenever and wherever they

were told to in the next day or so. The second thing that
happened was a surprise to Tim Chen. Sometime during all
of the discussions and the reaching out, Tim was elevated to
the de facto leader of this movement. His name was used
over and over and once Sam let it slip that Tim Chen was
the 'researcher' the U.S. president was referring to, he
became an icon, a leader who could deliver the people out of
their oppression. A modern-day Moses. Tim really didn't
grasp this until the next morning.

The coalition was holding and China was virtually locked
down. Li Wei's directive to the Chinese agents to find
alternative ways across the border actually worked. Small
private jets were able to skirt radar by flying very low and
then, once over the border, they found countries they could
land at and drop their cargo, the agents, who then got on
other international flights to the U.S. A few agents also
made it across the border by foot, horse, or 4-wheel drive
vehicles and into several cities, about ten in all. By this time
the agents were sick and wouldn't make it to see another full
day. They knew this and were good faithful countrymen.
They did everything they could to come in contact with as
many people as they could. All in all, about twenty agents
made it to other countries out of the original fifty that were
tasked. Four of the twenty made it to the U.S. One made it
into Russia and another two into Europe. The others made it
into other parts of Asia. If it wasn't for the international call

J RUSTY SHAFFER 274

for doctors to be on the lookout for pockets of deaths, they wouldn't have even reported them. The Chinese Politburo would never be able to celebrate how well their researchers made Virus Two and especially its vaccine. Those that avoided the public water supply, typically in small towns across the world, or where agents had infected people, died within thirty-six hours just as the Chinese scientists had predicted. Otherwise, those that were inoculated by the vaccine in the water supply simply got a mild case of the flu or a bad cold or nothing. The reports from the handful of hospitals around the world quickly made their way into the appropriate government hands. This was seen as real proof that the Chinese had indeed released a second virus on the world. Those new Virus Two deaths were tragic, but they served a purpose. The media couldn't now speculate that this whole thing was made up by the U.S. president or any other world leader. As the president entered the Situation Room, all stood to attention.

"Be seated. Where are we, Admiral?"

"Sir, it's remarkable. It would appear that the plan is working. We're getting a few reports of the new virus and some hospitalizations in various cities and countries, but the plan has worked!"

"How many deaths so far?"

Alden Scott spoke up. "We don't know yet, Sir. We think that they must have infected some of their agents and that some of them got through by foot or otherwise to other places and from there they spread the disease. But the good news is that those cases are isolated and there's no reason to believe they will infect others that have been inoculated from the vaccine in the public water supply. There will be some deaths, it's inevitable, but nothing like what we just went through."

CHAPTER 27

Thirty-six hours had gone by in a blink of an eye. Li Wei had not gone to his office since the Politburo meeting two days ago. He had reconciled his affairs and come to grips with what was going to happen today. He had cleaned his QSZ-92 handgun and loaded it. News of the last day and a half was actually worse. Not only did China fail in their plans, but world condemnation was coming fast and furious. There were no more flights to stop, no ships to stop, and the border crossings were virtually silent. He had been informed that several agents got through and were able to infect certain areas and groups of people in select cities, but because the vaccine had been distributed worldwide, the death toll was minimal. The numbers were so low that he surmised that more people drowned at the beaches every year than were dying from Virus Two. Though he accepted the failure, Wei still couldn't accept that his plan was in any way flawed.

There were rumblings from the Chinese people. There were demands for reform, demands for leaders to step down. There were many protests throughout China's cities and they were growing hourly. As he entered the Politburo building, he saw the large crowd building outside the gates. The president of China, who was a mere figurehead, hadn't been seen in the last two days. He had only been told about the plan a week ago and right after the president of the U.S. had spoken to the world, he had denied every accusation with aplomb. It was rather easy for him to lie because that was basically his job. There was a huge misconception in the West that the president of China had decision-making power. It was the opposite. He did what the Politburo members wanted and that was it. Aside from that, he was basically a hot air balloon, a front for the real power brokers in China. Li Wei joined the other Politburo members in the Chamber.

Xin spoke first, "Wei, the situation is worse, we must do something, we must decide on a course of action."

"We should fight our way out of this. If we have the military engage the forces off our coast at least we have a fighting chance that it will lead to some sort of stalemate and we can move forward."

Fu was resigned and spoke softly. "Min, we are finished. It is time for change and China will survive even though politically, we will not."

Wei remained silent. He could hear the protests and the crowd outside growing. He knew that he would not see tomorrow. He quietly responded to his colleagues, "Gentlemen, there is nothing to do. We have done enough damage for one lifetime. I believe it is now time for us to say our goodbyes."

Shou stood, "Wei, I cannot and will not accept that! Fu, please call General Liao and order him to use our forces to attack the Western forces in the South China Sea."

No one else spoke and Fu, after pausing for what seemed like the longest two seconds in world history, reluctantly made the call. It was a short call as General Liao had been briefed the day before that this call might come today. Within a few minutes, Chinese forces were moving, pilots running to planes, ships pulling anchor or moving toward their attack positions, and the Western forces, who were already on high alert, also instantly saw this movement and phone calls went up the chain of command just as fast and eventually to the White House.

"Mr. President, they need you in the Situation Room immediately."

The president nodded to the corpsman who had knocked and then entered the residence. Within four minutes, the president was telling his commanders and other personnel to be seated as he spoke, "What do we have?"

Admiral Reed gave him the update. "Sir, it appears Chinese officials have given the order to their military to engage coalition forces in the South China Sea. They are scrambling their jets and turning their ships toward our fleet."

"Damn. I was hoping that it wouldn't come to this. Admiral, put our forces on ready alert. Our forces are not to fire unless fired upon."

"Sir, maybe we should reach out diplomatically as well?"

"Reach out to who, Alden? It appears from the TV that the Politburo building is about to be overrun."

"Sir, we could try to reach out to their generals."

"Do it now, Admiral. See if you can get them to verify the order. With any luck, they won't be able to get in touch with their 'higher-ups' and we can talk them into not attacking."

"Yes Sir, right away."

Things were happening so fast that by the time Fu hung up the phone after giving the order to attack, the Politburo grounds had been breached and overrun. There were some military and police guards stationed to protect the entire compound, but they were simply the minimum protective detail that was posted there year-round. This detail was more for the cameras than actual protection against an armed insurrection.

In the Chamber, the members could hear the commotion outside the closed doors and it was growing louder. On TV, the overrun looked like the running of the bulls in Pamplona, Spain. Protests and forcible breaches were happening all over China at most government offices and the borders. The local police and military couldn't even

begin to engage the protestors. There were gunshots here
and there, and some of the protesters were injured and even
died, but that did not stop the crowd of about 500,000
strong. In the Chamber, it was apparent that the doors would
give way any second and Zhou Shou and Wu Xin took out
pistols and shot themselves in the side of the head. As the
doors to the Chamber buckled and strained under the
pressure of being opened against their will, Wei slipped out
a side door. Huang Fu and Zhang Min basically surrendered
once the doors were indeed breached and the protestors
entered and filled the Chamber. Reports were now coming
in on TV that the Chinese military had been scrambled and
was on its way to engage coalition forces. Even Chinese TV
reported this as there was chaos in the TV station. There
were no censors to filter what was going out on the
airwaves, so raw footage was going out to the world. The
censors, along with others sympathetic to the communist
regime, had fled the station and other private institutions all
over the country that had a government oversight function.
Anyone perceived as being friendly to the communist
government had fled their posts.

Tim Chen had led the charge in Beijing at the
Politburo. He was the perceived or *de facto* leader of this
revolution, or so they told him. The small group of people
he'd met two nights before were incredibly organized and
resourceful. They were able to marshal over five million
people nationwide within forty-eight hours for their cause.
Once inside the Chamber, the crowd calmed after about ten
minutes, Tim was told about the order from Fu to the
Chinese military. He grabbed Zhang Min and told him that

the Chinese communist government is being overthrown and to call the military and stop the attack. Zhang Min was a stubborn, but proud Chinaman. He ignored the young man's order. Tim grabbed a gun and put it to the head of Min and spoke, "I will count to three and then I will pull this trigger. One … Two …" Huang Fu then spoke, "Stop, don't kill him. I will call."

———————————————

U.S. Navy F/A-18F Super Hornet fighter aircraft flying their patrols were the first to see the blips on their radar screens. The lead pilot, Lieutenant Commander William 'Billy' McCord, spoke to the other four aircraft in his patrol. "Here they come boys, weapons hot, remember your training. Tally Ho!" It was really beautiful to see these pilots manipulate their aircraft. The coordinated dance of the 30,000-pound machines of war as they sliced through the air so effortlessly looked like seagulls diving for their dinner and it was incredible. As the Chinese aircraft approached, the F-15 group was ready and had already slid into attack formation. The Chinese Aircraft were still out of gun range, but had entered missile range. The rules of engagement were clear for the U.S. fighters. The order from the NCA, National Command Authority was *'Engage only after being fired upon.'* Just then, the wave of Chinese aircraft broke off their engagement and veered into a 180 degree turn back to the Chinese mainland. The U.S. fighters watched cautiously and Major McCord reported the situation to his commanders. Chinese ships were turning around, ground forces halted movement, and the E-2C airborne radar aircraft were earning their pay by detecting, documenting, and reporting all of the activity.

After Huang Fu had made the call to General Liao to stop the attack, he and Zhang Min were arrested. Tim Chen grabbed the phone before Fu could hang up so he could speak directly to General Liao and informed him that the communist government of China had been overthrown and was no longer in power and that a new government would be put in place soon. As the interim leader of this new Chinese government, Tim Chen reiterated the order to the General to stand down all forces and maintain a defensive posture only as to any invading force. For now, the General listened and complied. Tim then decided he had to address the world. Normally, Tim Chen was pretty quiet, but things happened so fast and he knew that he could form the requisite words so as to help calm down the situation and at the same time, give the Chinese people hope.

Chinese TV was on the scene and had never really had this kind of access to the Politburo Chamber before. Tim Chen, waved them over and yelled to everyone in the Chamber to be quiet. He asked the TV crew if they could broadcast live and they said yes. With no censorship in place, Tim had asked his new friends to put it out over social media that the feed could be picked up by all TV and radio stations and internet sites. He waited a couple of minutes, and then his friends nodded for him to speak.

"Dear citizens of China and the world. My name is Timothy Chen and I am a Chinese-American that was recently a lab technician at the Sunhexiang Bio Research lab. I was the one who discovered that the Chinese government planned to infect the world not once, but twice, in order to gain more power for China and its Politburo. I reported my findings to a friend of mine in the United States who took my evidence and helped unravel this terrible plan. She was then able to alert the U.S. government who, along with a coalition of other countries, took action against China to stop this mass killing. I am not a political leader. I have no aspirations of political life other than to live a peaceful life on the planet we all must inhabit. The Chinese citizens and the peaceful people of China have been loyal citizens to a regime that stifled freedom, the freedom that I took for granted as a U.S. citizen. I am here to report that the Chinese Politburo has been overthrown. I'm sure I can speak for most all Chinese citizens in saying to the world, that we are sorry for the actions of our government. I understand and rightly so, that China will now face scrutiny as to their behavior in the future. I am here to tell the world that China will need your help and guidance in becoming a friendly, free, and democratic nation."

With that last statement a roar of applause went up in the Chamber and outside. Tim Chen again motioned for quiet.

"This revolution happened because a small group of dedicated individuals cared enough about the future of their country, the world, and each other to risk their lives for freedom. Again, I am not a politician and I don't want to be. This group of dedicated people should act as the interim leadership for China. I am happy to provide any help I can, but China and the interim leaders will need the world's help in order to set-up free elections as soon as possible. I'm asking the world's leaders to immediately help us with this process. Once free elections are set-up, China will properly elect a government and new leader. The citizens of the world have seen first-hand how fragile life is. No man or government, free or not, should be able to ever put the world in this position again. I ask the Chinese people to be patient while this wonderful change takes place."

And with that, amidst the roar and cheering of the crowd, Tim motioned to end the broadcast.

————————————————

Most nations' leaders had been watching on TVs and computer screens all over the world. The president was in the Oval watching with Alden Scott and Admiral James Reed.

"I'll be damned!" said President Hunter. "They finally wanted freedom bad enough. See, if you leave it up to the people, they will do the right thing eventually. *We The People* … Get it?"

Alden acknowledged him. "Yes sir, we don't need the history lesson, we get it."

"Admiral, I want a transition plan in place for China. First, we need to make sure that any rogue sympathizers don't have access to their nuclear weapons."

"Yes sir, already on it. We'll have teams ready to go from the Gerald Ford within the hour."

"Alden, I need you to get back to the Situation Room and come up with a plan for transitioning China to a democratic and free country. They have asked for our help and we cannot let them down."

"It's going to be a massive undertaking, but we'll do our best Sir."

"I need to address the nation tonight, put it out to the news channels and get Ms. Parker Hall over here. That guy, Tim Chen, is her friend, right? Set up a meeting with her ASAP … oh, and I guess we need to get Mr. Chen's cell phone number from her?"

"Yes sir, that appears to be what we need to do."

CHAPTER 28

L i Wei had not heard Tim Chen and the worldwide broadcast. It didn't matter, he could surmise as much from what was going on. He knew that if he was caught, he would be arrested. He had other plans. During the chaos, no one had noticed that he was gone from the Politburo Chamber and he walked to his favorite place on the grounds, the Water Clouds Pavilion. There was chaos all over the place, but he essentially blended in with every other Chinamen. He hadn't worn his uniform, so he was in casual business attire. Once at his favorite bench, he sat down and tried to focus on the beauty that nature had provided rather than the various pillars of smoke and chaos from the protests. He had led a good life. He had no regrets. He reflected on his youth and wondered if his time in the West had contributed at all to the failure of his plan. *No*, he thought, *the plan was always sound. So where was the failure?* Wei knew that if the Politburo members had chosen not to proceed with Virus Two, China probably would have continued, in a slightly better position in the world, but the same political issues would have also been present. No, he knew the decisions he and the others had made were the right ones in order to achieve China's long-term objectives. He also knew that the phrase, 'China's long-term objectives,' would now change meanings and he didn't want to be around to see that. Though he had enjoyed his time in the West as a young man and student, he knew he was being corrupted every day under the guise of freedom. He remembered feeling tempted by many things, materialistic or otherwise. He wondered if he'd find the answers after he ended his life. *Why, under a free society, are humans tempted to do bad things or stray from principles and norms?* Well, he couldn't answer those questions, but he'd find out soon enough. With that, he grabbed his weapon and cocked the hammer. He took one last look at the glistening water and beautiful foliage on the island. Then he put the gun to his head and pulled the trigger.

Parker Hall couldn't speak, even though Josh was high-fiving everyone in the room at Homeland Security. Parker saw her friend on TV, but that was not the same guy from the emails or school. He looked the same, a little tired, but pretty much the same. *Holy crap*, she thought. She knew he had never had any political aspirations but to hear him speak from the Politburo Chamber was amazing. She couldn't wait to hear the full story, but she didn't know what footing they were on at this point. Timothy was pretty abrupt in his last email and kinda rude. *'Too many women to count'–yeah right. Maybe he's pissed at me*, she thought. The double entendre of the signature, *'Mr. Frank,'* was a dead giveaway. Could her previous email have been interpreted wrong? That's it, no more damn emails! I'll give him a few days and then I will call him. Just then she heard singing in a corner of the room. Several people, including Josh, were singing *Celebration* by Kool and the Gang: *'Cel-a-brate good times, come on!'*. Josh was going nuts; he found a bottle of champagne and was getting very drunk. Parker's phone was blowing up, too. Elliott was texting, Professor Short was texting, her father was texting. Then another text came in. This one she had to answer right away. It was from the White House. She typed, 'Absolutely, I will be there at 9 am.' She'd answer the other texts in a bit. She sat back in her chair, still not believing what Timothy had done. She just realized the time; it was now nearly 10:00 pm. She needed to get home and get a good night sleep for tomorrow's meeting. She was tempted to text or email Timothy, but she knew there was no way he'd have the time to thoughtfully respond. With all the commotion in the room, she slipped out and headed to her car.

―――――――――――――

"Ah, Ms. Hall, good morning!"
          "Good morning Mr. President."

"You must be very proud of yourself, I certainly am."

"Well thank you Sir, but it was a team effort, really."

"I'm sure it was, but you my dear, led the charge and we all owe you a debt of gratitude."

"Again, thank you Sir, but a lot of the credit goes to Timothy Chen."

"Yes, yes, and wow, who knew he was such an asset."

"Well sir, I doubt that he would refer to himself as an asset. He was merely being a good friend to me, a good American, and indulging my whims."

"Well, whatever you want to call him, he is an amazing young man. We are putting together a team to head over to China and meet with young Mr. Chen and his new friends and help put a government in place. The UK, Germany, and a couple of other countries are sending teams as well. I want you to be on the U.S. team and help with this transition. I'm not sure how long you'll be there, but certainly for a few weeks to start. How does that sound?"

"I would be honored Sir."

"Alden Scott is handling the team, so please see him for further details. I think you guys are leaving by the end of the week. That's all for now, thank you again, really."

"Thank you Mr. President."

As she was walking out of the Oval, the president spoke one last time from behind his desk. "Ms. Hall, when this is all done, I'd like you to think about coming to work for me."

Parker stopped and turned. "I don't know what to say Sir, I'd be honored."

"Have a good trip."

After she left the Oval Office, the president walked over to the Chief of Staff's office.

"Got a sec?"

"Yes Sir, what do you need?"

"I'm sending Parker Hall over to China with the transition team."

"No problem, I'll see to it."

"Make sure that the team understands that she is there at my request. Understood?"

"I understand Sir, I will make sure the team gets the message loud and clear."

Less than a week later, several teams from all over the world came together in Beijing. The interim 'government,' if it could be called that, had decided to accomplish several key things before the transition help arrived. They needed to have the Chinese military leaders trust and believe in their power. This was tricky, but they had identified several generals who were more sympathetic to reform and put them in charge of keeping things quiet. Next were local police forces throughout the country. This was a bit easier because most police departments took orders locally. The reformists, who were now new government officials, were able to reach out to others in their cause so they could immediately meet with local officials. Some of the local officials were thrown out of their jobs as communist sympathizers and those that were more in-line with democratic reform remained. In either case, an official friendly to the revolution was in contact and control of each city's local police force. They did this throughout China. Lastly, they still had to deal with Virus Two, and though the vaccine was working in China, there were still hospitalizations and deaths. They got a handle on what was needed and where to send it. The effort of these reformists was actually extraordinary, given that they were probably singing at a Karaoke bar a week ago.

As Parker got off the plane after the 16-hour flight, she immediately started to look for Timothy, but she was inundated with introductions to the 'new interim government leaders' who had met them at their gate. Tim had remained at the Politburo headquarters in order to help prepare for the transition teams. Parker, exhausted, politely smiled, shook hands, and followed the rest of the team to get their luggage and then to the busses. It would be a long day. She was disappointed that Timothy had not been there.

As they got into Beijing, she noticed that for the most part, things looked normal. You'd never know that this communist country had just gone through a revolution. Apparently, the plan was for the team to have meetings first and then they would go to their hotels after. All she could think about was hot bath and a good night's sleep. She grabbed her computer bag and shuffled off the bus, stepping into a crowd of team members and new government officials. As she took in the scene, she felt a tap on her shoulder. She turned around and there was Timothy. She instantly smiled and reached her arms out to hug him. She was actually tearing up a bit, but wiped her eyes before Timothy could tell. Neither of them said a word for another thirty seconds while they embraced. It was surreal. She pulled back and all she could think to say was "Hi!". Tim responded in kind and after the awkwardness of some small talk was over, they both felt more relaxed. They would have plenty of time to get reacquainted. She felt something different after seeing him. She'd make sure to rekindle the friendship first before even thinking about anything else, but for the first time in her relationship with Timothy Chen, she felt that there was a real hope of something more.

Transitioning to a democracy was no simple feat. Even if all the parties got consensus and China had a clear direction toward a new democratic government, there were forces inside China, including the Chinese military, that were not going to sit idly by and watch their regime disappear after thousands of years of communist rule. Outside forces, namely Russia, also resisted the idea of a democratic China. These forces stayed clandestine for the meantime but were very powerful. They would rear their ugly heads in the weeks and months to come. The democratic reformists may have won a big battle, but it was still up for grabs as to who would win the 'war.' Transition, if there was going to a transition, would take months if not longer. One thing was certain. The world had a vested interest in trying to prevent any rogue nation from using what could only be called a biological weapon of mass destruction from ever being turned loose on the world's population again.

CHAPTER 29

As the world adapted to a new China, at least for now, the leadership of Iran was hard at work. A lone scientist in full PPE gear was looking through a microscope when someone knocked on the main window to the lab. The scientist turned and looked and waved, then held up one finger. The person at the window nodded and mouthed, *'Ok.'* After a couple of minutes, the scientist went through the airlock and de-sterilization process in order to make his way into the non-sterile office. The person at the window was Iran's Minister of Infectious Disease. As the scientist entered the room, he used a fresh towel to wipe his head which was covered in sweat.

"Minister Karami, how are you?"

"I should ask you the same thing, Ebrahim."

"Even though the air conditioning in the suits is very good, they still get hot enough to sweat through one's clothes."

"So tell me, how is our progress?"

"Progress is very good. I believe I have found a way around the vaccine."

"Wonderful Ebrahim, please explain."

"As you know we were able to isolate the virus in a dying patient and then of course, the United States government distributed the vaccine to us and everyone else in the world. So, if you remember your biology and chemistry from your school days, most vaccines work by training one's immune system to recognize and battle a certain pathogen, either a virus or bacteria. By injecting a controlled amount of antigens into the body, the immune system can safely learn to recognize the antigens as unfriendly intruders. As a response to the intruders, the body produces antibodies and then "codes" them for recall and deployment in the future."

"I was following until your last statement."

"Think of it this way. The body identifies and catalogs the intruder and then makes, or creates, a fighter to fight the intruder. The fighter is called an antibody. The antibody is always standing by, now or anytime in the future, to fight the particular intruder when identified by the body."

"I see. And so, what is your "way around" this fighter?"

"The way around it, Minister Karami, is to prepare the intruder to look like a fighter. A sort of "slight-of-hand" so that the intruder can exist amongst the fighter and attack the host body without the fighter knowing the host is being· attacked."

"Would it be too simplified to suggest that you've found a way to "blind" the fighter Ebrahim?"

"No, that's exactly correct. I believe we can certainly blind the fighter temporarily, time enough for the intruder to destroy the host body. That's what we're working on now, trying to determine how much time the intruder might have before being detected, if at all, by the fighter. But Minister, this breakthrough allows us to use it in an opposite manner as well, for a good use. If we know how to 'blind the fighter,' that means we can also 'blind the intruder.' We can begin to eradicate any diseases that the body might encounter."

"Excellent, Ebrahim. I will let you get back to work. Is there anything you need?"

"No, nothing at present. Thank you. Understand that we still have many months of work, testing, and trials before this chemical is actually ready for deployment."

Dariush Karami smiled and patted Ebrahim on the back. As he left the secure facility, the guards saluted him. Without acknowledging them, he walked to his car. He knew that the esteemed Doctor Ebrahim Heydari was right, but the Mullahs would never see the 'good use' that could be had from this breakthrough, only the weapon it could and would be.

ABOUT THE AUTHOR

J Rusty Shaffer is an entrepreneur, CEO, and attorney with over thirty years of experience in all aspects of business including international sales, marketing, and manufacturing around the world – specifically in China. Rusty is the inventor of the Fretlight Guitar, which incorporates a lighted learning system into the fretboard of a real guitar. He is the named inventor on eight patents relevant to various facets of the Fretlight technology.

Rusty has recorded two albums and also played on stage over the years with various music greats, including the Grammy award-winning band America. Before inventing the Fretlight Guitar, Rusty was a commercial flight instructor. Rusty is a consultant to various businesses and mentors young entrepreneurs in the Reno/Tahoe area. He is currently an adjunct professor in the entrepreneurship department at the University of Nevada, Reno.

CPSIA information can be obtained
at www.ICGtesting.com
Printed in the USA
JSHW030738080720
6497JS00001B/1

9 781735 189406